勘誤表 (4X26)

頁碼	行	原	應改為
50	第 11 行	(3) *聊著等著，捷運站就到了。	註腳說明 An asterisk (*) is used to mark sentences which are ungrammatical.
76	第 8 行	……，我已經 ＿＿＿ （計畫）了。	……，我已經計畫好了。
76	第 9 行	……，因為網路還 ＿＿＿ （裝）。	……，因為網路還沒裝好。
76	第 10 行	……，所以作業 ＿＿＿ （寫）。	……，所以作業還沒寫好。
82	倒數第 3 行	……，多吉利啊！	……，多吉利呀！
83	第 3 行	對啊，我怎麼……	對呀，我怎麼……
84	第 2 行	…, duó jíli a!	…, duó jíli ya!
84	第 8 行	Duì a, …	Duì ya, …
87	短語 2	jíle	jí le
		…liang	…liang

頁碼	行數	原文	修正
106	第 2 行	…gùshi…	…gùshi…
157	語法點二：第 9 行	如：他對養生很有/沒有研究。	如：他對養生〔很有/沒有〕研究。
159	第 10 行	4. 如果後句省略主語，所省略的是指前句的第一個主語。	*加上英文說明 If the subject of the second sentence is omitted, the omitted subject refers to the subject of the previous one.
209	第 9 行	gùshi	gùshi
210	第 10 行	jile	jí le

印度臺灣華語教育中心——
國立清華大學計畫辦公室　策劃

主編／陳淑芬

編寫教師／張箴、劉殿敏、陳慶華

Incredible Mandarin
不可思議華語

五南圖書出版公司 印行

序一

2009 年我非常榮幸能安排吳前部長清基訪問印度，這是中華民國第一次有部長訪問印度。吳前部長清基及印度前人力資源部 Kapil Sibal 部長會面，當時 Kapil Sibal 部長要求中華民國派一萬名華語老師前往印度，因此，我們認知到華語教育在印度可大有所為。

返國後國立清華大學（以下簡稱本校）正式接受中華民國教育部委託在印度成立臺灣教育中心（Taiwan Education Center in India，簡稱 TEC）。起初我努力向本校的姊妹校詢問拓展 TEC 的意願，然因我國和印度沒有正式外交關係，而本校的姊妹校多為國立大學，故談判困難重重。直至 2011 年，非常感念經由印度駐臺代表 Mr. Rawat 的介紹在私立大學 O. P. Jindal Global University 成立了在印度的第一座 TEC，簡稱 TEC-JGU。因緣際會下我在杜拜教育展認識了印度最大的私立大學 Amity 大學創辦人的長公子，進而促成於 2012 年在 Amity 大學成立了在印度的第二座 TEC，簡稱 TEC-Amity。

在兩間私立大學成立 TEC 之後，在時任國立伊斯蘭大學（Jamia Millia Islamia，JMI）T. C. A. Rangachari 教授的協助下，於 2013 年 5 月簽成了我們在印度第一個國立大學成立的 TEC，簡稱 TEC-JMI。Rangachari 教授係前印度駐德國和法國的大使，曾在中華民國在大陸執政時前往學習華語，能說流利的中文。

2013 年同年本校也在印度理工學院—馬德拉斯分校（Indian Institute of Technology Madras, IITM）成立了在印度的第四座 TEC，簡稱 TEC-IITM。IITM 係本校陳文村前校長於 2009 年率團前往印度後簽訂姊妹校，才能於 2013 年在該校成立 TEC。

接著 2015～2017 之間本校分別於國立尼赫魯大學（Jawaharlal Nehru University，JNU）、SRM 大學（Sri Ramaswamy Memorial University，SRM 大學，後改名為 SRM Institute of Science and Technology, SRMIST）及印度理工學院—孟買分校（Indian Institute of Technology Bombay, IITB）成立 TEC，分別簡稱為 TEC-JNU、TEC-SRMIST 和 TEC-IITB。

自 2011 年一路走來平均一年成立一個 TEC，中心據點詳如後表所示。隨後，教育部認為我們可以暫緩設置新的 TEC，然而吉特卡拉大學（Chitkara University）於 2018

年和本校聯絡並表示願意提供所有費用讓本校在該校成立 TEC，教育部順勢同意，於 2019 年本校於吉特卡拉大學成立在印度的第八座 TEC，簡稱 TEC-Chitkara。後來因為教育部政策的轉變，2020 年本校於 SRM-AP 大學（SRM University, Andhra Pradesh）成立在印度的第九座 TEC，簡稱 TEC-SRMAP，教育部也同意本校繼續在印度增設 TEC。

成立 TEC 能夠協助臺灣各大專院校和我們駐點的學校建立合作關係，也藉由教授正體字，將臺灣的文化介紹給印度學生，並讓學生對臺灣有更進一步的了解；同時駐點學校也很周到安排宿舍及其他相關福利，長期以來雙方配合成效良好。

經過將近五、六年的運作後，我們漸漸發現在印度書店裡找不到任何臺灣的出版品，主要是因為印度政府對於印度自身出版業的保護，再加上臺灣和印度並無外交關係，業者都認為要把臺灣的出版品引進印度根本難上加難。臺灣目前有許多優良的華語教材但皆非為印度人設計，然我們認為學習語言會因國情不同所需要的教材也不同。所以我們在教育部的支持下自 2017 年起已舉辦三屆印度—臺灣印度華語教材雙邊共構論壇，蒐集全印度對華語教學有興趣的印度學校資訊與需求後，奠定了我們開發印度生專用華語教材的信心，同時也認知到臺灣出版的書籍出口到印度的價格偏高，故我們決定要在印度當地尋求出版社協助印刷、發行及銷售教材。

經過長時間的努力，我們成功爭取到臺灣目前最好的華語教材《當代中文課程》是由國立臺灣師範大學編輯，目前已在印度印刷、發行及銷售。前前後後費時一年半取得聯經出版社在印度的獨家授權，也經由 Yaoindia 創辦人印度尤（尤芷薇）的介紹，認識了 Sanctum Books 的副主理人，並將教材出版之印刷、出版和銷售事宜交與他們處理。在此之前，臺灣與印度從未進行過這樣跨國出版的合作，成品印刷十分精美，也特別為印度制訂售價，現在已經在印度 Amazon 上架。目前所有 TEC 一律使用這本書籍當作正式教材，希望未來所有在印度的華語老師和學習華語的學生都能採用此本教材。

於此同時，我們也籌備了針對印度人設計的華語教材。我們邀請了國立清華大學中文系的陳淑芬教授擔任主編，並邀請了劉殿敏、陳慶華及張箴教授等多位老師成立編輯委員會，在一年內完成校對和試教，也就是您現在手上這本 *Incredible Mandarin*。然這只是個開端，目前我們正持續開發更多印度華語文教材，不只是印度日常生活需

要用到的內容，還有專業領域的華語，讓臺灣能更有力在印度推動華語教學。

除此之外，我們也嘗試在印度的大學開設商業華語的課程，可是因為缺乏優良的教材加上印度 FRRO 的簽證限制，經過好一陣子的努力 TEC 華語老師仍無法在學校之外的場地授課，但我們深知印度商業華語有其大量需求，因此我們另外也委託國立清華大學信世昌副校長組織團隊進行商用華語教材的編纂。

我們非常高興能邀請信副校長進行商業華語教材之編纂，信副校長得知後也一口答應。信副校長為世界華語教材編輯權威，具編輯德語、西語和法語華語教材之經驗，他所編之教材廣受市場歡迎，預計在短期之內完成這一系列華語教材。

相信在我們的努力之下，有了好的華語教材，加上我們熱情的華語老師，還有駐點學校的大力支持，我們可以把印度的華語教學做得更好。

接下來我們的目標如前所述，我們要在印度更多適當的地點成立更多的 TEC，邀請臺灣有志於印度教授華語的華語講師，或是對印度文化有興趣的人士多多前往印度，擴大臺灣華語教學在印度的影響，也進一步吸引更多優秀的印度學生來臺灣深造，強化兩國各方面的關係。我們也希望藉由在印度的華語教學，促進語言上的溝通，同時也希望兩國在經濟、科技、學術和國防等各方面的合作，更能因為語言方便，使合作更臻順暢及擴大，也期盼我國政府和教育部能夠繼續支持 TEC 的運作。

此外，我們現在還要服務臺灣在印度的企業，讓印度員工來臺灣工作前，可以先在 TEC 學好華語再赴臺任職，並訓練外派印度前的臺灣員工先了解印度，甚至近年來我們也邀請臺灣的企業參與已舉辦近十年的印度臺灣高等教育展，充分發揮產學合作之加乘效果。未來我們也將協助 Amity 大學成立印度私立大學中的第一個應用華語文學系，期望能培養更多的印度學生幫助印度政府及臺灣在經商和遊學等方面成為兩國之間的助力。

印度臺灣華語教育中心—國立清華大學計畫辦公室

主任 王偉中

Preface I

In 2009, I was very honored to arrange the former Minister, Dr. Ching-Ji Wu's visit to India. It was the first time a minister from the Republic of China (Taiwan) visited India. The former Minister, Dr. Wu and the former Minister of the Ministry of Human Resource Development, India (MHRD) had a meeting. Minister, Mr. Kapil Sibal asked Taiwan to send 10,000 Mandarin Chinese instructors to India. It was then we understood how broad a future Mandarin Chinese language education has in India.

After returning to Taiwan, National Tsing Hua University (NTHU) officially accepted the mission from the Ministry of Education (MOE), Taiwan, to establish Taiwan Education Centers in India (TEC). In the very beginning, I tried to contact sister universities of NTHU in India; however, the negotiation process was very challenging, as most were national institutions and there were no formal diplomatic relations between Taiwan and India. It wasn't until 2011 that Mr. Rawat, former Representative of India in India-Taipei Association (ITA) then, introduced a private university, "O.P. Jindal Global University", to establish the first Taiwan Education Center in India, known as TEC-JGU. In addition, it was very lucky that, in Dubai Education Fair, I happened to come across the son of the Founder of Amity University, the largest private university in India. This has led us to set up the second TEC in India, also known as TEC-Amity.

After two TECs in private universities in India have been established, with the help of Prof. T.C.A. Rangachari in Jamia Millia Islamia (JMI), the first TEC in national university was founded in May 2013, also known as TEC-JMI. Professor Rangachari speaks fluent Mandarin Chinese which he acquired in the Republic of China before 1949. Professor Rangachari was the former Indian Ambassador to Germany and France

In the same year, 2013, the 4th TEC was established in Indian Institute of Technology Madras (IITM), also known as TEC-IITM. If it wasn't for the MoU of sister universities signed during the former NTHU President, Dr. Wen-Tsuen Chen's, visit to India in 2009 this would not have been possible.

During 2015 to 2017, NTHU has further established TEC in Jawaharlal Nehru University (JNU), SRM University (Sri Ramaswamy Memorial University, which was renamed as SRM Institute of Science and Technology, SRMIST), and Indian Institute of Technology Bombay (IITB). These three branches namely TEC-JNU, TEC-SRMIST, TEC-IITB.

Since 2011, one TEC has been established each year on an average (details shown in table 1). Later MOE suggested that we could slow down our pace. Nevertheless, Chitkara University contacted us in 2018, expressing that they would like to support NTHU to set up a TEC in their campus and offered to cover all the expenses required. The 8th TEC was still much supported by MOE in Chitkara University, and hence, TEC-Chitkara was established in 2019. The Ministry of Education altered its previous policy and acceded to NTHU to continue establishing TEC in India. In this regard, the 9th TEC in India in SRM University, Andhra Pradesh, was established, also known as TEC-SRMAP.

The establishment of TEC assists institutions around Taiwan to collaborate with the Indian universities. With the education of Traditional Chinese characters, it was possible to introduce Taiwanese culture to Indian students and helps them to have better understandings of Taiwan. The Indian-Taiwan bilateral collaboration has been fruitful with the partner universities' support in providing our instructors' staff quarters and other necessities.

After running TEC for about 5 to 6 years, we came to notice that there are no books from Taiwan in India. For one, the Indian government protects the press and publication industries in India. For another, without formal diplomatic relations between Taiwan and India, it is very difficult for publishers to issue Taiwanese books to India. Moreover, though there are many great Mandarin Chinese language teaching materials by Taiwanese publishers, they are not designed for Indians. We think learning a language requires adaptive materials designed based on learners' cultural background. With the support from MOE, we have organized three "India-Taiwan Bilateral Forum on Mandarin Chinese Teaching Materials for Indian Learners" since 2017. We have gathered opinions and requirements on the needs of Mandarin Chinese teaching and learning from institutions around India.

This provides us much confidence in developing a new Mandarin Chinese learning material dedicated to Indian. At the same time, we came to understand that exporting books to India cost tremendously. Consequently, we decided to search for local publishers for printing, publishing and selling new material.

With years of sustained effort, we have gained sole license to edit, print, publish and sell the best-selling Mandarin Chinese textbook, *A Course in Contemporary Chinese*, in Taiwan edited by National Taiwan Normal University (NTNU). It took us a year and a half to acquire an exclusive license from "Linking Publishing Company" to publish this textbook in India. Thanks to the Founder of Yaoindia, Ms. Chih-Wei Yu, who introduced us to "Sanctum Books" to handle related works of printing, publishing and sales. Before this, Taiwan and India had no such international collaboration. The printing quality is exquisite and the price is also tailored to the Indian market. This textbook *A Course in Contemporary Chinese* is now on sale on Amazon India online. All TEC now are using this textbook as official teaching and learning material. We hope this material will become a popular choice among teachers and learners of Mandarin Chinese language in India.

In the meanwhile, we are preparing a Mandarin Chinese learning material designed for Indian learners. We invited Prof. Shu-Fen Chen, from Department of Chinese Literature, NTHU, to be the Editor in Chief leading the team with Instructor Diane Dien-Min Liu, Instructor Ching-Hua Chen, Prof. Felicia Zhen Zhang and other specialists to co-edit, review, proofread and trial teach this textbook you're holding - *Incredible Mandarin*. This is just the beginning. At the moment, we continue to develop more Mandarin Chinese teaching and learning materials for India. Not only do we work on contents that cover daily life inquisition but also Mandarin Chinese used in professional fields. This would facilitate instructors/teachers from Taiwan to improvise Mandarin Chinese teaching in India greatly.

Apart from above-mentioned tasks, we are also trying to set-up Business Mandarin Chinese courses in Indian universities. However, a shortage of adaptive teaching and learning materials and also restrictions from FRRO and visa regulations, TEC instructors are still not permitted to teach courses off-campus. Indeed, we know that there is a huge demand for learning Business Mandarin Chinese in India. With this in mind, we invited Senior Vice President at NTHU, Prof. Shih-Chang Hsin, to form a team to edit further Business Chinese teaching and learning materials in India.

We are really glad to have Prof. Shih-Chang Hsin, accepting this mission, without any hesitation, to head the editorial of this book. As a leading specialist in Mandarin Chinese education and material development, Prof. Hsin has profound experiences in editing popular Mandarin Chinese textbooks for German, Spanish and French speakers. He has plans to complete this series of teaching and learning material in the near future.

I believe that we could take teaching Mandarin Chinese language in India to the next level with great efforts going into developing better Mandarin Chinese language teaching and learning materials, our professional and passionate instructors in teaching, and strong support from partner universities.

Our future goal is, as described, to establish more TEC in suitable places around India, to invite more Mandarin instructors who are interested in teaching in India, to encourage more people fond of Indian culture to visit India, and to expand the influence of language education of Taiwanese Mandarin Chinese in India. Meanwhile, we introduce higher education in Taiwan to excellent Indian students for further studies, bringing a stronger relationship between Taiwan and India. We also hope to inspire cross-cultural communication through Mandarin Chinese language education in India. Meanwhile, stimulating collaborations in economics, technology, national defense and academics between Taiwan and India. Without language barriers, collaboration can be direct and at larger scales. We hope our government and the Ministry of Education will continue to support the operation of TEC.

Furthermore, we plan to serve Taiwan companies in India to train their Indian staffs with Mandarin Chinese courses provided by TEC before they take up their positions in Taiwan and to help Taiwanese staffs to gain better understandings about India before they expat to India. In recent years, we have invited the industries to join Taiwan Higher Education Fair, fully utilizing the synergistic effect of industry-academia collaboration. In the future, we will assist Amity University in setting up the first Bachelor Degree program of Mandarin Chinese. We wish to assist and nurture more Indian students who will become a major boost between India and Taiwan in business, education and various aspects.

Wei-Chung Wang
Director, Program Office for Taiwan Education Center in India at NTHU
National Tsing Hua University, TAIWAN

表一　印度臺灣華語教育中心列表

Table 1: List of Taiwan Education Centers in India

分部 Office	合作大學 Collaborating Institutions	據點 Location
TEC-JGU (08.2011)	O. P. Jindal Global University 金德爾全球大學	Delhi
TEC-Amity (07.2012)	Amity University 亞米堤大學	Delhi
TEP-JMI (05.2013)	Jamia Millia Islamia 國立伊斯蘭大學	Delhi
TEP-IITM (09.2013)	Indian Institute of Technology Madras 印度理工學院－馬德拉斯分校	Chennai
TEP-JNU (03.2015)	Jawaharlal Nehru University 國立尼赫魯大學	New Delhi
TEC-SRMIST (09.2016)	SRM Institute of Science and Technology SRMIST 大學	Chennai
TEC-IITB (09.2017)	Indian Institute of Technology Bombay 印度理工學院－孟買分校	Mumbai
TEC-Chitkara (12.2019)	Chitkara University 吉特卡拉大學	Punjab
TEC-SRMAP (09.2020)	SRM University, Andhra Pradesh SRM-AP 大學	Andhra Pradesh

序二

　　自 2011 年伊始，國立清華大學印度中心王偉中主任奉派在印成立「印度臺灣華語教育中心」，至今已有九所印度大學與臺灣教育部合作，由臺灣外派的華語教師開設華語課程。鑑於印度大學目前使用的華語教材相當老舊，且與印度國情與文化有頗大差距，故印度臺灣華語教育中心亟思在教學與教材上有所改善。於是在王主任和國立高雄師範大學華語文教學研究所鍾鎮誠所長共同推動下，先後於 2017 年 3 月於尼赫魯大學（Jawaharlal Nehru University）舉辦了「第一屆印度華語教材雙邊共構論壇」；2018 年 5 月於亞米堤大學（Amity University）舉行第二屆論壇；第三屆論壇原計畫於 2020 年 4 月再次於印度舉辦，無奈新冠肺炎疫情嚴峻，只得暫停召開會議。不過，印度中心並未放棄推動華語教學工作，於 2020 年 3 月 9 日在清華大學舉辦了「第三屆印度華語教材雙邊共構論壇」的籌備會議，會中決議編寫一套國別化教材，為印度學習者編寫一套適用的華語教材，並推舉本人為主編。

　　本人有感於教學工作不能耽擱，於是前置作業完成後，旋及於 6 月 30 日旋即召開了第一次的「印度華語教材編寫」會議。會中邀請到國立臺灣師範大學國語中心陳慶華老師和劉殿敏老師，以及中國文化大學華語文教學碩士學位學程張箴老師來共同編寫此教材。此外並邀曾任教於印度臺灣華語教育中心（Taiwan Education Center in India）的八位華語教師——鄒宛育、蔡翎芸、王皓誠、蕭懿璱、吳佳玲、王潔予、賴佳吟和袁筱惠，共同構思貫穿全書的各課主軸。

　　本書以幽默有趣的故事內容，串起這本華語課本的十課，並以文化對比的角度來介紹臺灣和印度的文化特色。書中以四位主人翁串起故事，為顛覆性別刻板印象，以臺灣珠寶公司的女性經理和男性祕書來到印度出差為主軸，進行一周的 incredible 印度之旅。課文中男性祕書王偉中，正是以印度中心同名同姓的王偉中主任為取材原型。王主任是個道地的「印度通」，為了臺印兩國的交流，至今來往臺印共 44 次，不僅在印度如此艱困環境下推動華語教學，讓數千名印度學生學習繁體字華語，更鼓勵並協助許多印度學子跨海來臺就讀。王主任雖非華語教學專業，卻是將臺灣華語教學引入印度的最大幕後功臣之一。編者與曾任教於印度的教師，感佩王主任對印度華語教學的無私奉獻，均希冀於本書出版的同時，將王偉中主任的名字在印度華語教材留名，

以為傳承和感謝他為臺印交流真誠地付出與貢獻。

　　本書的主要學習對象為在印度大學學習華語第二年的大學生。第一年教材，使用聯經出版的《當代中文課程》第一冊，以奠定學生通用化一般詞彙與內容。清華大學印度中心已經得到聯經出版社的版權，在印度九個臺灣華語教育中心使用。因此，本書對詞性的分類，採取鄧守信教授編《當代中文課程》的系統，讓學生在學習上有連續性。本書的學習者定位參考「歐洲共同語言參考標準」CEFR，為 A2-B1 華語程度的印度學生，以文化比較與語言學習為主軸，設計在地化的教材。每一課分為七個部分：

1. 課程目標及課文屬性：每課皆指出該課的課程目標及課文屬性，並提供與課文相關之情境圖片，作為引導學生進入該課主題。

2. 課文對話：每課的對話約 14-18 個話輪。十課的對話部分的內容為一系列故事的連串，從周經理和王祕書在臺灣準備出訪印度開始，期間在印度經歷的不同文化體驗，一直到準備從印度回到臺灣。藉由活潑有趣的故事，引發學生主動學習的動機。

3. 短文：每課短文約 300 字左右，內容為跟該課課文屬性相關主題的短文。主要介紹臺灣文化的各個面向，有些則比較臺印文化之異同，讓學生從語言學習中，進行跨文化的反思，提升對多元文化的了解與尊重。

4. 生詞、專有名詞和短語：每課的課文對話和短文都列有生詞、專有名詞和短語，生詞一和生詞二數量維持在 40 個以內。生詞和短語的解釋以出現在該課的意思為主，每個生詞皆列出漢語拼音、詞性和英文翻譯。

5. 語法：每課從課文對話與短文選出四至五個語法點，進行有系統的語法說明，適時比較相似的語法點。並提供多個例句，以及多樣性的語法練習，以幫助學生熟悉運用。

6. 跨文化延伸：此部分以英文為主，讓學生能更加了解臺印文化之異同，培養國際觀與多元觀點。並在附錄三中提供中文版本，作為進階的閱讀補充教材。

7. 語言任務：每課規劃兩個語言任務，利用語法點設計任務型教學活動，提供多樣性的溝通活動，學習實用的華語，增進其口語能力。

本書各課負責編寫的教師如下：
- 張箴：第一、二課
- 劉殿敏：第三、五、六、七課
- 陳慶華：第四、八、九、十課

　　雖然各課有負責編寫的老師，但每一課的內容都是三位主筆老師和主編一起共同討論，開過近 20 次的教材編寫會議；另外，主編也跟三位老師無數次個別開會討論一些課文和文法的細節，經多方琢磨而定稿。本書特別感謝三位審查人 ── 美國 Williams College 亞洲研究系顧百里教授、臺灣師範大學華語文教學研究所葉德明榮譽教授和臺灣大學華語教學碩士學位學程張莉萍教授，他們提供了非常寶貴的修改意見，讓本書更臻完善。此外，本書的英文翻譯由張箴老師所完成，並經由顧百里老師審訂。為了不僅編一本編者觀點的語言書，更希望編一本學習者適用的工具書。於是雖於 Covid-19 疫情期間，本書仍進行了試教。試教的學生是由印度中心由 396 位報名的印度學生中，面試挑選出 26 位，經由 9 位華語講師分組線上上課。另外，本書編寫教師之一的劉殿敏老師也試教兩組學生，共 7 名印度學生。主編和三位編寫教師依據學生和講師們對本教材的建議，再次斟酌修改課文。

　　編寫一套教材過程繁瑣艱辛，絕非一人之心力所能完成，相信許多先進均能感同身受。故此，感謝所有參與此華語教材編寫的老師和審查委員，試教課程中的華語老師和印度學生。劉殿敏老師和陳姿靜老師提供本書許多印度景點的相片，跨院國際碩士學位學程華教組碩士生林怡秀小姐協助校對與排版，印度中心專案經理鍾睿婕小姐及蔡恩祥先生提供完善的行政支援，以及王潔予老師當我們團隊的印度文化顧問，在此致上由衷的謝意。此外，感謝教育部經費的支持，和王偉中主任大力促成此書的編寫，終於完成此系列書籍的初試與探索。希望此書在印度華語教材和臺印文化交流上扮演著領頭羊的角色，更期盼拋磚引玉，更多華語教學界的學者共同朝向此目標前進，能專門為在印度學習華語的學習者編寫更多元、更適性的華語教材，是為所祈。

主編 陳淑芬

辛丑秋初謹識於國立清華大學中文系

Preface II

As early as 2011, Prof. Wei-Chung Wang, Director of Center for India Studies, National Tsing Hua University (NTHU), was assigned the mission to establish "Taiwan Education Center in India" (TEC). Till date, nine institutions are hosting the operation of TEC, collaborating with the Ministry of Education, R.O.C. (Taiwan), which dispatches Mandarin Chinese language instructors from Taiwan to offer courses in higher education in India. Given that the Mandarin textbooks currently used by Indian universities are quite outdated, bearing a large gap with the Indian culture and condition of the nation, TEC has been proactive in advancing pedagogies and teaching materials. Prof. Wang, in a joint effort with Prof. Chen-Cheng Chun, former Director of Graduate Institute of Teaching Chinese as a Second/Foreign Language, National Kaohsiung Normal University (NKNU), organized "The First India-Taiwan Bilateral Forum on Mandarin Chinese Teaching Materials for Indian Learners" in Jawaharlal Nehru University (JNU) in March 2017, and "The Second India-Taiwan Bilateral Forum on Mandarin Chinese Teaching Materials for Indian Learners" in Amity University in May 2018. The third forum, initially planned to be held in India in April 2020, was later suspended due to the difficult situation of the COVID-19 pandemic. Yet, the Center for India Studies did not give up on promoting Mandarin Chinese education. Instead, the center held a preparatory meeting for "The Third India-Taiwan Bilateral Forum on Mandarin Chinese Teaching Materials for Indian Learners" at NTHU on 9 March 2020. During this meeting, we decided to compile country-specific Mandarin Chinese teaching materials specially designed for Indian learners, and I was elected as the editor-in-chief.

Concerning that teaching tasks were not to be hindered another second, after preliminary work, we immediately called for the first meeting for compiling a Mandarin Chinese language textbook for India. We invited Instructor Ching-Hua Chen and Instructor Diane Dien-Min Liu from Mandarin Training Center, National Taiwan Normal University (NTNU), and Prof. Felicia Zhen Zhang from the Master Program of Teaching Chinese as a Second Language, Chinese Culture University (CCU), to co-author this textbook. In addition, eight Mandarin instructors from TEC: Ms. Woanyuh Zoë Tsou, Ms.Ling-Yun Tsai, Mr. Hao-Cheng Wang, Ms.Yi Ying Hsiao, Ms. Chia-Ling Wu, Ms. Jessica Wang, Ms.Chia-Yin Lai, and Ms.Hsiao-Hui Yuan, also joined us for an initial discussion on the central theme and the main topics of the textbook.

The ten lessons of this textbook are threaded by an interesting story, introducing cultural highlights of Taiwan and India through cross-culture comparison. The four leading characters in the story overturn our stereotypical impression. The female manager and the male secretary of a Taiwan jewelry company go on a week's business trip to "Incredible India". In the textbook, the male secretary Mr. Wei-Chung Wang is based on the current Director of the Center for Indian Studies with the same name and surname, an actual "India Expert," having traveled between India and Taiwan 44 times so far to facilitate interactions between the two countries. He promoted Mandarin Chinese language education under harsh situations in India. Thousands of Indian students are learning Mandarin in traditional characters, and many Indian students are encouraged to study overseas in Taiwan. Although Prof. Wang is not an expert in Mandarin Chinese and language teaching, he is undoubtedly the meritorious contributor to Taiwan's Mandarin Chinese language education in India. Editors and instructors who contributed their teaching career in India would like to carve a niche for Prof. Wang's name and publish this textbook to appreciate the selfless dedication and sincere contribution Prof. Wang has devoted to the exchanges between Taiwan and India.

The target audience of this textbook is designed for university students who are learning Mandarin Chinese for the second year in India. The material before this textbook is *A Course in Contemporary Chinese, Volume 1*, published by Linking Publishing. It would provide a foundation in common vocabulary and usages for the learner. With an exclusive license NTHU has received from Linking Publishing, all nine TEC offices use *A Course in Contemporary Chinese* around India. In accordance, this textbook adopts the same system for parts of speech in *A Course in Contemporary Chinese*, which Prof. Shou-Hsin Teng has edited, for better cohesion in learning. This textbook is targeted at students with Chinese skills at A2-B1 levels of the Common European Framework of Reference for Languages (CEFR) and designed with localized content aiming at cultural comparison and language learning for communication. Each lesson is divided into seven parts:

1. Lesson Objectives and Topics: Each lesson has lesson objectives and a particular topic and provides a contextual picture related to the lesson as a guide to introduce students to the topic of the lesson.

2. Dialogues: The dialogue for each lesson is about 14-18 turn-takings between interlocutors. Content of the dialogues in each of the ten lessons are developing plots to the story. Starting with Manager Zhou and Secretary Wang preparing for their India visit, venturing a very different cultural experience in India, and finally heading back to Taiwan. The lively dialogues are to motivate students' autonomous learning through these interesting plots.

3. Readings: The essay for reading in each lesson is about 300 words. The content is related to the topic of the lesson, mainly introducing various aspects of Taiwanese culture. Some compare the similarities and differences between Indian and Taiwanese cultures, and some provide critical thinking in cross-cultures, allowing students to understand and respect more about cultural diversity from language learning.

4. Vocabulary, Proper Nouns, and Phrases: New vocabulary and phrases are listed after the dialogue and reading of each lesson. The number of the vocabulary in each lesson is maintained within 40. Moreover, the explanations of new words and phrases are based on the meanings that appear in the lesson. Hanyu Pinyin, part of speech, and English translation are listed for each vocabulary.

5. Grammar: Four to five grammar points are selected from the dialogue and reading for each lesson. Systematic explanations, examples, various practices, and comparisons to similar usages are provided to assist students' acquisition and proficiency.

6. Cross-Cultural Extension: This section is written mainly in English for students to understand the cultural differences between India and Taiwan, fostering international perspectives and diverse visions. A Chinese version is provided in Appendix III as a

supplementary for advanced reading.

7. Language Tasks: Two language tasks are designed for each lesson. The authors use grammar points of each lesson to design task-based teaching activities and provide a variety of communicative language tasks. In this way, students can learn practical usages of the language and improve their oral proficiency.

The teachers responsible for writing each lesson of the books are as follows:

- Felicia Zhen Zhang: Lessons 1 and 2.
- Diane Dien-Min Liu: Lessons 3, 5, 6, and 7.
- Ching-Hua Chen: Lessons 4, 8, 9, and 10.

Despite there being one author responsible for each lesson, nearly 20 editorial meetings were held for the content of each lesson by the three authors and me. In addition, I have also held numerous individual meetings with each of the three authors to discuss the details of the texts and grammar points before finalizing the draft. Special thanks to the three reviewers: Prof. Cornelius C. Kubler, Department of Asian Languages, Literatures, and Cultures, Williams College, U.S., Professor Emeritus Teh-Ming Yeh, Department of Chinese as a Second Language, NTNU, and Prof. Li-Ping Chang, Graduate Program of Teaching Chinese as a Second Language, National Taiwan University (NTU), for reviewing and proofreading, providing invaluable editorial suggestions in perfecting this textbook. This textbook is translated into English by Prof. Felicia Zhen Zhang and proofread by Prof. Cornelius C. Kubler.

Although most language textbooks are written from the authors' perspectives, we want this textbook to be a handy tool book for learners; thus, we still managed to conduct pilot courses to test this textbook during the severe situation under the COVID-19 pandemic. Twenty-six students were elected and interviewed out of 396 Indian students who signed up as participants for our pilot courses. These 26 students are grouped and dispatched among nine Mandarin Chinese instructors' online courses. One of the authors, Ms. Diane Dien-Min Liu, also taught two groups, with seven Indian students in total. The editor-in-chief and the three co-authors revised the content according to the pilot courses' feedback from students and instructors.

I believe pioneers and others in the field would share the same thought that compiling a teaching material is straining and arduous and that it would be impossible with the effort of a single person. Therefore, I am thankful to all co-authors, consultants, and reviewers, as well as students and the Mandarin Chinese instructors from the pilot courses, and all who participated in the editorial of this Mandarin Chinese textbook. Thanks to seamless administrative support from Ms. Sophie Chung, Senior Program Manager and Mr. Jim Tsai, Program Manager of Program Office for TEC in India at NTHU, and Yi-Xiu Lin, MA student of International Intercollegiate Program, MA Teaching Chinese as a Second/Foreign Language at NTHU in assisting with proofreading and typesetting. A hearty appreciation to our Indian culture consultant, Ms. Jessica Wang, and the many pictures of India provided by Ms. Diane Dien-Min Liu and Ms. Ginger Chen. Furthermore, we would like to express our gratitude towards the financial sponsorship from the Ministry of Education and Prof. Wei-Chung Wang's vigorous effort in the making of this textbook. We have finally started the trial and set foot on the expedition of language education materials for Indian learners. For an even better cross-cultural communication between India and Taiwan, we sincerely hope this textbook would lead more scholars to join us in developing and providing more diverse and adaptive teaching materials for learners in India.

Chief Editor
Shu-Fen Chen
Department of Chinese Literature, NTHU, 2021

Scope and Sequence

各課重點

課數	標題	課文屬性	課程目標
第一課	印度，我們來了！	出訪前準備	1. 能說明出訪前準備。 2. 能了解並比較臺灣與印度的送禮習俗。 3. 能了解臺灣和印度兩國女性就業的情況。
第二課	接風	餐桌禮儀	1. 能了解印度和臺灣安排座位的禮節。 2. 能了解在印度做客的禮節。 3. 能了解臺灣與印度社群媒體（LINE vs. WhatsApp）使用的差異。
第三課	自由行	交通	1. 能介紹印度大城市的主要交通工具。 2. 能介紹臺灣和印度都會地鐵的特點。 3. 能介紹一般平民化的交通工具。
第四課	熱鬧的排燈節	節日慶典	1. 能了解排燈節對印度人的意義。 2. 能了解排燈節的活動內容。 3. 能比較印度排燈節點油燈與臺灣春節點光明燈的異同。 4. 能適時、適地使用中文的祝賀語。
第五課	去喝喜酒	婚禮文化	1. 能使用有關婚禮的相關詞彙。 2. 能介紹印度婚禮新娘的服飾、繞火堆等傳統。 3. 能了解參加印度婚禮的服飾、禮金等習俗。 4. 能說明臺灣現代婚禮形式。
第六課	古蹟的故事	古蹟巡禮	1. 能概略介紹泰姬瑪哈陵。 2. 能簡單說明印度陵寢的設計文化。 3. 能概略介紹兵馬俑。 4. 能對古蹟維護表示感謝。

語法	跨文化延伸
1. A 離 B 2. V 過 3. 會……的 4. 為了	女性就業
1. V＋「到1」和「到2」 2. V 著 3. 正/在/正在 4. 把……V＋在/到2/給	臺印社群媒體使用差異（LINE vs.WhatsApp）
1.「被」字句 2. V 著 V 著，就……了 3. 差不多 4. V 來 V 去	三輪車跑得快
1. ……呢 2. V＋得／不＋結果補語／趨向補語 3. 一點都／也不 4. V 好	中文的祝賀語
1. Vs 極了、Vs 得不得了、Vs 得很 2. V 起來1 3. 連……都／也…… 4. 越……，越……	婚禮昏禮
1. 只要……，就…… 2. V 起 3. 趨向動詞＋來／去 4. 才1／才2	古蹟的科學

課數	標題	課文屬性	課程目標
第七課	逛逛市集	民俗文化	1. 能說明印度市集的概況。 2. 能了解市集是印度人民的重要經濟活動。 3. 能比較印度市集與臺灣夜市的異同。
第八課	養生的方法	健康養生	1. 能了解印度傳統的養生方法。 2. 能比較兩種人或事物的異同。 3. 能了解中醫與阿育吠陀的共同點。
第九課	伴手禮	文化禮俗	1. 能知道印度特產及如何挑選適合的伴手禮。 2. 能了解印度的珠寶文化和中國的玉文化。 3. 能了解伴手禮所代表的意義及其效應。
第十課	歡送會	惜別	1. 能明白惜別會的意義。 2. 能聊惜別會中的相關話題。 3. 能知道珠寶展覽會怎麼宣傳。 4. 能了解臺灣、印度不同的商務談判方式。

Lesson	Title	Topic	Lesson Objectives
Lesson 1	India, Here We Come!	Pre-departure Preparation	1. Students can explain what to prepare before departure. 2. Students can understand and compare the customs of gift-giving in both Taiwan and India. 3. Students can understand employment situations for females in both Taiwan and India.
Lesson 2	Holding a Welcome Reception	Table Manners	1. Students can understand etiquette for the seating arrangements in restaurants in India and in Taiwan. 2. Students can understand the etiquette of being a guest in an Indian home. 3. Students can understand the differences in social networking tools in Taiwan and India (Line vs. WhatsApp)

語法	跨文化延伸
1. 什麼的 2. 一邊……，一邊…… 3. 幾 4. 然後 5. 雙音節狀態動詞重疊（ABAB 式）	臺印的素食文化
1. 不但……，而且…… 2. 對……有…… 3. A 跟 B 比起來 4. V 起來$_2$	中醫與阿育吠陀
1. 除了……以外，還 / 也…… 2. 雙音節動詞重疊（ABAB 式） 3. 只有……，才$_3$…… 4. V 完	中國的玉文化
1. 不但……，還 / 也…… 2. V 上 3. 才$_3$ 4. 從來 + 不 / 沒	臺印不同的商務談判方式

Grammar	Cross-Cultural Extension
1. Distance from with 離 *lí* 2. Verb with Experience Particle 過 *guò* 3. To offer assurance with 會 *huì* ……的 *de* 4. 為了 *wèile* in order to	Female Employment
1. Resultative complement V + 到$_1$ *dào*$_1$ and Destination Marker 到$_2$ *dào*$_2$ 2. Manner of an Action with V + 著 *zhe* 3. Progressive, on-going actions 正 *zhèng*/在 *zài*/正在 *zhèngzài* 4. To dispose of Something with 把 *bǎ* ……V + 在 *zài* / 到$_2$ *dào*$_2$/給 *gěi*	Differences in the Use of Social Media Tools in Taiwan and India (Line vs. WhatsApp)

Lesson	Title	Topic	Lesson Objectives
Lesson 3	Self-organized tours	Transport	1. Students can introduce the primary means of transport used in big cities in India. 2. Students can introduce the special characteristics of Taiwan and Indian city subways. 3. Students can introduce the means of transport used by ordinary people.
Lesson 4	The Lively Diwali	Festival Celebrations	1. Students can understand the meaning of Diwali for Indian people. 2. Students can understand the content and activities of the Diwali festival. 3. Students can compare the differences between "lighting oil lamps" on Diwali in India and "lighting the good-fortune lamps" on Chinese New Year in Taiwan. 4. Students can use Chinese congratulatory phrases on suitable occasions.
Lesson 5	Going to a Wedding Reception	The Wedding Culture	1. Students can use vocabulary related to weddings. 2. Students can introduce traditions such as newlywed's costumes, dancing around the fire, etc. 3. Students can understand the customs of attending Indian weddings, such as costumes and gift money. 4. Students can describe modern wedding forms in Taiwan.
Lesson 6	Stories of Ancient Monuments	A Tour of Ancient Monuments	1. Students can briefly introduce the Taj Mahal. 2. Students can explain the design and culture associated with Indian mausoleums. 3. Students can introduce the Terracotta Army. 4. Students can learn to be thankful for the preservation of such ancient sites.

Grammar	Cross-Cultural Extension
1. Passive sentences with 被 *bèi* 2. "While doing A, B happens" with V 著 *zhe* V 著 *zhe*, 就 *jiù*... 了 *le* 3. 差不多 *chàbuduō* Almost 4. V 來 *lái* V 去 *qù* 　　V come V go	Tricycles Run Fast
1. ……呢 *ne* 2. V + 得 *de* / 不 *bu* + resultative complements or directional complements 3. Emphatic Negation with 一點 *yìdiǎn* 都 *dōu* / 也 *yě* 不 *bù* 4. Complement with V 好 *hǎo*	Congratulatory Phrases in Chinese
1. Adverbial Complements 極了 *jí le*, 得不得了 *de bùdéliǎo*, 得很 *de hěn* 2. Judgmental V 起來 *qǐlái₁* it's my assessment that…… 3. 連 *lián*……都 *dōu*/也 *yě* even 4. 越 *yuè* ……，越 *yuè* …… 　　the more……, the more ……	The Wedding Ceremony
1. 只要 *zhǐyào* ……，就 *jiù* …… *As long as* ..., 2. V + Verb Particle 起 *qǐ* to touch upon 3. Directional Verbs + 來 *lái* / 去 *qù* 4. 才₁ *cái₁* / 才₂ *cái₂* 　　(1) merely, only; 　　(2) longer/later than expected	The Science of Monuments

Lesson	Title	Topic	Lesson Objectives
Lesson 7	Going to the market	Folk Culture	1. Students can explain an overview of the Indian market. 2. Students can gain an understanding of the market being an important economic activity for the people of India. 3. Students can compare the similarities and differences between Indian bazaars and night markets in Taiwan.
Lesson 8	Ways of Keeping Healthy	Health and Wellness	1. Students can learn about traditional Indian health methods. 2. Students can compare the similarities and differences between two kinds of people or things. 3. Students can understand what Chinese medicine and Ayurveda have in common.
Lesson 9	Souvenirs	Cultural Etiquette	1. Students can know about Indian local specialties and choose the right souvenirs. 2. Students can gain information about India's jewelry culture and China's jade culture. 3. Students can understand the meaning and effect of souvenirs.
Lesson 10	The Farewell Dinner	Saying Goodbye	1. Students can understand the meaning of a farewell dinner. 2. Students can chat about relevant topics at the farewell party. 3. Students can understand how jewelry is advertised at the jewelry fair. 4. Students can learn about the different ways of negotiating business in Taiwan and India.

Grammar	Cross-Cultural Extension
1. 什麼的 *shénmede* things like (that), etc. 2. 一邊 *yìbiān*……一邊 *yìbiān* two simultaneous actions with 3. 幾 *jǐ* a few, several 4. 然後 *ránhòu* "then" 5. Reduplication of Disyllabic Adjectives (AABB)	The Vegetarian Cultures of Taiwan and India
1. 不但 *búdàn* ……，而且 *érqiě* ……not only……, but also…… 2. 對 *duì* ……有 *yǒu* …… towards …… 3. A 跟 *gēn* B 比起來 *bǐqǐlái* A compared with B 4. Inchoative Meaning with V 起來₂ *qǐlái*	Traditional Chinese Medicine and Ayurveda
1. 除了 *chúle* ……以外 *yǐwài*，還 *hái* / 也 *yě* …… in addition to ……, besides …… 2. Tentative Action with Reduplicated Disyllabic Verbs ABAB 3. 只有 *zhǐyǒu* ……，才₃ *cái*₃ …… cannot……, unless…… 4. Completion of an Action with V + 完 *wán*	China's Jade Culture
1. 不但 *búdàn*……，還 *hái* / 也 *yě* ……not only……, but also…… 2. Verb particle *shàng* 3. 才₃ *cái*₃ then and only then 4. 從來 *cónglái* + 不 *bù* / 沒 *méi* Never	Different Ways of Business Negotiation Between Taiwan and India

詞類表 Parts of Speech

Eight Major Parts of Speech in Chinese

Abbreviations	Parts of Speech	Chinese Terms	Examples
N	noun	名詞	經理、合約、禮盒、貴賓、家鄉、甜點
V	verb	動詞	送、整理、了解、建議、邀請、報名、欣賞
Adv	adverb	副詞	很、不、相當、難怪、不久、順便、特地
Conj	conjunction	連詞	和、而、而且、雖然、可是、所以、如果
Prep	preposition	介詞	從、給、在、跟、趁、按照、透過
M	measure	量詞	個、張、罐、節、套、趟、伏特
Ptc	particle	助詞	的、得、了、嗎、吧、把、被
Det	determiner	限定詞	這、那、每、哪、各、其他、另外

Verb Classification

Abbreviations			Classification	Chinese Terms	Examples
V	V		transitive action verbs	及物動作動詞	招待、拜訪、舉辦
	Vi	Vi	intransitive action verbs	不及物動作動詞	走、接風、做客
		V-sep	intransitive action verbs, separable	不及物動作離合詞	殺價、塞車、敬酒
Vs	Vs	Vs	intransitive state verbs	不及物狀態動詞	飽、擠、成功、熱情
		Vs-attr	intransitive state verbs, attributive only	唯定不及物狀態動詞	主要、一般、頂級
		Vs-pred	intransitive state verbs, predicative only	唯謂不及物狀態動詞	多、少、夠、差

Abbreviations			Classification	Chinese Terms	Examples
		Vs-sep	intransitive state verbs, separable	不及物狀態離合詞	放心、生氣、傷心
	Vst		transitive state verbs	及物狀態動詞	喜歡、尊重、吸引
	Vaux		auxiliary verbs	助動詞	會、能、可以、應該
Vp	Vp	Vp	intransitive process verbs	不及物變化動詞	死、消失、結束
		Vp-sep	intransitive process verbs	不及物變化離合詞	結婚、生病、畢業
	Vpt		transitive process verbs, separable	及物變化動詞	發現、離開、忘記

Default Values of the Verbs

Abbreviations	Default values
V	action, transitive
Vs	state, intransitive
Vp	process, intransitive
V-sep	separable, intransitive

主要人物介紹
Introduction to the Main Characters

周經理
Manager Zhou

周依琳，珠寶公司經理。約 45 歲，長髮飄逸，總是穿著套裝，高跟鞋；個性爽朗，為人率真，是個工作狂。

Yi-Lin Zhou is the manager of a jewelry company. She is about 45 years old with long, flowing hair. She likes to wear suits and high heels. She has an open personality, is sincere and straightforward, and is a workaholic.

王祕書
Secretary Wang

王偉中（綽號小鮮肉），對印度十分了解，去過印度 44 次，有瑜珈證照。38 歲，喜歡印度文化，西裝頭，穿著時尚，喜愛粉紅色襯衫。為人熱情幽默，喜歡開玩笑。

Wei-Zhong Wang (nicknamed "the Hunk") is a real India expert. He has been to India 44 times and has a yoga license. He is a 38-year-old who loves Indian culture. He sports a Western-style haircut and is fond of wearing the latest fashionable clothes, such as a stylish pink shirt. He is very warm and humorous and likes to joke a lot.

韋經理
Manager Wei

韋夏爾（Vishal），北印人，長期跟臺灣有生意往來，娶了臺灣太太，會說中文。將近 60 歲，戴眼鏡，穿傳統印度服裝，戴頭巾，拿公事包。個性謹慎，不愛說話。

Vishal is a North Indian male who has had long-term business dealings with Taiwan and has a Taiwanese wife. He is fluent in Chinese. He is nearly 60 years old, wears glasses, and is always in traditional Indian garb with a headscarf. He is always seen with a brief-case in hand, cautious and reticent in his speech.

桑吉
Sanji

桑吉，40 多歲家族珠寶企業的經理，長相帥氣，內涵不錯，受過西式教育，勇於追求愛情，希望和周經理發展姊弟戀。

Sanji is in his 40s and is the manager of a family jewelry business. He is a handsome and good-natured man with a Western-style education. He has the courage to pursue love and hopes to develop a sister-brother loving relationship with Manager Zhou.

目錄
Contents

第一課 印度，我們來了！
Lesson 1 India, Here We Come!

課程目標：

Topic：出訪前準備

    1. 能說明出訪前準備。

    2. 能了解並比較臺灣與印度的送禮習俗。

    3. 能了解臺灣和印度兩國女性就業的情況。

Lesson Objectives：

Topic：Pre-departure Preparation

    1. Students can explain what to prepare before departure.

    2. Students can understand and compare the customs of gift giving in both Taiwan and India.

    3. Students can understand employment situations for women in both Taiwan and India.

Lesson 1

在臺灣公司辦公室，周經理與王祕書討論，該買什麼見面禮。

In the office of the Taiwan company, Manager Zhou and Secretary Wang are discussing what they should buy as gifts for when they first meet people.

對話 Dialogue 🎧

周經理：去印度，我們應該帶什麼禮物？

王祕書：因為宗教的關係，我們不能送皮類和酒類的東西。

周經理：那應該送什麼？

王祕書：我們多帶幾罐臺灣烏龍茶好了！

周經理：好。現在新德里是春天嗎？

王祕書：是的，不冷不熱，帶一件薄外套就好了。

周經理：電壓是跟臺灣一樣是 110 伏特嗎？插頭是什麼形狀的？

王祕書：電壓是 220 伏特，插頭是三孔圓形的。

周經理：從臺北到新德里要坐多久的飛機？

王祕書：臺灣離印度有一點遠，不過，大概七個小時能到。

周經理：最重要的是別忘了帶合約。

王祕書：沒問題。文件我都整理好了。

周經理：辛苦了。有人來接我們嗎？

王祕書：放心，有人會來接我們的。

課文漢語拼音 Text in Hanyu Pinyin

Zhōu jīnglǐ :	Qù Yìndù, wǒmen yīnggāi dài shénme lǐwù?
Wáng mìshū :	Yīnwèi zōngjiào de guānxì, wǒmen bù néng sòng pílèi hàn jiǔlèi de dōngxi.
Zhōu jīnglǐ :	Nà yīnggāi sòng shénme?
Wáng mìshū :	Wǒmen duō dài jǐ guàn Táiwān wūlóngchá hǎole!
Zhōu jīnglǐ :	Hǎo. Xiànzài Xīn Délǐ shì chūntiān ma?
Wáng mìshū :	Shì de, bùlěng búrè, dài yí jiàn bó wàitào jiù hǎole.
Zhōu jīnglǐ :	Diànyā shì gēn Táiwān yíyàng shì yìbǎi yīshí fútè ma? Chātóu shì shénme xíngzhuàng de?
Wáng mìshū :	Diànyā shì liǎngbǎi èrshí fútè, chātóu shì sān kǒng yuánxíng de.
Zhōu jīnglǐ :	Cóng Táiběi dào Xīn Délǐ yào zuò duōjiǔ de fēijī?
Wáng mìshū :	Táiwān lí Yìndù yǒu yìdiǎnyuǎn, búguò, dàgài qī ge xiǎoshí néng dào.
Zhōu jīnglǐ :	Zuì zhòngyào de shì bié wàngle dài héyuē.
Wáng mìshū :	Méi wèntí. Wénjiàn wǒ dōu zhěnglǐ hǎole.
Zhōu jīnglǐ :	Xīnkǔ le. Yǒu rén lái jiē wǒmen ma?
Wáng mìshū :	Fàngxīn, yǒu rén huì lái jiē wǒmen de.

Lesson 1

課文英譯 Text in English

Dialogue

Manager Zhou : What should we take when we go to India?

Secretary Wang : For religious reasons, we cannot give leather and alcoholic goods as presents.

Manager Zhou : What should we give them as presents then?

Secretary Wang : I think it would be best if we take a few cans of Taiwanese Oolong tea.

Manager Zhou : Good. Is it Spring in New Dehli now?

Secretary Wang : Yes, it's neither cold nor hot, taking a light jacket with you will be just fine.

Manager Zhou : Is the voltage 110 volts like in Taiwan? What shape is the plug?

Secretary Wang : The voltage is 220 volts. The plug has a round head with three holes.

Manager Zhou : How long does it take by plane from Taipei to New Dehli?

Secretary Wang : Taipei is a bit far from India. But it would probably take about seven hours to arrive.

Manager Zhou : The most important thing is not to forget to take the contract with you.

Secretary Wang : No problems. I have already organized all the documentation.

Manager Zhou : Thanks for all the hard work. Will someone meet us there?

Secretary Wang : Don't worry, someone will come and pick us up.

生詞一 Vocabulary I 🎧

編號	生詞	漢語拼音	詞性	英文翻譯
1.	經理	jīnglǐ	N	manager
2.	祕書	mìshū	N	secretary
3.	宗教	zōngjiào	N	religion
4.	關係	guānxì	N	reason, condition
5.	皮類	pílèi	N	leather type
6.	酒類	jiǔlèi	N	liquor type
7.	罐	guàn	M	measure word for a can
8.	薄	bó	Vs	thin
9.	電壓	diànyā	N	voltage
10.	伏特	fútè	M	volt
11.	插頭	chātóu	N	plug
12.	形狀	xíngzhuàng	N	shape
13.	孔	kǒng	N	hole
14.	圓形	yuánxíng	N	round shape
15.	合約	héyuē	N	contract
16.	文件	wénjiàn	N	document
17.	整理	zhěnglǐ	V	to put in order, to arrange

專有名詞 Proper Nouns

編號	生詞	漢語拼音	英文翻譯
1.	新德里	Xīn Délǐ	New Delhi

短語 Phrases

編號	生詞	漢語拼音	英文翻譯
1.	辛苦了	Xīnkǔ le.	You have been working so hard.

短文 Reading 🎧

見面禮

　　周經理是臺灣清華珠寶公司的業務經理，今年三月計畫去印度談合作案，這是她第一次去印度。雖然她的英文非常好，但是她對印度文化不太了解，更不會說印地語，需要一位有經驗的祕書一起去，所以她找了王偉中當祕書。王偉中是位印度通，不但去過印度44次，還會說印地語，也非常了解印度各地的風俗文化。

　　這次他們要去印度談珠寶設計的合作案，得帶見面禮給對方。周經理出發前在臺北買了一些合適的禮物。為了尊重當地的宗教信仰，酒類和皮類的禮物都不合適。所以王祕書建議買一些臺灣有名的茶葉禮盒送給對方。

課文漢語拼音 Text in Hanyu Pinyin

Jiànmiànlǐ

　　Zhōu jīnglǐ shì Táiwān Qīnghuá zhūbǎo gōngsī de yèwù jīnglǐ. Jīnnián sān yuè jìhuà qù Yìndù tán hézuò'àn. Zhè shì tā dì yī cì qù Yìndù, suīrán tā de Yīngwén fēicháng hǎo, dànshì tā duì Yìndù wénhuà bú tài liǎojiě, gèng bú huì shuō Yìndìyǔ, xūyào yí wèi yǒu jīngyàn de mìshū yìqǐ qù, suǒyǐ tā zhǎole Wáng Wěizhōng dāng mìshū. Wáng Wěizhōng shì wèi Yìndù tōng, búdàn qùguò Yìndù 44 cì, hái huì shuō Yìndìyǔ, yě fēicháng liǎojiě Yìndù gèdì de fēngsú wénhuà.

第一課　印度，我們來了！India, Here We Come!

Zhè cì tāmen yào qù Yìndù tán zhūbǎo shèjì de hézuò'àn, děi dài jiànmiànlǐ gěi duìfāng. Zhōu jīnglǐ chūfā qián zài Táiběi mǎile yìxiē héshì de lǐwù. Wèile zūnzhòng dāngdì de zōngjiào xìnyǎng, jiǔlèi hàn pílèi de lǐwù dōu bù héshì. Suǒyǐ Wáng mìshū jiànyì mǎi yìxiē Táiwān yǒumíng de cháyè lǐhé sòng gěi duìfāng.

課文英譯 Text in English

Introductory Gifts

Manager Zhou is the business manager of Taiwan Tsinghua Jewelry Company. In March this year, she plans to go to India to discuss a cooperative project. This is her first time to India. Although her English is very good, she does not know much about Indian culture, let alone speak Hindi. She needs an experienced secretary to go with her, so she is taking Wei-Zhong Wang along as secretary. Wei-Zhong Wang is an India expert. Not only has he been to India 44 times, he also speaks Hindi and knows the culture and social customs of various parts of India very well.

This time they are going to India to discuss a cooperative project in jewelry design, and they need to bring an introductory gift to give to their partner. Manager Zhou bought some suitable gifts in Taipei before leaving. As a show of respect for local religious beliefs, alcohol and leather gifts are not appropriate. Therefore, Secretary Wang suggested that they buy some famous tea gift boxes from Taiwan to give as gifts to the other party.

生詞二 Vocabulary II 🎧

編號	生詞	漢語拼音	詞性	英文翻譯
1.	珠寶	zhūbǎo	N	jewelry
2.	業務	yèwù	N	professional work, business
3.	計畫	jìhuà	V	to plan to
4.	談	tán	V	to discuss
5.	文化	wénhuà	N	culture
6.	了解	liǎojiě	V	to understand
7.	經驗	jīngyàn	N	experience
8.	各地	gèdì	N	in all parts of (a country); various regions
9.	風俗	fēngsú	N	social custom
10.	設計	shèjì	N	design
11.	對方	duìfāng	N	the other party
12.	合適	héshì	Vs	suitable
13.	尊重	zūnzhòng	Vst	to respect
14.	當地	dāngdì	N	local
15.	信仰	xìnyǎng	N	belief, faith
16.	建議	jiànyì	V	to suggest
17.	茶葉	cháyè	N	tea
18.	禮盒	lǐhé	N	gift box
19.	送	sòng	V	to give as a present

專有名詞 Proper Nouns

編號	生詞	漢語拼音	英文翻譯
1.	印地語	Yìndìyǔ	Hindi

短語 Phrases

編號	生詞	漢語拼音	英文翻譯
1.	合作案	hézuò'àn	cooperative project
2.	印度通	Yìndù tōng	someone who is an expert on India

語法 Grammar 🎧

一、A 離 lí B　　Distance from with 離 lí

說明：「離」是一個介詞，它的作用是標記著從 A 點和 B 點之間的距離，後面的主要謂語通常是表距離的狀態動詞，如「遠」或「近」。此外，跟大部分的介詞不一樣，「離」不能直接加否定詞「不」。在否定句中，「不」應該放在狀態動詞的前面。

Explanation：離 *lí* is a preposition whose function is to mark the distance between point A and point B. The main predicate in the back is usually a state verb that expresses distance, such as "far" 遠 *yuǎn* or "near" 近 *jìn*. In addition, unlike most prepositions, 不 *bù* cannot be directly added to 離 *lí*. In negative sentences, 不 *bù* should be placed before the state verb.

例句：

1. 我家離大學宿舍很遠。
2. 學校離咖啡店很近。
3. 新竹離臺北不太遠。
4. 學校離公車站有多遠？

Lesson 1

練習：請回答以下問題。

Exercise：Please answer the following questions.

    1. 你家離大學是不是很遠？

    2. 臺北離新德里有多遠？（4392 公里）

    3. 學校離商場遠不遠？

    4. 這個房子離捷運站有多遠？（100 公尺）（捷運站：jiéyùn zhàn, Metro station）

    5. 大學離書店很近嗎？

二、會⋯的 *huì...de*　　To offer assurance with 會 *huì*⋯的 *de*

說明：「會⋯的」表明說話者確信將來會發生什麼事情。「會」表示動作或狀態的可能性，而句末的語氣助詞「的」表示說話者斷言將來事情發生的可能性。

Explanation：會 *huì*⋯的 *de* indicates that the speaker confirms what will happen in the future. 會 *huì* means the possibility of an action or state, and the modal particle 的 *de* at the end of the sentence asserts the possibility of a future event.

例句：

    1. 你吃東西吃得太多，會胖的。

    2. 你放心，你說的話，我不會告訴別人的。

    3. 他會來參加舞會的。

練習：請用「會⋯的」完成下面的句子。

Exercise：Please use 會 *huì*⋯的 *de* to complete the following sentences.

1. A：媽媽已經病了三年了。

   B：放心，＿＿＿＿＿＿＿＿＿＿＿＿＿＿＿。

2. A：我覺得大家還不太注意文化不同的問題。

   B：＿＿＿＿＿＿＿＿＿＿＿＿＿＿＿。

3. A：學了這麼久的中文，我覺得沒進步。

   B：只要你多練習，＿＿＿＿＿＿＿＿＿＿＿＿＿＿＿。

4. A：我在臺北找房子找了這麼久，什麼時候能找到啊！

   B：你放心，你一定＿＿＿＿＿＿＿＿＿＿＿＿＿＿＿。

5. A：怎麼辦？這幾個字學生們總是念錯。（明白）

   B：沒問題，多學幾次他們就＿＿＿＿＿＿＿＿＿＿＿＿＿＿＿。

三、V 過 *guò*　　Verb with Experience Particle 過 *guò*

說明：「過」是動態助詞，「V 過」描述過去對那個動作的經歷。跟經驗有關的句子通常會包括時間的長短度，頻率和非特定的過去時間。在這個句型的否定式中，僅能使用「沒」。

Explanation：過 *guò* is an aspect particle. V *guò* describes the past experience of the action. Sentences related to past experience usually include the length of time, frequency, and unspecified time in the past. In the negative of this sentence pattern, only 沒 *méi* can be used.

例句：

1. 我去過印度 44 次。
2. 我沒喝過臺灣烏龍茶。
3. 你在印度買過珠寶嗎？

練習：下列的詞重新排列為有意義的順序。

Exercise：Please rearrange the following sequences of words into meaningful sentences.

1.	學	過	臺灣	我	去	中文
2.	英文	也	我	過	教	
3.	住	三年	也	我	在	英國 過
4.	點心	我	這	吃	種	沒 過
5.	了	你	印度	看	電影	過 沒有

四、為了 *wèile*　　in order to

說明：「為了」是介詞，是指出要達到的目的，後面可接動詞短語或名詞短語。「為了」的賓語可以是名詞短語或動詞短語。在否定句中，僅能用「別」或「不是」。

Explanation：為了 *wèile* is a preposition, which points out the purpose to be achieved. It can be followed by a verb phrase or a noun phrase. The object of 為了 *wèile* can be a noun phrase or a verb phrase. In a negative sentence, only 別 *bié* or 不是 *bú shì* can be used.

例句：

1. 為了了解印度，我們應該查些資料。
2. 她不是為了錢工作，是為了經驗。
3. 你是不是為了出去玩，所以不來上課？
4. 別只為了他去美國。

練習：請用「為了…」完成下面的句子。

Exercise：Please use 為了 *wèile* ... to complete the following sentences.

1. 你們為什麼學中文？
2. 你們為什麼要去印度？
3. 醫生為什麼說別喝太多可樂？
4. 你們為什麼都買了新衣服？
5. 我們為什麼要住在市中心？

跨文化延伸 Cross-Cultural Extension

Female Employment

You may be a little bit curious; Manager Zhou, who is going to discuss business in India, is a woman! In fact, the working rights of men and women are roughly equal in Taiwan. Many women in Taiwan start working as soon as they graduate from school. There are women in almost every profession, such as female engineers, female managers, female bus drivers, female tour guides, etc.

According to statistics, one out of every ten women in Taiwan is a college graduate. In addition, more and more new service industries are springing up, thus providing women with even more job opportunities. Because of this, the government is also paying attention to their welfare. For example, for female employees to raise their children with peace of mind, eight weeks of paid maternity leave after giving birth is provided for. After taking maternity leave, you can also apply for parental leave without pay. Even for female employees with babies under one year old, time is allocated for them to feed or collect milk every day in the workplace. Such benefits allow married women to work at ease.

In India, from 2005 to the present, not only has the number of women over 15 years old who have a job not increased, it has decreased. Some studies point out the traditional culture of India might be related to this phenomenon. India is a society where "men make decisions." Some reports mentioned that if Indian women have as many job opportunities as Indian men, India's productivity will increase substantially in the future.

語言任務 Language Tasks

一、學生兩個人一組，依照表格中所提供的資訊互相訪問。

Students should form groups of two and interview each other according to the information provided in the table.

	景點名稱（英文）	景點名稱（中文）	景點名稱（拼音）	景點距離（distances）
1.	Janpath market	市民大道商店街	Shìmín Dàdào Shāngdiàn Jiē	0.25 km
2.	Agrasen ki baoli	阿格森階梯水井	Āgésēn Jiētī Shuǐjǐng	0.9 km
3.	Jantar mantar	天文館	Tiānwén Guǎn	0.2 km
4.	Indira Gandhi Airport	甘地夫人機場	Gāndìfūrén Jīchǎng	13 km
5.	Sri Bangla Sahib Gurudwara	錫克教廟	Xíkèjiào Miào	0.73 km
6.	Wenger's	Wenger's 甜點老店	Wenger's tiándiǎn lǎodiàn	0.5 km

例句：A：市民大道商店街離飯店有多少公里？遠不遠？

B：市民大道商店街離飯店有 0.25 公里，不遠，很近。

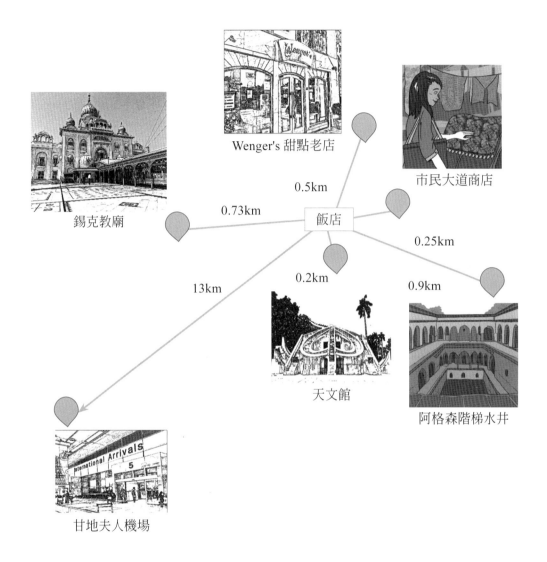

Wenger's 甜點老店

市民大道商店

錫克教廟

飯店

0.5km

0.73km

0.25km

13km

0.2km

0.9km

天文館

阿格森階梯水井

甘地夫人機場

二、用「V 過」討論個人的經驗。

Use V + 過 *guò* to discuss personal experiences.

任務：學生兩個人一組，互相訪問，並將「回答」寫在表格上。

Task：Students should form groups of two, interview each other and then write the answers in the form. This first one has been done for you.

例句：A：你<u>去過</u>臺<u>灣</u>嗎？
　　　B：我<u>去過</u>臺<u>灣</u>。
　　　　 我<u>沒去過</u>臺<u>灣</u>。

	V 過	沒 V 過
去臺灣	去過	沒去過
坐飛機		
吃漢堡		
坐火車		
看中國電影		
學日文		

第二課　接風
Lesson 2　Holding a Welcome Reception

課程目標：

Topic：餐桌禮儀備

    1. 能了解印度和臺灣安排座位的禮節。

    2. 能了解在印度做客的禮節。

    3. 能了解臺灣與印度社群媒體（LINE vs. WhatsApp）使用的差異。

Lesson Objectives：

Topic：Table Manners

    1. Students can understand the etiquette for the seating arrangements in restaurants in India and in Taiwan.

    2. Students can understand the etiquette of being a guest in an Indian home.

    3. Students can understand the differences in social networking tools in Taiwan and India (Line vs. WhatsApp)

對話 Dialogue 🎧

韋經理：周經理，請您坐在門對面。

周經理：謝謝您的座位安排。

韋經理：哪裡，哪裡！您是主要的貴賓，按照禮節應該坐這個位子。

周經理：這裡也有這樣的規矩啊，臺灣也有。

韋經理：您想喝紅葡萄酒還是白葡萄酒？

周經理：我們喝紅葡萄酒吧。

韋經理：好。祝您身體健康，也祝我們合作愉快。

周經理：謝謝您。請問，印地語的乾杯怎麼說？

韋經理：我們跟英文一樣，也說：「Cheers」。

周經理：各位請舉杯，為我們的友誼和合作成功乾杯！

韋經理：我們今天吃到的是新德里有名的奶油咖哩雞（Murgh
　　　　Makhani）。

周經理：好，我嚐一嚐。

韋經理：周經理，飯菜還可口吧？

周經理：道地的 Murgh Makhani 味道真好！

韋經理：那就多吃點。一會兒還有甜點呢。

周經理：謝謝。小王，你還想吃甜點嗎？

王祕書：不好意思，我已經吃飽了，不能再吃了。

周經理：那你就看著我們吃吧！

【電話響了。】

韋經理：對不起，我先接電話。

　　　　喂，我們正在吃飯呢。吃完飯，就去找你。

課文漢語拼音 Text in Hanyu Pinyin

Wéi jīnglǐ：Zhōu jīnglǐ, qǐng nín zuò zài mén duìmiàn.

Zhōu jīnglǐ：Xièxie nín de zuòwèi ānpái.

Wéi jīnglǐ：Nǎlǐ, nǎlǐ! Nín shì zhǔyào de guìbīn, ànzhào lǐjié yīnggāi zuò zhège wèizi.

Zhōu jīnglǐ：Zhèlǐ yě yǒu zhèyàng de guījǔ a, Táiwān yě yǒu.

Wéi jīnglǐ：Nín xiǎng hē hóng pútáojiǔ háishì bái pútáojiǔ.

Zhōu jīnglǐ：Wǒmen hē hóng pútáojiǔ ba.

Wéi jīnglǐ：Hǎo. Zhù nín shēntǐ jiànkāng, yě zhù wǒmen hézuò yúkuài.

Zhōu jīnglǐ：Xièxie nín. Qǐng wèn, Yìndì yǔ de gānbēi zěnme shuō?

Wéi jīnglǐ：Wǒmen gēn Yīngwén yíyang, yě shuō: "Cheers".

Zhōu jīnglǐ：Gèwèi qǐng jǔ bēi, wèi wǒmen de yǒuyì hàn hézuò chénggōng gānbēi!

Wéi jīnglǐ：Wǒmen jīntiān chīdào de shì Xīn Délǐ yǒumíng de nǎiyóu kālǐjī (Murgh Makhani).

Zhōu jīnglǐ : Hǎo, wǒ cháng yì cháng.

Wéi jīnglǐ : Zhōu jīnglǐ, fàncài hái kěkǒu ba?

Zhōu jīnglǐ : Dàodì de Murgh Makhani wèidào zhēn hǎo!

Wéi jīnglǐ : Nà jiù duō chī diǎn. Yìhuǐr háiyǒu tiándiǎn ne.

Zhōu jīnglǐ : Xièxie. Xiǎowáng, nǐ hái xiǎng chī tiándiǎn ma?

Wáng mìshū : Bùhǎoyìsī, wǒ yǐjīng chī bǎo le, bù néng zài chī le.

Zhōu jīnglǐ : Nà nǐ jiù kànzhe wǒmen chī ba!

[Diànhuà xiǎng le.]

Wéi jīnglǐ : Duìbùqǐ, wǒ xiān jiē diànhuà.

Wèi, wǒmen zhèngzài chīfàn ne. Chīle fàn, jiù qù zhǎo nǐ.

課文英譯 Text in English

Dialogue

Manager Wei : Manager Zhou, please sit opposite the door.

Manager Zhou : Thank you for your seating arrangement.

Manager Wei : Not at all, not at all! You are our honored guest. According to the etiquette, this is the seat that you should sit in.

Manager Zhou : You also have this kind of custom here. We have the same in Taiwan.

Manager Wei : Would you like to drink red wine or white wine?

Manager Zhou : Let's have the red wine.

Manager Wei : Good. We wish you good health and a happy collaboration with us.

Manager Zhou : Thank you. Could I ask you how you say "bottoms up" in Hindi?

Manager Wei : We say the same as in English: 'Cheers!'

Manager Zhou : Everybody, please raise your glasses to wish our friendship and collaboration success.

Secretary Wang : Manager Wei, today's dish is very special.

Manager Wei : We will eat New Delhi's famous Murgh Makhani today.

Manager Zhou : Good, I'll try it.

Manager Wei : Manager Zhou, are the dishes delicious?

Manager Zhou : The taste of authentic Murgh Makhani is really good!

Manager Wei : Then you should eat more. There is still dessert in a while.

Manager Zhou : Thanks, Xiao Wang. Do you still want to eat dessert?

Secretary Wang : Excuse me, I am already full. I can't eat anymore.

Manager Zhou : In that case, you can watch us eat!

[The phone rings.]

Manager Wei : I am sorry; I need to take the call first. Hello, we are eating. After eating, I will go and find you.

生詞一 Vocabulary I 🎧

編號	生詞	漢語拼音	詞性	英文翻譯
1.	接風	jiēfēng	Vi	to hold a welcome reception
2.	座位	zuòwèi	N	seat, a place to sit
3.	安排	ānpái	N/V	arrangement; to arrange
4.	貴賓	guìbīn	N	honored guest, distinguished guest

編號	生詞	漢語拼音	詞性	英文翻譯
5.	按照	ànzhào	Prep	according to
6.	禮節	lǐjié	N	etiquette, courtesy
7.	規矩	guījǔ	N	rule, custom
8.	葡萄酒	pútáojiǔ	N	(grape) wine
9.	愉快	yúkuài	Vs	happy, cheerful
10.	各位	gèwèi	N	everybody
11.	友誼	yǒuyì	N	friendship
12.	成功	chénggōng	Vs	successful
13.	嚐	cháng	V	to taste
14.	飯菜	fàncài	N	dishes, food
15.	可口	kěkǒu	Vs	delicious
16.	道地	dàodì	Vs	authentic, genuine
17.	味道	wèidào	N	taste
18.	飽	bǎo	Vs	to be full in the stomach

短語 Phrases

編號	生詞	漢語拼音	英文翻譯
1.	哪裡，哪裡	Nǎlǐ, nǎlǐ	You are welcome. Lit. "Where? Where?"
2.	身體健康	Shēntǐ jiànkāng	Good health.
3.	乾杯	gānbēi	Cheers! Bottoms up! Lit. "dry cup"
4.	舉杯	jǔbēi	to propose a toast
5.	奶油咖哩雞	nǎiyóu kālǐjī	butter chicken, Murgh Makhani
6.	一會兒	yìhuǐr	in a moment

短文 Reading 🎧

在印度做客的禮節

印度人請外國朋友到家裡吃晚餐，是一種熱情的表示。印度人大部分信印度教，不吃牛肉；伊斯蘭教不吃豬肉，所以羊肉常常用來招待貴賓。咖哩是印度菜的主角，非常好吃。

印度南方人和北方人吃的習慣也不太一樣，北方人的主食是烤餅，用叉子，南方人喜歡吃米飯，而且覺得用手抓著吃更好吃。當然如果有興趣，客人也可以一起用右手吃吃看。主人會把檸檬水放在桌上，給大家洗手。

臺灣人請吃晚飯，一般都會約在晚上六、七點。但在印度，因為午餐時間是一點，所以九點左右，才是他們晚餐的時間。客人到得太早了，主人可能還正在準備，或穿著不太正式的衣服，這樣就不禮貌了。

課文漢語拼音 Text in Hanyu Pinyin

Zài Yìndù zuòkè de lǐjié

Yìndù rén qǐng wàiguó péngyǒu dào jiā lǐ chī wǎncān, shì yì zhǒng rèqíng de biǎoshì. Yìndù rén dà bùfèn xìn Yìndùjiào, bù chī niúròu; Yīsīlánjiào bù chī zhūròu, suǒyǐ yángròu chángcháng yònglái zhāodài guìbīn. Kālǐ shì Yìndù cài de zhǔjiǎo, fēicháng hǎo chī.

Yìndù nánfāng rén hàn běifāng rén chī de xíguàn yě bú tài yíyàng, běifāng rén de zhǔshí shì kǎobǐng, yòng chāzi, nánfāng rén xǐhuān chī mǐfàn, érqiě juéde yòng shǒu zhuāzhe chī gèng hǎo chī. Dāngrán rúguǒ yǒu xìngqù, kèrén yě kěyǐ yìqǐ yòng yòushǒu chīchi kàn. Zhǔrén huì bǎ níngméngshuǐ fàng zài zhuō shàng, gěi dàjiā xǐshǒu.

Lesson 2

Táiwān rén qǐng chī wǎnfàn, yìbān dōu huì yuē zài wǎnshàng liù-qī diǎn. Dàn zài Yìndù, yīnwèi wǔcān shíjiān shì yì diǎn, suǒyǐ jiǔ diǎn zuǒyòu, cái shì tāmen wǎncān de shíjiān. Kèrén dào de tài zǎo le, zhǔrén kěnéng hái zhèng zài zhǔnbèi, huò chuānzhe bú tài zhèngshì de yīfú, zhèyàng jiù bù lǐmào le.

課文英譯 Text in English

Etiquette of Being a Guest in India

When Indians invite foreign friends to have dinner at home, it is a sign of hospitality. Most Indians believe in Hinduism and do not eat beef; Islamic people do not eat pork, so lamb is often used to entertain VIP guests. Curry is the protagonist of Indian cuisine, and it is very delicious.

Southern and northern Indians have different eating habits. The staple food of northerners is baked flatbread, and they like to use a fork to eat. Southerners like to eat rice and feel that food tastes better if you eat with your hands. Of course, if they are interested, guests can also use their right hand to eat with them together. The host will put a bowl of lemon water on the table for you to wash your hands with.

Taiwanese like to invite people to have dinner, usually around six or seven in the evening. However, in India, because lunch is at one o'clock, nine o'clock is dinner time for them. If the guest arrives too early, the host may still be preparing food or wearing informal clothes. In that case, it would be impolite.

生詞二 Vocabulary II 🎧

編號	生詞	漢語拼音	詞性	英文翻譯
1.	做客	zuòkè	Vi	to be a guest
2.	熱情	rèqíng	Vs	enthusiastic
3.	表示	biǎoshì	N	expression
4.	信	xìn	Vst	to believe
5.	豬肉	zhūròu	N	pork
6.	羊肉	yángròu	N	lamb
7.	招待	zhāodài	V	to receive guests
8.	咖哩	kālǐ	N	curry
9.	主角	zhǔjiǎo	N	protagonist, leading role
10.	主食	zhǔshí	N	the main course in a meal, staple food
11.	烤餅	kǎobǐng	N	baked flatbread
12.	叉子	chāzi	N	fork
13.	米飯	mǐfàn	N	rice
14.	抓	zhuā	V	to grab
15.	客人	kèrén	N	guest
16.	檸檬水	níngméngshuǐ	N	lemon water
17.	準備	zhǔnbèi	V	to prepare
18.	正式	zhèngshì	Vs	formal
19.	禮貌	lǐmào	Vs	polite, courteous

專有名詞 Proper Nouns

編號	生詞	漢語拼音	英文翻譯
1.	印度教	Yìndùjiào	Hinduism
2.	伊斯蘭教	Yīsīlánjiào	Islamism

短語 Phrases

編號	生詞	漢語拼音	英文翻譯
1.	有興趣	yǒu xìngqù	to be interested
2.	洗手	xǐshǒu	wash hands

語法 Grammar 🎧

一、V +「到$_1$」和「到$_2$」　　**Resultative complement V + 到$_1$ *dào1* and Destination Marker 到$_2$ *dào2***

說明：V +「到$_1$」中的「到」指的是一個動作的結果補語，是指那個動作已經達到了某個目標。V +「到$_2$」指的是一個東西被移動到標記的位置。

Explanation：The 到 *dào* in V + 到$_1$ *dào1* refers to the resultative complement of an action, which means that the action has reached a certain goal. V 到$_2$ *dào2* indicates that an object is moved to a marked position.

1. V +「到$_1$」表示動作成功或達到目標。

V + 到$_1$ *dào1* means that the action has been successful or the goal has been reached.

如：(1) 我今天買到票了。

(2) 他們今天吃到道地的印度菜了。

2. V +「到$_2$」表示一個東西被移動到標記的位置。在否定的句子中，「沒」會放在動詞的前面。

V + 到$_2$ *dào2* means that an object is moved to a marked position. In negative sentences, 沒 *méi* will be placed before the verb.

如：(1) A：你昨天是在高雄下飛機的嗎？

　　　B：不是，我昨天是在桃園下飛機的，沒坐到高雄。

(2) 昨天晚上她看書看到第 90 頁了。

(3) 我已經收到你的禮物了。

例句：

1. 他今天早上買到課本了。

2. 昨天晚上我見到我爸爸了。

3. 上禮拜他從臺北騎機車騎到新竹。

4. 我在德里就下飛機了，沒搭到孟買（Mumbai）。

5. 我的書，你明天會拿到學校給我嗎？

練習：請用「V ＋ 到」完成以下句子。

Exercise：Please use V ＋ 到 *dào* to complete the following sentences.

1. 我昨天已經＿＿＿＿＿＿印度菜了。
2. 在這裡可以＿＿＿＿＿＿臺北的夜景。
3. 生日蛋糕已經＿＿＿＿＿＿陳老師家了。
4. 昨天我跟我先生騎腳踏車＿＿＿＿＿＿銀行。
5. 昨天晚上我看書＿＿＿＿＿＿第 250 頁了。

二、V 著　　Manner of an Action with V ＋ 著 *zhe*

說明：當動作動詞後邊加「著」時，有下面兩種狀況。

Explanation：When 著 *zhe* is added after an action verb, there could be the following two situations.

1. 描述主要動作的持續進行狀況。

　It describes the continuation of the main action.

　如：(1) 我拿著一本書。

　　　(2) 她穿著紅色的裙子。

2. 表示「在做 A 動作的同時做 B 動作」，也就是兩個動作同時進行。

It means "do action B while doing action A." That is, two actions are performed at the same time.

如：(1) 我常聽著音樂開車。

　　(2) 你應該看著地圖找路吧。

例句：

1. 我生病了，媽媽一直陪著我。

2. 看著手機開車不安全。

3. 老師們常常是站著上課。

練習：請用「V 著」完成以下句子：

Exercise：Please use V 著 *zhe* to complete the following sentences.

---

1. 他＿＿＿＿＿跟客人聊天。

2. 在火車上，學生們一邊＿＿＿＿＿，一邊＿＿＿＿＿

3. 妹妹總愛＿＿＿＿＿開車。

4. 老師不是＿＿＿＿＿，她是＿＿＿＿＿上課。

5. 他是不是和朋友＿＿＿＿＿喝咖啡？

三、正 / 在 / 正在　　Progressive, on-going actions 正 *zhèng*/ 在 *zài*/ 正在 *zhèngzài*

說明：正 / 在 / 正在：表示「動作在進行中」或「狀態在持續中」語意基本相同，加上「呢」的時候，語氣會比較輕鬆。

Explanation：正 *zhèng*/ 在 *zài*/正在 *zhèngzài*: They all mean "the action is in progress," or "the state is continuing." The tone will be more relaxed when 呢 *ne* is added at the end of the sentence.

1.「正」著重於時間。

　　正 *zhèng* focuses on time.

如：(1) 下午我正睡覺（呢），他就打電話來了。

　　(2) 他昨天來找我的時候，我正看電視（呢）。

2.「在」著重於狀態。「在」否定句可用「不 / 沒（有）在＋V」或「不是在＋V」。

在 *zài* focuses on situations. The negative of 在 *zài* can be " 不 *bù* / 沒 *méi* (有 *yǒu*) 在 *zài* ＋ V" or " 不 *bú* 是 *shì* 在 *zài* ＋ V."

如：(1) A：爸爸在睡覺（呢），不要去吵他。

　　　 B：爸爸沒在睡覺，你去叫他吧。

　　(2) 她不是在寫功課，她在跟朋友聊天。

3.「正在」既指時間又指狀態，但「正在」的否定句只能用「不是」，不能用「不 / 沒（有）」。

正在 *zhèngzài* refers to both time and state, but the negative of 正在 *zhèngzài* can only be " 不 *bú* 是 *shì*," not " 不 *bù*/沒（有） *méi (yǒu)*."

如：(1) A：他給你打電話的時候，你正在做作業（呢）。

　　　 B：他給我打電話的時候，我不是正在做作業。

　　(2) 我正在訂飛機票，下個月就要去印度了。

例句：

1. 他早上十點來我家，我正準備出門。

2. 昨天他打電話給我的時候，我正上課呢！

3. 我在看電視。

4. 我剛剛沒（有）在吃飯，我在看書呢。

5. 我正在吃飯。

6. 我不是在洗澡，我正在看電視呢。

練習：請看看這些圖示，然後用「正 / 在 / 正在」造句。

Exercise：Please look at the pictures below, then use 正 *zhèng*/ 在 *zài*/ 正在 *zhèngzài* to make sentences.

騎機車、跳舞、睡覺、吃飯、看電視…等。

1.		
2.		
3.		
4.		
5.		

四、把…V＋在／到₂／給　　To dispose of Something with 把 *bǎ* …V＋在 *zài* ／到₂ *dào₂* ／給 *gěi*

說明：「把」字句是一種處置式（disposal construction）的用法，指主語
　　　（Subj）透過動作對賓語（Obj）做了什麼。「把…V＋在／到₂／給」用
　　　於表示對賓語（特定的人或事物）加上一個動作，使其發生一定的變
　　　化，如：位置的移動或所屬關係的轉移。

Explanation：The word 把 *bǎ* is a disposal construction, which refers to what the
　　　subject does to the object through actions. 把 bǎ …V＋在 *zài* ／到 *dào₂* ／

給 *gěi* is used to mean adding an action to the object (a specific person or thing) to make a certain change, such as a movement to a position or the transfer of relationships.

1. 當結構為「把⋯ V ＋ 在」：主語如果明確時可以省略。「在」後面是地點，「V 在」的 V 必須是放置動詞（placing V）。

   When the structure is 把 *bǎ*...V ＋ 在 *zài*: the subject can be omitted if it is clear. After 在 *zài* is the location, the Verb of V ＋ 在 *zài* must be a verb that places things somewhere (placing Verb).

   如：(1) 把床放在門的右邊。

   (2) 請把你的名字寫在本子上。

2. 當結構為「bǎ ⋯ Verb ＋ 到$_2$」：主語如果明確時可以省略。「到」後面是地點，「V 到」的 V 必須是移動動詞（moving V）。

   When the structure is 把 *bǎ*...V ＋ 到$_2$ *dào$_2$*, the subject can be omitted if it is clear. After 到 *dào* is a location, the Verb of V ＋ 到 *dào* must be a moving verb (moving V).

   如：(1) 他把禮物送到飯店去了。

   (2) 請把桌子搬到飯廳。

3. 當結構為「把⋯ V ＋ 給」：主語如果明確時可以省略。「給」後面是人。

   When the structure is 把 *bǎ*⋯V ＋ 給 *gěi*, the subject can be omitted if it is clear. Words referring to people should follow 給 *gěi*.

   如：(1) 請你把這本書拿給小明。

   (2) 她把這支手機賣給我了。

例句：

1. 我把洗衣機放在洗衣房了。
2. 請把電視搬到客廳去。
3. 明天別忘了把禮物送給經理。

練習：請用「把⋯V ＋ 在 / 到$_2$/ 給」重寫下面的句子。

Exercise：Please use 把 *bǎ* ···V + 在 *zài*/ 到 *dào₂*/ 給 *gěi* to rewrite the following sentences.

1.	今天	車	會	開	臺南	到	去	我	。		
2.	請	書	翻	第	55	到	頁	。			
3.	請	裡	在	書房	書架	放	到	。			
4.	放	請	床	在	臥室	裡	。				
5.	老師	發	本子	給	我們	。					
6.	可以	明天	還	你	書	我	給	嗎	？		

跨文化延伸 Cross-Cultural Extension

Differences in the Use of Social Media Tools in Taiwan and India (Line vs. WhatsApp)

To do business or travel, Taiwan and India use different communication software. "Line" is used most frequently in Taiwan, and some other countries also use "Line" as the primary communication software. "Line" can be used to chat and interact with good friends free at anytime, anywhere. It supports not only one-on-one chats but also group chats. "Line" provides free international voice and video calls, allowing users to keep in touch with their loved ones easily. "Line" also has the convenient and safe "Line Pay," which allows you to shop safely on the Internet at any time.

"WhatsApp" has many users in India, and its functions are similar to those of "Line." One of the advantages of "WhatsApp" is that even in areas where the Wi-Fi signal is not good, such as those with only 3G, the signal can still be received. Currently, "Line" and its services are free, and

"WhatsApp" is also free to download. Because "WhatsApp" comes from the United States and is a communication software in English, it is very popular in India.

語言任務 Language Tasks

一、兩個人一組，一人扮演臺灣貴賓，一人扮演印度主人，使用本課語法點「V + 到₁」。貴賓問主人在哪裡能「V + 到₁」在印度旅遊時的食物、東西或地方。

Form groups of two people. One person will role-play the Taiwanese guest, and the other role-play the Indian host. Please use the 「V + 到₁」grammar point in this lesson. The guests should ask the host where they can 「V + 到₁」eat Indian food, buy Indian things and visit places of interest in India when they travel in India.

例句：

A：請問到哪裡可以吃到印度有名的奶油咖哩雞（Murgh Makhani）？

B：你可以去舊德里或是 Zakir Nagar。那兩個地方的餐廳都有非常好吃的 Murgh Makhani。

| (a) Murgh Makhani | (b) Masala Chai（印度奶茶） | (c) 瑜伽課（yújiākè）（Yoga class） | (d) 伴手禮（bànshǒulǐ, souvenir） | (e) 板球賽（bǎnqiúsài, cricket match） |

二、在教室給同學過生日 Celebrate birthdays for classmates in the classroom

任務：兩個人一組，用「把…V + 在 / 到₂/ 給」編寫一段對話，描述過生日的情況。包括怎麼布置教室。

Task：Break students into groups of two. Each group writes a dialogue with 把 *bǎ* …V + 在 *zài*/ 到₂*dào₂*/ 給 *gěi* to describe the situation at the birthday party, including how to arrange the classroom.

Verbs that can be used are：搬、放、掛、貼、拿、寫、送…

Useful words：花、蛋糕、桌子、椅子、生日卡、氣球、禮物…

如：學生 A：……放在哪裡？

學生 B：……吧！/ 怎麼樣？

學生 A：……

學生 B：……

第三課　自由行
Lesson 3　Self-Organized Tours

課程目標：

Topic：交通

1. 能介紹印度大城市的主要交通工具。
2. 能介紹臺灣和印度都會地鐵的特點。
3. 能介紹一般平民化的交通工具。

Lesson Objectives：

Topic：Transport

1. Students can introduce the primary means of transport used in big cities in India.
2. Students can introduce the special characteristics of Taiwan and Indian city subways.
3. Students can introduce the means of transport used by ordinary people.

對話 Dialogue 🎧

【周經理和王祕書趁剛簽了合約比較沒事，打算自由行，在新德里到處逛逛。】

周經理：簽了合約，今天輕鬆一下吧！王祕書，你怎麼安排？

王祕書：沒坐過 auto 和地鐵，就不能說到過印度，搭車逛市區吧。

周經理：auto？你是說那種黃綠兩色的車？聽說不殺價就會被騙！

王祕書：對，印度 auto 大部分是黃綠兩色。價錢，有我在，請放心！

周經理：好，試試吧！印度每個地方的車，顏色都不同嗎？

王祕書：是的，auto 是平民的腿，沒了它很不方便，塞車也會更嚴重。

周經理：說著說著，就來了一輛，奇怪兩邊為什麼都掛著塑膠布？

王祕書：先上車吧，您馬上就能發現為什麼了。

【王祕書殺價以後，兩人坐上 auto 去地鐵站。】

周經理：我懂了，有塑膠布，不怕風也不怕空氣汙染。地鐵站到了。

王祕書：別急，班次很多，不過前面兩節車廂只給女生坐。

周經理：現在不擠，我們一起坐後面的車廂。

王祕書：您看每節車廂還有特別留給女生的位子，男生得讓座。

周經理：真的，坐在那裡的先生讓座了。對了，等一下回飯店試試
　　　　搭公車，怎麼樣？

王祕書：坐地鐵能用旅遊卡，公車又擠又得在車上買票，太麻煩了。

周經理：那可以坐火車玩玩嗎？

王祕書：印度人說：「再等一下，火車一定會來」，所以「有事」
　　　　別搭火車吧。

周經理：那回去我們坐坐三輪車。

課文漢語拼音 Text in Hanyu Pinyin

[Zhōu jīnglǐ hàn Wáng mìshū chèn gāng qiānle héyuē bǐjiào méishì, dǎsuàn zìyóu xíng, zài Xīn Délǐ dàochù guàngguang.]

Zhōu jīnglǐ : Qiānle héyuē, jīntiān qīngsōng yíxià ba! Wáng mìshū, nǐ zěnme ānpái?

Wáng mìshū : Méi zuòguò auto hàn dìtiě, jiù bù néng shuō dàoguò Yìndù, dā chē guàng shìqū ba.

Zhōu jīnglǐ : Auto? Nǐ shì shuō nà zhǒng huáng lǜ liǎng sè de chē? Tīngshuō bù shājià jiù huì bèi piàn!

Wáng mìshū : Duì, Yìndù auto dàbùfèn shì huáng lǜ liǎng sè. Jiàqián, yǒu wǒ zài, qǐng fàngxīn!

Zhōu jīnglǐ : Hǎo, shìshi ba! Yìndù měi ge dìfāng de chē, yánsè dōu bùtóng ma?

Wáng mìshū : Shì de, auto shì píngmín de tuǐ, méile tā hěn bù fāngbiàn, sāichē yě huì gèng yánzhòng.

Zhōu jīnglǐ : Shuōzhe shuōzhe, jiù láile yí liàng, qíguài liǎng biān wèishénme dōu guàzhe sùjiāo bù?

Wáng mìshū : Xiān shàng chē ba, nín mǎshàng jiù néng fāxiàn wèishénme le.

[Wáng mìshū shājià yǐhòu, liǎng rén zuò shàng auto qù dìtiě zhàn.]

Zhōu jīnglǐ : Wǒ dǒngle, yǒu sùjiāo bù, bú pà fēng yě bú pà kōngqì wūrǎn. Dìtiě zhàn dàole.

Wáng mìshū : Bié jí, bāncì hěn duō, búguò qiánmiàn liǎng jié chēxiāng zhǐ gěi nǚshēng zuò.

Zhōu jīnglǐ : Xiànzài bù jǐ, wǒmen yìqǐ zuò hòumiàn de chēxiāng.

Wáng mìshū : Nín kàn měi jié chēxiāng hái yǒu tèbié liú gěi nǚshēng de wèizi, nánshēng děi ràngzuò.

Zhōu jīnglǐ : Zhēn de, zuò zài nàlǐ de xiānshēng ràngzuò le. Duì le, děng yíxià huí fàndiàn shìshi dā gōngchē, zěnmeyàng?

Wáng mìshū : Zuò dìtiě néng yòng lǚyóu kǎ, gōngchē yòu jǐ yòu děi zài chē shàng mǎi piào, tài máfán le.

Zhōu jīnglǐ : Nà kěyǐ zuò huǒchē wánwan ma?

Wáng mìshū : Yìndù rén shuō: "Zài děng yíxià, huǒchē yídìng huì lái", suǒyǐ "yǒu shì" bié dā huǒchē ba.

Zhōu jīnglǐ : Nà huíqù wǒmen zuòzuò sānlún chē.

課文英譯 Text in English

Dialogue

[Manager Zhou and Secretary Wang wanted to use their free time after signing the contract to travel around freely in New Dehli.]

Manager Zhou : We have signed the contract. Let's relax a bit today! Secretary Wang, what have you arranged?

Secretary Wang : If one hasn't taken an auto or the subway, one cannot say that one has been to India. So, let's take the auto to drive around the city.

Manager Zhou : Auto? Do you mean the kind of car which has yellow and green colors on it? I heard that if you don't bargain, you might be cheated!

Secretary Wang : Correct, most of the Indian autos are yellow and green. As for the price, you have me here, don't worry!

Manager Zhou : Good, let's try it. Do cars from different areas of India have different colors?

Secretary Wang : Yes, the auto is the legs of ordinary citizen. Without it, it would be very inconvenient because the congestion would be much more severe.

Manager Zhou : Just as we speak, here comes a car. I am curious why both sides of the car have plastic sheets hanging over them?

Secretary Wang : Let's get in the car, then you will immediately discover why.

[After bargaining with the driver, Secretary Wang and Manager Zhou get into the auto to go to the subway station.]

Manager Zhou : I understand now. With the plastic sheets on both sides, we don't need to be afraid of the wind or air pollution. We've arrived at the metro station.

Secretary Wang : No need to hurry, there are many trains. But the front two carriages are reserved only for females.

Manager Zhou : It is not so crowded right now. Let's take the carriages behind (the front two) together.

Secretary Wang : You see, in every carriage, there are even special seats reserved for women. Men need to give up the reserved seats for women (if they are sitting in women-only seats).

Manager Zhou : Really, the gentleman who is sitting there has given up his seat. Oh yes, when we go back to the hotel, shall we try taking the bus, what do you think?

Secretary Wang : You can use the travel card when taking the subway. The bus is crowded, and you also must purchase a ticket on the bus. It is too troublesome.

Manager Zhou : In that case, can we try taking the train for fun?

Secretary Wang : Indians say: "Wait a little longer; the train will surely come." Therefore, if you have a business to attend to, it is better not to take the train.

Manager Zhou : In that case, we will return by rickshaw.

生詞一 Vocabulary I 🎧

編號	生詞	漢語拼音	詞性	英文翻譯
1.	趁	chèn	Prep	take advantage of 'opportunity, time, etc.'
2.	簽	qiān	V	to sign
3.	輕鬆	qīngsōng	Vs	relaxed
4.	地鐵	dìtiě	N	metro, subway
5.	殺價	shājià	V-sep	to bargain
6.	騙	piàn	V	to cheat
7.	價錢	jiàqián	N	price
8.	放心	fàngxīn	Vs-sep	to be at ease, not to worry
9.	平民	píngmín	N	ordinary people
10.	腿	tuǐ	N	legs
11.	塞車	sāichē	V-sep	to be congested with cars
12.	嚴重	yánzhòng	Vs	serious
13.	奇怪	qíguài	Vs	strange
14.	掛	guà	V	to hang up
15.	發現	fāxiàn	Vpt	to discover
16.	空氣	kōngqì	N	air
17.	汙染	wūrǎn	N	pollution
18.	班次	bāncì	N	the number of runs of scheduled buses, trains, flights
19.	節	jié	M	measure word for carriages
20.	車廂	chēxiāng	N	carriage
21.	擠	jǐ	Vs	crowded

編號	生詞	漢語拼音	詞性	英文翻譯
22.	留	liú	V	to reserve something for someone
23.	讓座	ràngzuò	V-sep	to give away a seat
24.	麻煩	máfán	Vs	troublesome

短語 Phrases

編號	生詞	漢語拼音	英文翻譯
1.	自由行	zìyóu xíng	self-organized free travel
2.	塑膠布	sùjiāo bù	plastic sheet
3.	地鐵站	dìtiě zhàn	metro station, subway station
4.	別急	bié jí	no need to hurry
5.	三輪車	sānlún chē	tricycles

印度的捷運卡《旅遊卡》
an Indian travel card

捷運上女生的特別座
Special seats for females on the subway

短文 Reading 🎧

臺北的交通工具

　　每個城市都有它主要的交通工具。印度的首都新德里，地鐵、uber、auto 和三輪車都非常重要，而臺灣的首都臺北，捷運差不多

就像城市的血管，一張悠遊卡，就能帶你輕鬆地到城市的每個地方。另外，機車、汽車、公車、計程車、uber，在交通和這個城市的發展上，也相當重要。

　　每天上下班時間，捷運站擠滿了人，三鐵共構的大站，搭車的人多得可怕，附近房子的價錢也非常貴。捷運的「博愛座」更是一大特色，老人、孕婦、行動不方便的人，可以先坐，不過看到身體不舒服的人，大家也都會馬上讓座給他們。

　　機車族是臺北另一個特色，每天一些重要路口的機車瀑布，讓人看了難忘，還有這幾年流行的外送服務，他們騎著機車在大街小巷裡鑽來鑽去，更讓城市熱鬧不少。

課文漢語拼音 Text in Hanyu Pinyin

Táiběi de jiāotōng gōngjù

　　Měi ge chéngshì dōu yǒu tā zhǔyào de jiāotōng gōngjù. Yìndù de shǒudū Xīn Délǐ, dìtiě, uber, auto hàn sānlún chē dōu fēicháng zhòngyào, ér Táiwān de shǒudū Táiběi, jiéyùn chàbuduō jiù xiàng chéngshì de xiěguǎn, yī zhāng yōuyóukǎ, jiù néng dài nǐ qīngsōng de dào chéngshì de měi ge dìfāng. Lìngwài, jīchē, qìchē, gōngchē, jìchéngchē, uber, zài jiāotōng hàn zhège chéngshì de fāzhǎn shàng, yě xiāngdāng zhòngyào.

　　Měitiān shàng-xiàbān shíjiān, jiéyùn zhàn jǐ mǎnle rén, sāntiě gònggòu de dà zhàn, dā chē de rén duō de kěpà, fùjìn fángzi de jiàqián yě fēicháng guì. Jiéyùn de bó'àizuò gèng shì yí dà tèsè, lǎorén, yùnfù, xíngdòng bù fāngbiàn de rén, kěyǐ xiān zuò, búguò kàndào shēntǐ bù shūfú de rén, dàjiā yě dōu huì mǎshàng ràngzuò gěi tāmen.

　　Jīchē zú shì Táiběi lìng yí ge tèsè, měi tiān yìxiē zhòngyào lùkǒu de jīchē pùbù, ràng rén kànle nánwàng, hái yǒu zhè jǐ nián liúxíng de wàisòng fúwù, tāmen qízhe jīchē zài dàjiē xiǎoxiàng lǐ zuān lái zuān qù, gèng ràng chéngshì rènào bù shǎo.

課文英譯 Text in English

Transportation in Taipei

Every city has its primary means of transportation. In New Delhi, the capital of India, subways, uber, auto, and tricycles are all very important, while in Taipei, the capital of Taiwan, the MRT is almost like the blood vessel of the city. A travel card can take you easily to every part of the city. In addition, motorcycles, cars, buses, taxis, and Uber are also significant in transportation and the development of the city.

The MRT station is crowded with people every day when commuting to and from work. Big stations with the three rail lines have so many people that it is frightening. The price of nearby houses is also very high. The MRT's "Priority seat" is even more unique. The elderly, pregnant women, and people with limited mobility can sit on them first. However, if people are seen as unwell, everyone will immediately give up their seats for them.

The "motorcycle family" is another characteristic of Taipei. At some important intersections every day, the sheer volume of motorcycles makes them look like a "motorcycle waterfall." The sight is simply unforgettable. There are also delivery services which have become popular in the past few years. They ride their motorcycles in and around the streets and alleyways, adding a lot of excitement to the city.

生詞二 Vocabulary II 🎧

編號	生詞	漢語拼音	詞性	英文翻譯
1.	交通	jiāotōng	N	transportation
2.	工具	gōngjù	N	tool
3.	城市	chéngshì	N	city
4.	主要	zhǔyào	Vs-attr	mainly
5.	首都	shǒudū	N	capital
6.	血管	xiěguǎn	N	blood vessel
7.	發展	fāzhǎn	N	development
8.	相當	xiāngdāng	Adv	relatively
9.	博愛座	bó'àizuò	N	priority seat
10.	特色	tèsè	N	special characteristic
11.	孕婦	yùnfù	N	pregnant women
12.	行動	xíngdòng	N	movement
13.	流行	liúxíng	Vs	popular
14.	外送	wàisòng	V	delivery

短語 Phrases

編號	生詞	漢語拼音	英文翻譯
1.	悠遊卡	yōuyóukǎ	Easy Card
2.	三鐵共構	sāntiě gònggòu	the convergence of the three rail systems
3.	機車族	jīchē zú	motorcycle generation
4.	機車瀑布	jīchē pùbù	motorcycle waterfall
5.	大街小巷	dàjiē xiǎoxiàng	big streets and small alleyways
6.	鑽來鑽去	zuānlái zuānqù	zigzaging in and out

Lesson 3

語法 Grammar 🎧

一、「被」字句　　Passive sentences with 被 *bèi*

說明：「被」字句一般用來表示被動式，語意不只表示受到影響，也常用在不好的事情上。句中謂語，動詞後面要有表示動作完結或結果的成分。

「被」字句的結構是「Obj＋被＋Subj＋V＋了／過／complement」。

Explanation：The word 被 *bèi* is generally used to express the passive form. The semantic meaning not only means that things have been affected, but also often in a bad way. The predicate in the sentence, after the verb, must have a component that indicates the end or result of the action.

1. 「被」字句的結構為「Obj＋被＋Subj＋V＋了／過／complement」。

　 The structure of a 被 *bèi* sentence is "Obj＋被 *bèi*＋Subj＋V＋了 *le*/過 *guò*/complement."

　 如：(1) 他在學校被同學打了。

　　　 (2) 我放在書桌上的東西被誰動過？

　　　 (3) 媽媽最喜歡的那個杯子，被弟弟打破了。

2. 「被」後面的施事者如果不明確，可以省略。

　 If the agent behind 被 *bèi* is not clear, it can be omitted.

　 如：我的手機被（人）偷了。

3. 「被」字句可以用在過去、未來和習慣性的事情上。

　 The word 被 *bèi* can be used with past, future, and habitual events.

　 如：(1) 昨天晚上那家銀行被偷了。（過去）

　　　 (2) 如果爸爸知道你沒去上學，你一定會被罵。（未來）

　　　 (3) 每次有新的東西都被他先拿走。（習慣）

4. 否定詞要放在「被」前面。

　 Negative words should be placed in front of 被 *bèi*.

　 如：(1) 剛才地鐵上很擠，還好我的錢沒被偷。

　　　 (2) 在這裡買東西要殺價，別被騙了。

5. 「把」字句和「被」字句的比較

此處「把」字句和「被」字句的主、被動以及結構，都是以施事者和受事者的觀點來做比較。

Comparison of 把 *bǎ* and 被 *bèi* Sentences

Here, the active and passive structure of the 把 *bǎ* sentence and the 被 *bèi* sentence are compared from the perspective of the agent and recipient.

「把」字句 把 *bǎ* sentences	1. 把字句為主動式。 2. 表示主語透過動作對賓語做了什麼，是處置式。 3. 賓語一般是名詞，必須是確指的，如「那輛車」「這把傘」。 4. 否定句或其他成分，放在「把」前面。 5. 句中謂語，動詞後面要有表示動作完結或結果的成分。 6. 結構為「Subj＋把＋Obj＋V＋complement（了／過／在／到／給）」 　　例：(1) 我把咖啡喝了。 　　　　(2) 他把手機放在桌上／拿到客廳／送給我。 1. 把 *bǎ* sentences are active sentences. 2. It means what the subject does to the object through actions and describes a disposition imposed upon the object. 3. The object is generally a noun, which must be definite, such as "that car" and "this umbrella." 4. Negative sentences or other elements are placed in front of 把 *bǎ*. 5. In the predicate, there must be an element after the verb that indicates the end or result of the action. 6. The structure is Subj＋把 *bǎ*＋Obj＋V＋complement (*le /guò / zài /dào /gěi*)
「被」字句 被 *bèi* sentences	1. 被字句為被動式。 2. 語意表示受到影響，常用在不好的事情上。 3. 後面的主語如果不明確，可以省略。 4. 否定句或其他成分，放在「被」前面。 5. 句中謂語，動詞後面要有表示動作完結或結果的成分。 6. 結構為「Obj＋被＋Subj＋V＋了／complement」。

<table>
<tr>
<td></td>
<td>

例：(1) 我的咖啡被他喝了。

(2) 他不寫功課，所以被媽媽罵了。

1. The 被 *bèi* sentence is passive.
2. The meaning of the expression is that something or someone has been affected and often in a bad way.
3. If the subject following 被 *bèi* is not clear, it can be omitted.
4. Negative sentences or other elements are placed in front of 被 *bèi*.
5. In the predicate, there must be an element after the verb that indicates the end or result of the action.
6. The structure is "Obj + 被 *bèi* + Subj + V+ /complement".

</td>
</tr>
</table>

有時「把」字句可以轉換成「被」字句。

Sometimes 把 *bǎ* sentences can be converted into 被 *bèi* sentences.

(1) 我把我臺北的房子賣了。→ 我臺北的房子被我賣了。

(2) 我把老朋友的生日忘了。→ 老朋友的生日被我忘了。

例句：

1. 他吃東西沒付錢，被老闆發現了。
2. 星期六逛夜市的時候，我的錢包被偷了。
3. 圖書館的位子，常被人放東西，真討厭。
4. 那個男的早就有太太，小美被騙了。
5. 今天被老闆罵的事，希望別被我女朋友知道。
6. 誰把桌上的那塊蛋糕吃了？
7. 太吵了，把電視關了。
8. 媽媽回家前，妳別把車子賣了。

練習一：請用「被」字句（被 -construction）重寫下面的句子。

Exercise 1：Please use 被 *bèi* sentences (被 *bèi*-constructions) to rewrite the following sentences.

1. 媽媽知道他跟人借錢的事了。

   →＿＿＿＿＿＿＿＿＿＿＿＿＿＿＿＿＿。

2. 孩子們把王太太家的窗戶打破了。

   →＿＿＿＿＿＿＿＿＿＿＿＿＿＿＿＿＿。

3. 誰喝了他的咖啡？

   →＿＿＿＿＿＿＿＿＿＿＿＿＿＿＿＿＿。

4. 上個週末，朋友把他的腳踏車騎壞了。

   →＿＿＿＿＿＿＿＿＿＿＿＿＿＿＿＿＿。

5. 去看棒球比賽要小心，要是球打到會很疼。

   →＿＿＿＿＿＿＿＿＿＿＿＿＿＿＿＿＿。

練習二：請用「把」字句（把 -construction）重寫下面的句子。

Exercise 2：Please use 把 *bǎ* sentences (把 *bǎ* -constructions) to rewrite the following sentences.

1. 睡覺以前記得吃藥。

   →＿＿＿＿＿＿＿＿＿＿＿＿＿＿＿＿＿。

2. 書下星期一要還給圖書館。

   →＿＿＿＿＿＿＿＿＿＿＿＿＿＿＿＿＿。

3. 媽媽的車他開到學校去了。

   →＿＿＿＿＿＿＿＿＿＿＿＿＿＿＿＿＿。

4. 他已經看完那本書了。

   →＿＿＿＿＿＿＿＿＿＿＿＿＿＿＿＿＿。

5. 他肚子不舒服，沒吃完麵，就不吃了。

   →＿＿＿＿＿＿＿＿＿＿＿＿＿＿＿＿＿。

Lesson 3

二、V 著 V 著，就…了　　"While doing A, B happens" with V 著 *zhe* V 著 *zhe*, 就 *jiù*... 了 *le*

說明：「V 著 V 著，就…了」是指當前面一個動作還在連續進行時，後面的情況也不知不覺地就發生了。

Explanation：V 著 *zhe* V 著 *zhe*, 就 *jiù*... 了 *le* means that while the previous action is still in continuous progress, the latter happens unknowingly.

1. 「V 著 V 著」的 V，必須使用同一個動詞。

The V in V 著 *zhe* V 著 *zhe* must be the same verb.

如：(1) 說著說著，車子就來了。

(2) 聊著聊著，捷運站就到了。

(3) *聊著等著，捷運站就到了。

2. 「V 著 V 著」的後面不可以接賓語，如果語境不清楚，可以補充條件來說明。

Objects are not allowed after V 著 *zhe* V 著 *zhe*. If the context is not clear, you can add conditions to explain it.

如：(1) 她走著走著，就迷路了。

(2) 她剛搬家，附近有很多小巷子，她常走著走著，就迷路了。

(3) *她常走著走著路，就迷路了。

3. 「V 著 V 著」的 V 如果是及物動詞，它的賓語不可在動詞後，必須往前移當主題。

If the V in V 著 *zhe* V 著 *zhe* is a transitive verb, its object cannot be after the verb and must be moved forward as the subject.

如：(1) 臺灣話，我聽著聽著就會說了。

(2) 包子，我看著看著就會包了。

例句：

1. 我寫作業的時候，常常寫著寫著，就想睡覺了。

2. 好久沒回國了，她看著家人的照片，看著看著，就哭了。

3. 沒人教我做飯，我是看媽媽做飯，看著看著，就會了。

練習：請用「V 著 V 著，就…了」，回答下面的問題。

Exercise：Please use V 著 *zhe* V 著 *zhe*, 就 *jiù...* 了 *le* to answer the following questions.

---

1. A：看好玩的電影，你會笑嗎？

   B：看好玩的電影，＿＿＿＿＿＿＿＿＿＿＿＿＿＿＿

2. A：你怎麼會騎腳踏車的，有人教你嗎？

   B：沒有人教我，＿＿＿＿＿＿＿＿＿＿＿＿＿＿＿。

3. A：你們不是在聊男朋友嗎？她怎麼哭了？

   B：是啊，＿＿＿＿＿＿＿＿＿＿＿＿＿＿＿＿。

4. A：你昨天不是去爬山嗎？今天怎麼就感冒了？

   B：我們去的時候天氣還很好，＿＿＿＿＿＿＿＿＿＿。（爬、下雨）

5. A：你先生說昨天下班回家沒有飯吃，你怎麼沒做飯呢？

   B：我跟朋友上網聊天，＿＿＿＿＿＿＿＿＿＿＿。（聊、時間）

三、差不多 *chàbuduō*　　**Almost**

說明：「差不多」是一個概略而且模糊的用語，所表示的意思可概分為「大約」、「幾乎一樣」、「幾乎完成」三種。

Explanation：差不多 *chàbuduō* is an approximate and vague term, and its meaning can be roughly divided into "approximately," "almost the same" and "almost complete."

1. 表示「大約」，當狀語。

   It means "approximately" when it is used as an adverbial.

   如：(1) 我家在學校附近，走路差不多五分鐘就到了。

   　　　(2) 我們差不多六點半去吃飯，怎麼樣？

2. 表示「幾乎一樣」，當謂語。

   It means "almost the same" when it is used as a predicate.

如：(1) 風景區賣的東西都差不多。

(2) 這幾天的天氣都差不多，下午都會下雨。

3. 表示「幾乎完成」，當補語。

It means "almost finished" when it is used as a complement.

如：(1) 明天的考試，我準備得差不多了。

(2) 這次的活動計畫得差不多了。

4. 也可只用「差不多」簡短回答。

You can also answer just with 差不多 *chàbuduō*.

如：(1) A：給奶奶過八十歲生日的事，都準備好了嗎？

B：差不多了。

(2) A：去印度要帶的禮物都買好了嗎？

B：差不多了。

練習：請用「差不多」，完成下面的句子。

Exercise：Please use 差不多 *chàbuduō* to complete the following sentences.

---

1. A：從你幫我訂的飯店到火車站開車要多久？

   B：很近，＿＿＿＿＿＿＿＿＿＿＿＿。

2. A：你每天幾點到家？

   B：我下班搭公車，＿＿＿＿＿＿＿＿＿＿＿＿。

3. A：跟德里比，臺北捷運的班次多不多？

   B：＿＿＿＿＿＿＿＿＿＿＿＿。

4. A：我騎摩托車還是坐計程車去比較快？

   B：＿＿＿＿＿＿＿＿＿＿＿＿。

5. A：臺北冬天沒有這裡冷吧？我得帶大衣嗎？

   B：你還是帶著吧，臺北的冬天和＿＿＿＿＿＿＿＿，一下雨就很冷。

---

6. A：在臺北坐捷運真的去哪裡都最方便嗎？

　　B：沒錯，捷運＿＿＿＿＿＿＿＿＿＿＿＿心臟。

7. A：明天早上七點的飛機，你的東西都準備好了嗎？

　　B：＿＿＿＿＿＿＿＿＿＿＿＿＿＿。

8. A：考試時間還有三分鐘，同學們都寫完了嗎？

　　B：＿＿＿＿＿＿＿＿＿＿＿＿＿＿。

四、V 來 *lái* V 去 *qù*　　V come V go

說明：表示一個動作重複很多次，用法如下：

Explanation：V 來 *lái* V 去 *qù* expresses the repetition of one action many times. The usage is as below:

1. 單純指一個動作不斷地重複。

　　In its pure form, it means one action is being continuously repeated.

　　如：(1) 外送東西的機車常在路上鑽來鑽去。

　　　　(2) 每次去餐廳吃飯，孩子們吃幾口就開始跑來跑去。

2. 說話者經過反覆思考，然後做出評論或決定。

　　The speaker thinks about something over and over and then makes a comment or decision.

　　如：(1) 我覺得臺灣水果，吃來吃去還是芒果最好吃。

　　　　(2) 這些茶葉，我想來想去，還是買大罐的便宜。

3. 如果有賓語，要將賓語提前。

　　If there is an object, it needs to go to the front of the sentence.

　　如：(1) 這麼多錢，別帶來帶去，存銀行吧。

　　　　(2) 交通工具，坐來坐去，還是 auto 最方便。

例句：

　　1. 小朋友常常吵來吵去，但是一會兒就好了。

　　2. 聽來聽去，還是這個歌手唱得最好聽。

　　3. 你的背包，別背來背去，放在旅館吧。

Lesson 3

練習：請選用下列合適的動詞，用「V 來 V 去」完成句子。

Exercise：Please choose a suitable verb from the following list and then use V 來 *lái* V 去 *qù* to complete the sentences.

（吃、用、喝、住、逛、念、洗）

1. _____ ，還是這個名字最好聽又有意思。
2. 這件衣服，_____ ，還是不乾淨。
3. 臺北的小籠包_____ ，還是學校旁邊的那家最好吃。
4. _____ ，這幾家店的手機，價錢都差不多，就在這裡買吧。
5. _____ ，我最喜歡那家窗外是大海的旅館。

跨文化延伸 Cross-Cultural Extension

Tricycles Run Fast

"Tricycles can run fast." This nursery rhyme describes the early traffic conditions in Taiwan. It was because alleys were narrow, and everyone was economically not well-off. A mother who had collected her children along with bags of big and small things bought for the family had to call a tricycle to squeeze the whole family in. All the weight fell on the two legs of the tricycle man. It is very similar to the Indian rickshaws running around the street with a family of young and older people carrying their purchases.

In the progress of the times, with the availability of taxis, tricycles have become a nostalgic tool for tourist attractions in Taiwan. Taiwan's taxis are all yellow, so they are also called "little yellow." The color of autos in each city in India is different, but all have been designed for easy identification and management.

The Central Mountain Range is in the middle of Taiwan. In the early days, it was inconvenient for the east-west traffic. In the 1950s, the government let the veterans bomb mountains and build roads, sacrificing their lives in the project. Eventually, the east-west highway opened. The "Taroko National Park" is at the beginning of this road. Now there are high-speed railways in the west of Taiwan and trains and buses in the east, which are very convenient.

There are many people in India. At present, trains are the primary means of transportation throughout India. However, in general, over-crowding and frequent delays are most inconvenient for people. Although there are also well-equipped and punctual trains, they are extremely expensive. Therefore, cheap and comfortable trains are the Indian people's biggest wish.

臺北的機車瀑布
Taipei's motorcycle waterfall

印度三輪車
Indian rickshaw

臺灣觀光三輪車
Taiwan's tourist tricycle

語言任務 Language Tasks

一、看圖說故事：

Look at the pictures and then tell stories.

學生依據每組圖片要求的語法「被」字句或「Ｖ著Ｖ著，就…了」，兩

人一組練習描述圖片情境，說一個小故事。

Students should use 被 *bèi* sentences or V 著 zhe V 著 *zhe*, 就 *jiù*... 了 *le* sentences to practice describing the situation in each card in groups of two students.

例句：(1) 好吃的都被他拿走了。

(2) 我覺得中文歌不難，我常常聽著聽著就會唱了。

例子	造句	說一個小故事
	被 好吃的東西都被哥哥拿走了。	媽媽買的甜點，好吃的都被哥哥拿走了。爸爸一回家小玉就跟爸爸說哥哥好壞，她說著說著就哭了。
1.	被	
2.	被	
3.	「V 著 V 著，就…了」 弟弟看書， _____。	

例子	造句	說一個小故事
4.	「V 著 V 著，就⋯了」 妹妹在游泳池玩水， ＿＿＿＿＿＿＿＿。	
5.	「V 著 V 著，就⋯了」 先生滑手機， ＿＿＿＿＿＿＿＿。	

二、角色扮演 Role Play：

　　學生兩人一組，扮演朋友，討論自由行、買東西、送禮、旅行、買房子、看什麼電影、穿什麼衣服等主題。或是自己設計一個話題，用「V 來 V 去」、「差不多」互相否決對方的提議。

Students work in pairs to role-play friends discussing topics such as self-organized tours, shopping, giving gifts, traveling, buying a house, what movies to watch, and what clothes to wear. Or you can design a topic by yourself by using V 來 *lái* V 去 *qù* and 差不多 *chàbuduō* to reject each other's proposals.

　　如：A：小偉生日，我們送他一個水果蛋糕，怎麼樣？

　　　　B：沒意思，每年送來送去都差不多，你能不能想一個不一樣的禮物？

第四課 熱鬧的排燈節
Lesson 4 Lively Diwali

課程目標：

Topic：節日慶典

　　1. 能了解排燈節對印度人的意義。

　　2. 能了解排燈節的活動內容。

　　3. 能比較印度排燈節點油燈與臺灣春節點光明燈的異同。

　　4. 能適時、適地使用中文的祝賀語。

Lesson Objectives：

Topic：Festival Celebrations

　　1. Students can understand the meaning of Diwali for Indian people.

　　2. Students can understand the content and activities of the Diwali festival.

　　3. Students can compare the differences between "lighting oil lamps" on Diwali in India and "lighting the good-fortune lamps" on Chinese New Year in Taiwan.

　　4. Students can use Chinese congratulatory phrases on suitable occasions.

Lesson 4

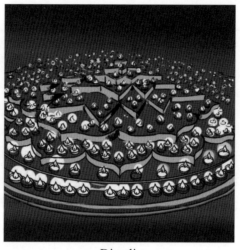

Diwali

對話 Dialogue 🎧

【今天是印度排燈節，印度珠寶公司韋經理邀請周經理和王祕書到家裡作客。】

韋經理：歡迎，歡迎，請進。這是我太太，她是臺灣人。

周經理：你們好。在這裡看到家鄉的人，好開
　　　　心！

印度甜點

韋經理：我太太看到你們更高興呢！請嚐嚐她
　　　　做的甜點。

王祕書：真不錯！不同國家口味的甜點要做得
　　　　好，不容易吧？

韋經理：我太太按照食譜做，她說一點也不難。

【外面傳來很大的鞭炮聲。】

周經理：外面鞭炮的聲音好大！真熱鬧。

韋經理：這幾天是排燈節，是印度教的節日，跟過新年一樣。

王祕書：謝謝您邀請我們到你家吃飯。

韋經理：不客氣。你們來印度，就像是我們的家人。

周經理：排燈節你們跟家人一起吃飯，還做什麼事呢？

韋經理：這個節日大概三天到五天，我覺得最有意思的是點油燈。

王祕書：我看過！你們在家門口、河邊…點著小油燈。

韋經理：是啊！意思是希望平安。我們也穿新衣、
放鞭炮、迎財神。

王祕書：我也看過我的印度朋友帶禮物去她姐妹
家拜訪。

韋經理：這跟臺灣春節大年初二，我太太回娘家
一樣的意思吧！

周經理：沒錯！很晚了，我們該走了。謝謝招待，
再見。

印度財神

課文漢語拼音 Text in Hanyu Pinyin

[Jīntiān shì Yìndù Páidēngjié, Yìndù zhūbǎo gōngsī Wéi jīnglǐ yāoqǐng Zhōu jīnglǐ hàn Wáng mìshū dào jiālǐ zuòkè.]

Wéi jīnglǐ : Huānyíng, huānyíng, qǐng jìn. Zhè shì wǒ tàitai, tā shì Táiwān rén.

Zhōu jīnglǐ : Nǐmen hǎo. Zài zhèlǐ kàndào jiāxiāng de rén, hǎo kāixīn!

Wéi jīnglǐ : Wǒ tàitai kàndào nǐmen gèng gāoxìng ne! Qǐng chángchang tā zuò de tiándiǎn.

Wáng mìshū : Zhēn bú cuò! Bù tóng guójiā kǒuwèi de tiándiǎn yào zuò de hǎo, bù róngyì ba?

Wéi jīnglǐ : Wǒ tàitai ànzhào shípǔ zuò, tā shuō yìdiǎn yě bù nán.

[Wàimiàn chuán lái hěn dà de biānpào shēng.]

Zhōu jīnglǐ : Wàimiàn biānpào de shēngyīn hǎo dà! Zhēn rènào.

Wéi jīnglǐ : Zhè jǐ tiān shì Páidēngjié, shì Yìndùjiào de jiérì, gēn guò Xīnnián yíyàng.

Wáng mìshū : Xièxie nín yāoqǐng wǒmen dào nǐ jiā chīfàn.

Wéi jīnglǐ : Búkèqì. Nǐmen lái Yìndù, jiù xiàng shì wǒmen de jiārén.

Zhōu jīnglǐ : Páidēngjié nǐmen gēn jiārén yìqǐ chīfàn, hái zuò shénme shì ne?

Wéi jīnglǐ : Zhège jiérì dàgài sān tiān dào wǔ tiān, wǒ juéde zuì yǒu yìsi de shì diǎn yóudēng.

Wáng mìshū : Wǒ kànguò! Nǐmen zài jiā ménkǒu, hé biān...diǎnzhe xiǎo yóudēng.

Wéi jīnglǐ : Shì a! Yìsi shì xīwàng píng'ān. Wǒmen yě chuān xīn yī, fàng biānpào, yíng cáishén.

Wáng mìshū : Wǒ yě kànguò wǒ de Yìndù péngyǒu dài lǐwù qù tā jiěmèi jiā bàifǎng.

Wéi jīnglǐ : Zhè gēn Táiwān Chūnjié Dànián chū'èr, wǒ tàitai huí niángjiā yíyàng de yìsi ba!

Zhōu jīnglǐ : Méi cuò! Hěn wǎn le, wǒmen gāi zǒule. Xièxie zhāodài, zàijiàn.

課文英譯 Text in English

Dialogue

[Today is Diwali in India. Manager Wei of the Indian jewelry company invited Manager Zhou and Secretary Wang to be guests at home.]

Manager Wei : Welcome, welcome, please come in. This is my wife; she is Taiwanese.

Manager Zhou　: Hello. I am so happy to see people from my hometown here!

Manager Wei　: My wife is more than happy to see you! Would you please try the desserts she made, Indian desserts?

Secretary Wang　: That's great! It's not easy to make desserts with different flavors in different countries, right?

Manager Wei　: My wife made it according to the recipe, and she said it was not difficult at all.

[There is a loud sound of firecrackers outside.]

Manager Zhou　: The sound of firecrackers outside is so loud! It's so lively.

Manager Wei　: We are in Diwali, a Hindu festival; it's just like celebrating Chinese New Year.

Secretary Wang　: Thank you for inviting us to dinner at your house.

Manager Wei　: You are welcome. When you come to India, you are like our family.

Manager Zhou　: You have dinner with your family on Diwali. What else do you do?

Manager Wei　: There are about three to five days in the festival. I think the most interesting thing is lighting the oil lamps.

Secretary Wang　: I have seen it! You light a small oil lamp at the door of your house, by the river, etc.

Manager Wei　: Yes! It means to hope for peace. We also wear new clothes, set off firecrackers, and welcome the God of Wealth.

Secretary Wang : I have also seen my Indian friend bringing gifts when visiting her sister's house.

Manager Wei : This has the same meaning as my wife returning to her family on the second day of the Lunar New Year in Taiwan!

Manager Zhou : That's right! It's late; we should go. Thank you for your hospitality and goodbye.

生詞一 Vocabulary I 🎧

編號	生詞	漢語拼音	詞性	英文翻譯
1.	熱鬧	rènào	Vs	lively, bustling with noise and excitement
2.	家鄉	jiāxiāng	N	homeland
3.	高興	gāoxìng	Vs	happy
4.	甜點	tiándiǎn	N	sweets
5.	口味	kǒuwèi	N	flavor, taste
6.	食譜	shípǔ	N	recipe
7.	鞭炮	biānpào	N	firecrackers
8.	聲音	shēngyīn	N	sound
9.	節日	jiérì	N	festival
10.	邀請	yāoqǐng	V	to invite
11.	意思	yìsi	N	meaning
12.	拜訪	bàifǎng	V	to pay a visit
13.	春節	Chūnjié	N	Spring Festival (Chinese New Year)
14.	走	zǒu	Vi	to leave

專有名詞 Proper Nouns

編號	生詞	漢語拼音	英文翻譯
1.	排燈節	Páidēngjié	Diwali

短語 Phrases

編號	生詞	漢語拼音	英文翻譯
1.	點油燈	diǎn yóudēng	to light oil lamps
2.	放鞭炮	fàng biānpào	to let off firecrackers
3.	迎財神	yíng cáishén	to welcome the God of Wealth
4.	大年初二	Dànián chū'èr	the second day of the Chinese New Year
5.	回娘家	huí niángjiā	married women returning to their parents' home

短文 Reading 🎧

印度的油燈與臺灣的光明燈

　　點油燈是印度排燈節的重要習俗，而點光明燈是臺灣春節的重要習俗。

　　排燈節是印度的重要節日，也是著名的印度教節日。排燈節在每年的十月或十一月舉辦。在五天的慶祝活動中，最特別的是：很多人在家、在商店和辦公室的門上，放著小油燈，希望「燈」的光明帶給他們平安和財富。排燈節和臺灣的春節一樣，是和家人在一起的節日。

　　「燈」在佛經中是光明、智慧的意思。臺灣人點光明燈是為了祈求光明與平安。大概是過春節的時候，很多人會去寺廟付錢點光

明燈，希望新的一年都平安健康、事事如意。點光明燈的方法很容易，寫好姓名、生日和地址就可以了。點完以後，每個月的初一、十五，寺廟的人都會為他們念經。

　　印度排燈節的「點油燈」和臺灣的「點光明燈」雖然不一樣，但是點燈的人，他們的想法是一樣的，都希望年年健康如意。

課文漢語拼音 Text in Hanyu Pinyin

Yìndù de yóudēng yǔ Táiwān de guāngmíngdēng

　　Diǎn yóudēng shì Yìndù Páidēngjié de zhòngyào xísú, ér diǎn guāngmíngdēng shì Táiwān de zhòngyào xísú.

　　Páidēngjié shì Yìndù de zhòngyào jiérì, yěshì zhùmíng de Yìndùjiào jiérì. Páidēngjié zài měi nián de shí yuè huò shíyī yuè jǔbàn. Zài wǔ tiān de qìngzhù huódòng zhōng, zuì tèbié de shì: Hěn duō rén zài jiā, zài shāngdiàn hàn bàngōngshì de mén shàng, fàngzhe xiǎo yóudēng, xīwàng "dēng" de guāngmíng dài gěi tāmen píng'ān hàn cáifù. Páidēngjié hàn Táiwān de Chūnjié yíyàng, shì hàn jiārén zài yìqǐ de jiérì.

　　"Dēng" zài fójīng zhōng shì guāngmíng, zhìhuì de yìsi. Táiwān rén diǎn guāngmíngdēng shì wèile qíqiú guāngmíng yǔ píng'ān. Dàgài shì guò Chūnjié de shíhòu, hěn duō rén huì qù sìmiào fù qián diǎn guāngmíngdēng, xīwàng xīnde yì nián dōu píng'ān jiànkāng, shìshì rúyì. Diǎn guāngmíngdēng de fāngfǎ hěn róngyì, xiě hǎo xìngmíng, shēngrì hàn dìzhǐ jiù kěyǐ le. Diǎn wán yǐhòu, měi ge yuè de chūyī, shíwǔ, sìmiào de rén dōu huì wèi tāmen niànjīng.

　　Yìndù Páidēngjié de "diǎn yóudēng" hàn Táiwān de "diǎn guāngmíngdēng" suīrán bù yíyàng, dànshì diǎn dēng de rén, tāmen de xiǎngfǎ shì yíyàng de. Dōu xīwàng niánnián jiànkāng rúyì.

課文英譯 Text in English

Lighting Oil Lamps in India and Lighting the Good-Fortune Lamps in Taiwan

Lighting oil lamps is an essential custom on Diwali in India, while lighting the good-fortune lamps is important for the Chinese New Year in Taiwan.

Diwali is an important festival in India and a famous Hindu festival. Diwali is held in October or November every year. In the five-day celebration, the most remarkable event is that many people put small oil lamps on the doors of homes, shops, and offices, hoping that the light of the "lamps" will bring them peace and wealth. Diwali, like the Spring Festival in Taiwan, is a holiday for families to get together.

The word "lamp" means light and wisdom in Buddhist scriptures. Lighting the lamps is to pray for light and peace. Around the time of the Chinese New Year, many people will go to the temple to pay for the lighting of good-fortune lamps, hoping that the year will be safe and healthy and everything goes as one wishes. The method is easy: just write down your name, birth date, and address. After that, on the first and fifteenth days of every month, people in the temple will recite sutras for you.

Although Diwali's "lighting the oil lamp" in India and "lighting the good-fortune lamp" in Taiwan are not the same, the people who light the lamp have the same idea: hope to be healthy every year.

春節團圓

排燈節的小油燈

光明燈

生詞二 Vocabulary II 🎧

編號	生詞	漢語拼音	詞性	英文翻譯
1.	與	yǔ	Conj	and
2.	光明燈	guāngmíngdēng	N	good-fortune lamp
3.	重要	zhòngyào	Vs	important
4.	習俗	xísú	N	custom, convention, tradition
5.	而	ér	Conj	and, and yet, but
6.	著名	zhùmíng	Vs	famous
7.	舉辦	jǔbàn	V	to hold a ceremony
8.	慶祝	qìngzhù	V	to celebrate
9.	平安	píng'ān	N	safe
10.	財富	cáifù	N	wealth
11.	佛經	fójīng	N	Buddhist sutras
12.	光明	guāngmíng	N	bright
13.	智慧	zhìhuì	N	wisdom
14.	祈求	qíqiú	V	to pray for
15.	寺廟	sìmiào	N	temples

編號	生詞	漢語拼音	詞性	英文翻譯
16.	地址	dìzhǐ	N	address
17.	初一	chūyī	N	first day of a month
18.	十五	shíwǔ	N	the fifteenth day of a month
19.	念經	niàn jīng	V-sep	to chant Buddhist scripture
20.	想法	xiǎngfǎ	N	ways of thinking

短語 Phrases

編號	生詞	漢語拼音	英文翻譯
1.	事事如意	shìshì rúyì	Everything goes as you wish.

語法 Grammar 🎧

一、⋯呢 ne

說明：「呢」是助詞，一般用於句末。表示疑問、強調前述行為或事實是說話者的觀點或表示動作持續或進行。

Explanation：呢 *ne* is an auxiliary word, which is generally used at the end of a sentence to express doubts, emphasizing that actions or facts mentioned are before from the speaker's point of view. It can also indicate that the action continues or proceeds.

1. 表示疑問，用於「是非問句」以外的問句。

呢 *ne* expresses a question; it is used for questions other than "choice questions."

(1) 用於句中有疑問詞「哪、誰、什麼、怎麼」等。

呢 *ne* is used in sentences with question words "which, who, what, how," etc.

如：(a) 你放假要去哪裡玩呢？

(b) 你怎麼回家呢？

(c) 誰要喝咖啡呢？

(d) 你想吃什麼呢？

(2) 「呢」前面也可以只有一個名詞性成分。

There can also be only one nominal component in front of 呢 *ne*.

如：(a) 我的手機呢？

(b) 你的外套呢？

(c) 我要喝咖啡，你呢？

(3) 用於選擇問句的兩個項目後面，常用「還是」連接兩個項目。後項可不用「呢」。

The two items in a choice question sentence are often connected with 還是 *háishì*. The second item does not need to use 呢 *ne*.

如：(a) 你要喝咖啡呢？還是喝茶（呢）？

(b) 你要坐 auto 呢？還是坐地鐵（呢）？

2. 表示強調。To express emphasis.

如：(a) 我覺得他穿的衣服很好看呢！

(b) 印度甜點真的很好吃呢！

3. 動作持續或進行。When an action is continuing or in progress.

如：(a) 他在門口等著你呢！

(b) 我正在跟朋友一起吃飯呢！

例句：

1. A：你週末要做什麼呢？

   B：我要去游泳。

2. A：我覺得中文很難學。

   B：可是我覺得學中文很有意思呢！

3. A：我們去運動。

   B：外面下著雨呢！

練習：請用「呢」完成下面的問題。

Exercise：Please use 呢 *ne* to complete the following questions.

---

1. A：你晚飯想吃什麼呢？

　　B：＿＿＿＿＿＿＿＿＿＿＿＿＿＿＿。

2. A：臺灣菜和印度菜都很好吃。

　　B：我覺得＿＿＿＿＿＿＿＿＿＿＿！（A 比 B 更…呢！）

3. A：他今天也點了小籠包嗎？

　　B：不是，他今天點＿＿＿＿＿＿＿！

4. A：聽說小李生病了。

　　B：我正在他家＿＿＿＿＿＿＿＿！（陪著）

5. A：你在家嗎？

　　B：我一直在＿＿＿＿＿＿＿＿！（學校門口、等你）

二、V＋得／不＋結果補語／趨向補語　V＋得 *de* ／不 *bù* ＋ resultative complements or directional complements

說明：在動詞與結果補語或趨向補語的中間插入「得」或「不」，表示其結果可能或不可能達成。

Explanation：Insert 得 *de* or 不 *bù* in the middle of the resultative verb-complement or directional verb-complement to indicate that the result may or may not be achieved.

1. 動結式：V＋得／不＋結果補語 (RE)

　　Verb + Resultative complement form: V + 得 *de* ／不 *bù* + resultative complement (RE)

　　如：(1) 老師說的話，有些我聽不懂。

　　　　(2) 這種菜的做法不難，我一定做得好。

　　　　(3) 車上的人太多了，我聽不見你說什麼。

　　　　(4) 印度吃得到道地的臺灣菜嗎？

2. 動趨式：V+ 得 / 不 + 趨向補語 (DV)

Verb + Directional complement form: V + 得 *de* / 不 *bù* + directional complement (DV)

如：(1) 他感冒了，早上起不來，所以沒去上班。

(2) 下班時間車子這麼多，你半個小時回得來嗎？

(3) 這把椅子太重了，我拿不起來。

(4) 這座山有點高，你的車開得上去開不上去？

「V₁ 不 V₂」和「沒 V₁V₂」的用法不同。「V₁ 不 V₂」是指不具潛在能力（potential form），表示結果不可能達成；「沒 V₁V₂」是強調結果沒達成的事實（actual form）。

The usage of V₁ 不 *bù* V₂ and 沒 *méi* V₁V₂ are different. V₁ 不 *bù* V₂ refers to the lack of ability (potential form), which means that the result cannot be achieved; 沒 *méi* V₁V₂ emphasizes the fact that the result has not been achieved (actual form).

1. 我沒學會游泳。（Actual form）

2. 我怕水，所以學不會游泳。（Potential form）

3. 我沒買到回臺灣的機票。（Actual form）

4. 這家店東西不多，買不到合適的禮物。（Potential form）

例句：

1.「不」這個字很容易寫，每個人都學得會。

2. 你點這麼多菜，我們吃不完。

3. 日文的語法太難了，你學得下去嗎？

4. 我手機上的字很小，媽媽說她看不見。

練習：請用「V + 得 / 不 + 結果補語 / 趨向補語」完成下面的句子。

Exercise：Please use V + 得 *de* / 不 *bù* + resultative complement/directional complement to complete the following sentences.

1. A：這本中文書，你看得懂嗎？

　　B：我的中文不好，_____。

2. A：老師剛剛説什麼？

　　B：下課時間太吵了，我_____。（聽見）

3. A：用英文寫合約，你學得會學不會？

　　B：_____。我從小就學英文，所以沒問題。（學會）

4. A：我們明天早上六點去運動，你_____嗎？（起來）

　　B：我晚上早一點睡，應該_____。

5. A：你日本同學説的日文，你_____？（聽懂）

　　B：我只學過一點日文，他們説什麼我常_____。

三、一點都／也不　Emphatic Negation with 一點 *yìdiǎn* 都 *dōu* / 也 *yě* 不 *bù*

說明：「一點也不」強調強烈否定後面的情況。像英文的「not at all…」或「not a bit…」。「也」可以用「都」取代，否定的語氣更強，但是「一點也不」使用的頻率比較高。

Explanation：一點 *yìdiǎn* 都 *dōu* / 也 *yě* 不 *bù* emphasizes the strong negation of the situation that follows. Like the English "not at all" or "not a bit...", 也 *yě* can also be replaced with 都 *dōu* but with a stronger negative tone. However, 一點 *yìdiǎn* 也 *yě* 不 *bù* is used more frequently.

1. 後面可接動作動詞（V）或狀態動詞（Vs）。

　　The expression can be followed by action verbs (V) or state verbs (Vs).

　　如：(1) 我現在一點也不想睡覺。（V）

　　　　(2) 我今天一點都不累。（Vs）

　　　　(3) 你說的話，我一點都不懂。（V）

　　　　(4) 這部電影一點也不好看。（Vs）

2. 如果有賓語（O），賓語可放在句首當作話題。（O，S＋一點都／不）

If there is an object (O), the object can be placed at the beginning of the sentence as a topic. (O, S + 一點 *yìdiǎn* 都 *dōu*/ 不 *bù*)

如：(1) 臭豆腐，我一點也不想吃。

(2) 電視，我今天一點都不想看。

(3) 印度歌，我一點也不會唱。

(4) 甜點，他一點都不愛吃。

3. 如果有賓語（O），也可以放在「一點」的後面。（一點 + O + 都 / 不）

If there is an object (O), it can also be placed after 一點 *yìdiǎn*. (一點 *yìdiǎn* + object + 都 *dōu* / 不 *bù*)

如：(1) 我一點臭豆腐都不喜歡吃。

(2) 我今天一點電視也不想看。

(3) 我一點印度歌也不會唱。

(4) 他一點甜點都不愛吃。

4.「一點都 / 也不 + V」表示拒絕做某事。

一點 *yìdiǎn* 都 *dōu* / 也 *yě* 不 *bù* + V means refusing to do something.

如：(1) 我一點咖啡也不喝。

(2) 他剛剛不開心，一點飯都不吃。

(3) 我沒帶錢，所以一點東西都不買。

(4) 他不懂中文，所以一點中文書都不看。

5.「一點都 / 也沒 + V」表示否定過去的事件。（non-happening in the past）

一點 *yìdiǎn* 都 *dōu* / 也 *yě* 沒 *méi* + V means to deny past events. (non-happening in the past)

如：(1) 我昨天一點咖啡也沒喝。

(2) 他剛剛一點飯都沒吃。

(3) 我昨天晚上一點功課也沒寫。

(4) 他這個禮拜一點書都沒看。

例句：

　　1. 我今天一點也不忙。

　　2. 她太累了，現在一點也不想出去。

　　3. 功課，我昨天一點也沒做。

　　4. 我不渴，一點水都不想喝。

　　5. 他一點辣的東西都不吃。

　　6. 她不舒服，昨天晚上一點書都沒看。

練習：請用「一點都／也不（沒）V/Vs」回答下面的問題。

Exercise：Please use 一點 *yìdiǎn* 都 *dōu/* 也 *yě* 不 *bù (*沒 *méi)* V/Vs to answer the
　　　　following questions.

---

1. A：我做了很多菜，你要不要吃一點？

　 B：謝謝，可是我現在＿＿＿＿＿＿＿＿＿＿＿＿。

2. A：你出門要多帶一件外套。

　 B：不必帶吧！今天＿＿＿＿＿＿＿＿＿＿＿。

3. A：週末我們去打籃球，怎麼樣？

　 B：籃球，我＿＿＿＿＿＿＿，我們去看電影吧。

4. A：你有打工的經驗嗎？

　 B：我＿＿＿＿＿＿＿＿＿＿。

　 A：你吃早餐了嗎？

　 B：我＿＿＿＿＿＿＿，現在很餓。

四、V 好　Complement with V 好 *hǎo*

說明：「好」是表示結果的助詞，當動詞補語，意思是動作圓滿完成。

Explanation：好 *hǎo* is the auxiliary word that expresses the result. When this
　　　　　　 verb complement is used, it means that the action has been successfully

completed.

1. 「好」前面可結合的動詞如：買、做、搬、寫、想、計畫。可以是指
事實（actual form）或指潛在可能（potential form）。如下表：
The verbs that can be combined with 好 *hǎo* include 買 *mǎi* , 做 *zuò* , 搬
bān , 寫 *xiě* , 想 *xiǎng*, 計畫 *jìhuà*. They can refer to facts (actual form)
or refer to potential form. Please see the following table:

	Actual		Potential	
	V 好	沒 V 好	V 得好	V 不好
買	✓	✓	✕	✕
做	✓	✓	✓	✓
搬	✓	✓	✓	✓
寫	✓	✓	✓	✓
想	✓	✓	✕	✕
計畫	✓	✓	✓	✓

例句：

1. 出國旅行的事，我已經_____（計畫）了。
2. 我最近不能上網，因為網路還_____（裝）。
3. 我今天很忙，所以作業_____（寫）。

練習：請選用下列的動詞搭配「好」，完成下面的問題或句子。

Exercise：Please combine the following verbs with 好 *hǎo* to complete the
following questions or sentences.

（計畫、搬、買、做、裝 *zhuāng*: to install）

1. A：颱風快來了，我們得去超市買一些吃的東西。

　B：放心，我已經_____了。

2. A：去旅行的事，你_____了沒有？

　B：還沒，我還要再想想。

3. A：媽媽，我肚子很餓。

　B：快_____了，等一下就可以吃了。

4. 熱水器還沒_____，所以現在還不能用。

5. 很多朋友幫我搬家，所以很快就_____了。

跨文化延伸 Cross-Cultural Extension

Congratulatory Phrases in Chinese

"Congratulations" means to celebrate and congratulate. "Congratulatory words" are words quoted when congratulating each other on special holidays or days. These words are all targeted at special events or individuals and are full of emotional content.

Chinese people attach great importance to interpersonal relationships. They all hope to appropriately express their concern and congratulations on appropriate occasions, such as the Spring Festival, the opening of a company, housewarming, marriage, and birthdays. Most of these congratulatory words are "Four-Character Idioms."

A "four-character idiom" is an idiom composed of four Chinese characters and has a fixed meaning. Commonly used four-character congratulatory words for marriage are "a match made in heaven" (天作之合 *tiānzuòzhīhé*); "a union of one heart forever" (永結同心 *yǒngjié-tóngxīn*); "a good match for a hundred years" (百年好合 *bǎinián-hǎohé*); and "wish you to live to old age together" (白頭偕老 *báitóuxiélǎo*). New Year's greetings are "Congratulations on getting rich" (恭喜發財 *gōngxǐ-fācái*); "have a peaceful year" (歲歲平安 *suìsuì-píng'ān*); "all the best" (萬事如意 *wànshì-rúyì*) and "may all your wishes come true" (心想事成 *xīnxiǎng-shìchéng*). Birthday greetings include "May you live a long life up to hundred years old" (長命百歲 *zhǎngmìng-bǎisuì*); "be safe and healthy" (平安健康 *píng'ān-jiànkāng*); "smooth sailing" (一帆風順 *yìfānfēngshùn*), and "we wish you happiness" (幸福快樂 *xìngfú-kuàilè*). Among them, the one that applies on all occasions is: "We wish that everything goes as you wish, and everything you want comes true" (萬事如意，心想事成 *wànshì-rúyì*, *xīnxiǎng-shìchéng*).

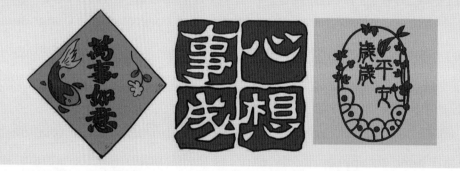

語言任務 Language Tasks

一、學生兩人一組，依提示各表示自己的看法。

Break students into groups of two and then according to the instructions, express each other's opinions.

任務：A 依提示說出看法，B 用「一點都 / 也不（沒）V/Vs＋呢！」說出不同情況或觀點。

Task：A expresses an opinion, then B uses " 一點 *yìdiǎn* 都 *dōu* / 也 *yě* 不 *bù*（沒 *méi)* V/Vs＋呢 *ne* ！" to present a different point of view from A.

提示語	A 的看法	B 不同的看法
1. 電影 / 好看	我們昨天去看的那部電影真不錯！	我覺得那部電影一點都 / 也不好看呢！
2. 沒看到你 / 很忙	好幾天沒看到你了，你最近很忙嗎？	
3. 吃甜點 / 怕（胖）	你吃這麼多甜點，不怕胖嗎？	
4. 做功課 / 想睡覺		
5. 冷氣 / 好冷		
6. 考試 / 念好		

二、學生兩個人一組，用「V + 得 / 不 + 結果補語 / 趨向補語」、「V 好」聊「學開車、學中文、寫漢字、做甜點、搬家、旅行、買禮物、裝冷氣⋯。」

可用的動詞，如：聽、看、學、想、回、做、搬、買、裝、計畫、決定、準備

Break students into groups of two, then use "V + 得 *de* / 不 *bù* + resultative complement/directional complement" and "V 好 *hǎo*" to chat about learning how to drive, learning Chinese, character writing, making desserts, moving, traveling, gift buying, and installing air conditioners, etc.

例句：1. A：我最近很想學開車。可是我怕學不會。

　　　 B：別擔心！多花一點時間，常常練習一定學得會。

　　 2. A：明天要送印度朋友的禮物，你買了嗎？

　　　 B：放心，已經買好了。

第五課　去喝喜酒
Lesson 5　Going to a Wedding Reception

課程目標：

Topic：婚禮文化

　　　1. 能使用有關婚禮的相關詞彙。

　　　2. 能介紹印度婚禮新娘的服飾、繞火堆等傳統。

　　　3. 能了解參加印度婚禮的服飾、禮金等習俗。

　　　4. 能說明臺灣現代婚禮形式。

Lesson Objectives：

Topic：Wedding Culture

　　　1. Students can use vocabulary related to weddings.

　　　2. Students can introduce traditions such as the bride's costumes, circling around the fire, etc.

　　　3. Students can understand the customs of attending Indian weddings, such as costumes and gift money.

　　　4. Students can describe modern forms of wedding in Taiwan.

Wedding Costumes in India

對話 Dialogue 🎧

周經理：王祕書，你再幫我看看，今天穿這套紗麗合適嗎？

王祕書：都到了，您還在擔心？紗麗是印度正式的禮服，不會錯的。

桑　吉：看起來真是美極了！兩位好，我是新郎的弟弟桑吉，替哥哥來招待貴賓。

周經理：您好！我們來自臺灣，麻煩您了。（轉身）王祕書，你看，我穿藍色的禮服會不會跟新娘的一樣？

桑　吉：不會的！印度新娘傳統的禮服大部分是紅的、白的加金色。

周經理：謝謝。對了，王祕書，等一下給新娘的紅包和金飾帶了沒有？

王祕書：都帶了，紅包在這兒，一共是八千塊，發、發、發，多吉利啊！

周經理：太好了，我們快進去參加婚禮吧！

桑　吉：慢點，先換個紅包袋吧。

周經理：怎麼了？為什麼要換？

桑　　吉：因為我們送尾數是「一」，不送尾數是「零」的禮金。

王祕書：對啊，我怎麼忘了？只想到按照臺灣的文化，「八」是最好的祝福。

桑　　吉：在印度「一」表示新人兩人一心，從「一」開始，未來家運興旺。

周經理：所以紅包袋上黏一塊盧比，尾數就一定是「一」了。

王祕書：快看，新郎新娘開始繞火堆了，聽說得繞七次…。

桑　　吉：對，是希望平安、健康、永遠愛對方。晚上喜宴能請兩位一起跳舞嗎？

課文漢語拼音 Text in Hanyu Pinyin

Zhōu jīnglǐ：Wáng mìshū, nǐ zài bāng wǒ kànkan, jīntiān chuān zhè tào shālì héshì ma?

Wáng mìshū：Dōu dào le, nín hái zài dānxīn? Shālì shì Yìndù zhèngshì de lǐfú, bú huì cuò de.

Sāngjí：Kàn qǐlái zhēn shì měi jí le! Liǎng wèi hǎo, wǒ shì xīnláng de dìdi Sāngjí, tì gēge lái zhāodài guìbīn

Zhōu jīnglǐ：Nín hǎo! Wǒmen láizì Táiwān, máfán nín le. (Zhuǎnshēn) Wáng mìshū, nǐ kàn, wǒ chuān lánsè de lǐfú huì bú huì gēn xīnniáng de yíyàng?

Sāngjí：Bú huì de! Yìndù xīnniáng chuántǒng de lǐfú dà bùfèn shì hóng de, bái de jiā jīnsè.

Zhōu jīnglǐ：Xièxie. Duì le, Wáng mìshū, děngyíxià gěi xīnniáng de hóngbāo hàn jīnshì dàile méiyǒu?

Wáng mìshū : Dōu dàile, hóngbāo zài zhè'er, yígòng shì bāqiān kuài, fā, fā, fā, fā, duó jílì a!

Zhōu jīnglǐ : Tài hǎo le, wǒmen kuài jìnqù cānjiā hūnlǐ ba!

Sāngjí : Màn diǎn, xiān huàn ge hóngbāodài ba.

Zhōu jīnglǐ : zěnmele? Wèishénme yào huàn?

Sāngjí : Yīnwèi wǒmen sòng wěishù shì "yī", bú sòng wěishù shì "líng" de lǐjīn.

Wáng mìshū : Duì a, wǒ zěnme wàng le? Zhǐ xiǎngdào ànzhào Táiwān de wénhuà, "bā" shì zuì hǎo de zhùfú.

Sāngjí : Zài Yìndù "yī" biǎoshì xīnrén liǎngrén yìxīn, cóng "yī" kāishǐ, wèilái jiāyùn xīngwàng.

Zhōu jīnglǐ : Suǒyǐ hóngbāodài shàng nián yí kuài lúbǐ, wěishù jiù yídìng shì "yī" le.

Wáng mìshū : Kuài kàn, xīnláng xīnniáng kāishǐ rào huǒ duī le, tīngshuō děi rào qī cì….

Sāngjí : Duì, shì xīwàng píng'ān, jiànkāng, yǒngyuǎn ài duìfāng. Wǎnshàng xǐyàn néng qǐng liǎngwèi yìqǐ tiàowǔ ma?

課文英譯 Text in English

Dialogue

Manager Zhou : Secretary Wang, can you help me again? Is this sari suitable for today?

Secretary Wang : We've already arrived. Are you still worried? Sari is a formal dress in India; you can't go wrong with that.

Sanji : It looks so beautiful! Hello, you two. I am Sanji, the bridegroom's younger brother. I will entertain distinguished guests for my brother.

Manager Zhou : Hello! We are from Taiwan. Thanks for the trouble. (Turns around) Secretary Wang, look, will my blue dress look like the bride's?

Sanji : Not at all! Indian brides' traditional dresses are primarily red and white with gold mixed in.

Manager Zhou : Thank you. By the way, Secretary Wang, did we bring our red envelope and gold jewelry that we need to give to the bride?

Secretary Wang : We brought it all. The red envelope is here; it contains 8,000 rupees in total. Fā, fā, and fā, it's so auspicious!

Manager Zhou : Great! Let's go to the wedding reception.

Sanji : One moment, please. It would be best if you change the red envelope first.

Manager Zhou : What's wrong with it? Why do we need to change the envelope?

Sanji : It's because we only give amounts that end in "one"; we don't give the amount of gift money that ends in "zero."

Secretary Wang : Oh, how did I forget it? I just thought that according to Taiwanese culture, "eight" is the best blessing.

Sanji : In India, the number "one" represents the two newly-weds becoming one heart, and starting with "one," their family fortunes will be prosperous in the future.

Manager Zhou : Therefore, if you stick one rupee on the red envelope, the total will become a number ending in "one."

Secretary Wang : Look, the bride and groom are starting to go around the fire. I heard that they must go around it seven times.

Sanji : Yes, it is to wish for a safe, healthy life and love each other forever. Oh yeah, for tonight's wedding banquet, can I invite both of you to dance with us?

生詞一 Vocabulary I 🎧

編號	生詞	漢語拼音	詞性	英文翻譯
1.	喜酒	xǐjiǔ	N	wedding feast
2.	紗麗	shālì	N	sari
3.	都	dōu	Adv	already
4.	禮服	lǐfú	N	formal dress, full dress
5.	新郎	xīnláng	N	bridegroom
6.	新娘	xīnniáng	N	bride
7.	加	jiā	V	to add
8.	金色	jīnsè	N	golden color
9.	紅包	hóngbāo	N	money wrapped in red as a gift, lit. "red envelope"
10.	金飾	jīnshì	N	gold jewelry
11.	發	fā	Vp	to sprout, to grow, to prosper

編號	生詞	漢語拼音	詞性	英文翻譯
12.	吉利	jílì	Vs	auspicious
13.	參加	cānjiā	V	to participate
14.	婚禮	hūnlǐ	N	wedding ceremony
15.	換	huàn	V	to change
16.	紅包袋	hóngbāodài	N	red envelope bags
17.	尾數	wěishù	N	the remainder of a number
18.	祝福	zhùfú	N/V	blessings; to wish sb. well
19.	黏	nián	V	to stick
20.	盧比	lúbǐ	N	rupee
21.	未來	wèilái	N	future
22.	家運	jiāyùn	N	family fortunes
23.	興旺	xīngwàng	Vs	prosperous, thriving
24.	喜宴	xǐyàn	N	wedding banquet

短語 Phrases

編號	生詞	漢語拼音	英文翻譯
1.	看起來	kànqǐlái	to look like
2.	極了	jíle	extremely
3.	繞火堆	rào huǒduī	go around the sacred fire

短文 Reading 🎧

臺灣婚禮

　　臺灣的婚禮有越來越多不同的形式，連跳傘、潛水或是騎著白馬的古代婚禮，都能見到。形式越特別，年輕人越喜歡。不過大部

分新人還是選在飯店舉行婚禮。

結婚這天，在鞭炮聲中，新郎一到新娘家，就得接受很多挑戰，才能見到新娘。離開娘家前，很多新娘都會捨不得地哭了。車子一開，她就得把扇子丟出窗外，丟掉壞習慣，開始新生活。到了新郎家，新娘得跨火爐，把平安吉祥帶到新家。

婚禮開始，新娘的父親把女兒交給新郎，然後新人的父母說些祝福的話，再請大家舉杯祝福新人。喜宴開始，客人吃著東西，看新人從小到大的影片。這時，新娘穿著另外一件漂亮的禮服，跟新郎和兩人的父母一起敬酒。除了敬酒，新人還會跟大家玩遊戲、送客人小禮物。最後新人拿著喜糖站在門口送客，客人開心地和新人照相，婚禮就在熱鬧的氣氛中結束了。

課文漢語拼音 Text in Hanyu Pinyin

Táiwān hūnlǐ

Táiwān de hūnlǐ yǒu yuè lái yuè duō bùtóng de xíngshì, lián tiàosǎn, qiánshuǐ huòshì qízhe báimǎ de gǔdài hūnlǐ, dōu néng jiàn dào. Xíngshì yuè tèbié, niánqīng rén yuè xǐhuān. Búguò dàbùfèn xīnrén háishì xuǎn zài fàndiàn jǔxíng hūnlǐ.

Jiéhūn zhè tiān, zài biānpào shēng zhōng, xīnláng yí dào xīnniáng jiā, jiù děi jiēshòu hěnduō tiǎozhàn, cái néng jiàndào xīnniáng. Líkāi niángjiā qián, hěnduō xīnniáng dōu huì shěbùdé de kū le. Chēzi yì kāi, tā jiù děi bǎ shànzi diūchū chuāngwài, diūdiào huài xíguàn, kāishǐ xīn shēnghuó. Dàole xīnláng jiā, xīnniáng děi kuà huǒlú, bǎ píng'ān jíxiáng dài dào xīnjiā.

Hūnlǐ kāishǐ, xīnniáng de fùqīn bǎ Nǚ'ér jiāo gěi xīnláng, ránhòu xīnrén de fùmǔ shuō xiē zhùfú de huà, zài qǐng dàjiā jǔ bēi zhùfú xīnrén.

Xǐyàn kāishǐ, kèrén chīzhe dōngxi, kàn xīnrén cóngxiǎo dào dà de yǐngpiàn. Zhèshí, xīnniáng chuānzhe lìngwài yí jiàn piàoliàng de lǐfú, gēn xīnláng hàn liǎng rén de fùmǔ yìqǐ jìngjiǔ. Chúle jìngjiǔ, xīnrén hái huì gēn dàjiā wán yóuxì, sòng kèrén xiǎo lǐwù. Zuìhòu xīnrén názhe xǐtáng zhàn zài ménkǒu sòng kè, kèrén kāixīn de hàn xīnrén zhàoxiàng, hūnlǐ jiù zài rènào de qìfēn zhōng jiéshù le.

課文英譯 Text in English

Taiwanese Weddings

There are more and more different forms of weddings in Taiwan; even parachuting, diving, or old-style weddings such as riding a white horse can be seen. The more exceptional the form, the more younger people like it. However, most new couples still choose to hold their wedding in a hotel.

On the wedding day, with the sound of firecrackers, once the bridegroom arrives at the bride's house, he needs to pass many challenges before he can see the bride. Before leaving their parents' home, many brides would cry because of their reluctance to leave their family home. As soon as the car starts to drive off, she would throw a fan out the window, signifying throwing away bad habits and starting a new life. Arriving at the groom's house, the bride needs to cross a hot stove to symbolize the bringing of peace and good fortune to her new home.

At the beginning of the wedding, the bride's father would hand over his daughter to the groom. Then the new couple's parents would say some words of blessings and ask everyone to raise their glasses to bless the couple. At the beginning of the wedding banquet, guests would watch videos of the new couple's journeys from childhood to adulthood while eating. At this time, the bride would wear another beautiful dress and toast with the bridegroom and their parents. In addition to the toasting, the couple will also play games with everyone and give small gifts to the guests. Finally, the couple would take the wedding candy and stand at the door to see the guests off. Guests would happily take photos with the couple, and the wedding would end in a lively atmosphere.

生詞二 Vocabulary II 🎧

編號	生詞	漢語拼音	詞性	英文翻譯
1.	形式	xíngshì	N	form
2.	跳傘	tiàosǎn	V-sep	to parachute
3.	潛水	qiánshuǐ	V-sep	to dive
4.	新人	xīnrén	N	newly-wed
5.	舉行	jǔxíng	V	to hold (a meeting, conference, etc.)
6.	結婚	jiéhūn	Vp-sep	to get married
7.	挑戰	tiǎozhàn	N	challenge
8.	離開	líkāi	Vpt	to leave
9.	吉祥	jíxiáng	N	auspiciousness, good luck
10.	敬酒	jìngjiǔ	V-sep	to make a toast with wine
11.	遊戲	yóuxì	N	game
12.	喜糖	xǐtáng	N	wedding candies
13.	氣氛	qìfēn	N	atmosphere

短語 Phrases

編號	生詞	漢語拼音	英文翻譯
1.	捨不得	shěbùdé	reluctant
2.	跨火爐	kuà huǒlú	to cross a hot stove

語法 Grammar 🎧

一、Vs 極了、Vs 得不得了、Vs 得很　　terribly, extremely

Adverbial Complements 極了 jí le, 得不得了 de bùdéliǎo, 得很 de hěn

說明：副詞補語「極了」、「得不得了」、「得很」表示效果與程度增強的補語，搭配在動詞後使用。這些與置於動詞前面的副詞「很」、「非常」、「相當」不同，程度補語表示的程度更強一些。但這些補語不能跟「比」的句子搭配使用。

Explanation：Adverbial complements such as 極了 *jí le*, 得不得了 *de bùdéliǎo*, 得很 *de hěn* indicate stronger in effect and are used after the verb. These are different from adverbs such as 很 *hěn*, 非常 *fēicháng* and 相當 *xiāngdāng* which are usually placed in front of the verb. Adverbial complements express stronger intensity in effect; however, they cannot be used in conjunction with 比 *bǐ* sentences.

1. 「極了」在形容某一狀態時，強度屬於最高等級，大多用在正面的意義，但也可用於負面。

   極了 *jí le* is the highest level of intensity when describing a certain state. It is mainly used in a positive sense, but it can also be used negatively.

   如：(1) 新娘穿著紅色的禮服，真是美極了。

   　　(2) 不能參加姐姐的婚禮，美美難過極了。

2. 「得不得了」也是強度最高等級的詞彙，多用於正面意義和口語，也有少部分用於負面意義。

   得不得了 *de bùdéliǎo* is, perhaps, the most powerful expression. It is mainly used in positive and spoken language, and on rare occasions, it has a negative meaning.

如：(1) 拿到很特別的喜糖，客人都開心得不得了。

(2) 剛買的手機就有問題，他氣得不得了。

3.「得很」，強度比前兩者稍低。

The intensity of 得很 *de hěn* is slightly lower than the previous two.

如：(1) 爸爸週末要帶我們去印度門玩，大家都開心得很。

(2) 一晚沒睡覺，我現在累得很。

4. 不可與「比」的句子搭配使用。

These adverb complements cannot be used in conjunction with the comparative pattern with 比 *bǐ*.

如：(1) *這裡春天的天氣比臺北冷極了。

(2) *弟弟拿到獎學金，媽媽比他開心得不得了。

例句：

1. 印度紗麗，有各種顏色，美極了。

2. 昨天大家給他過生日，玩得開心得不得了。

3. 跟自己喜歡的人結婚，她覺得幸福得很。

練習：請用「極了、得不得了、得很」回答句子。

Exercise：Please respond with 極了 *jí le*, 得不得了 *de bùdéliǎo*, 得很 *de hěn*.

---

1. A：聽說你要去新德里，到了車站有人接你嗎？。

   B：不用，那裡的捷運_____，我自己搭車就行了。（方便）

2. A：昨天去參加王經理婚禮的人多嗎？

   B：真是_____，還有些人沒位子坐呢。（多）

3. A：我下個月要去印度旅行，你覺得買紗麗怎麼樣？

   B：你一定要買，因為在印度買_____。（便宜）

---

4. A：你看，紅包袋上黏了一塊錢！

　　B：這個紅包袋的設計真的_____。（特別）

5. A：你怎麼了，不舒服嗎？

　　B：可能感冒了，昨天下雨我沒帶傘，現在頭_____。（痛）

6. A：很多臺灣人喜歡打棒球，在印度呢？

　　B：當然是板球，印度人覺得這種運動_____。（好玩）

7. A：臺灣的孩子非常愛滑手機，很多孩子還很小，眼睛就很差。

　　B：我國最近也一樣，孩子們的眼睛_____。（差）

二、V 起來₁　Judgmental V 起來 *qǐlái1*　it's my assessment that⋯

說明：「V 起來₁」是一個動詞補語，表達說話者對人事物或某種情況，透過人體動作、思考得出的看法、評價或判斷。其中的 V，所使用的動詞常常是感官動詞或動作動詞，這些評價或判斷通常是藉由我們的「眼、耳、口、鼻、手、身體」直接或間接產生的。如：看起來、聽起來、吃起來、喝起來、聞起來、摸起來、穿起來⋯等。

Explanation：V 起來 *qǐlái*₁ is a verb complement that expresses the speaker's views, evaluations, or judgments about people, things, or certain situations based on human actions and thoughts. The verbs used are often sensory verbs or action verbs. These evaluations or judgments are usually produced directly or indirectly through our "eyes, ears, mouth, nose, hands, and body," for example, 看起來 kàn qǐlái, 聽起來 tīng qǐlái, 吃起來 chī qǐlái, 喝起來 hē qǐlái, 聞起來 wén qǐlái, 摸起來 mō qǐlái, 穿起來 chuān qǐlái, etc.

1. 「V 起來₁」前面的主語，是動詞要評論的對象；「V 起來」後面的部分則是說話者的評論。

The subject before V 起來 *qǐlái*₁ is the object of the verb's comment; the part after V 起來 *qǐlái*₁ is the speaker's comment.

如：西方人覺得中文的四聲聽起來像唱歌。

2.「V 起來」前面的主語，一般應該加上限定詞「這、那、臺灣的⋯ 」等，所評論的對象才更清楚。

The subject in front of V 起來 *qǐlái*₁ should generally be added with the qualifier " 這 *zhè*, 那 *nà*, 臺灣的 *Táiwān de*," etc., to make the object of the comment clearer.

如：(1) 這件衣服你穿起來很漂亮。

(2) 這個西瓜吃起來好甜。

(3) 這家店的臭豆腐聞起來特別臭。

(4) 臺灣的烏龍茶喝起來很好喝。

3.「V 起來₁」結構本身沒有否定式，若有否定的意思可置於後面的內容。

如：這支手機用起來不太方便。

The V 起來 *qǐlái*₁ structure itself does not have a negative expression. If there is a negative meaning, it can be placed in the content following the expression.

例句：

1. 這杯茶聞起來很香。

2. 這件事聽起來有點可怕。

3. 這件禮服穿起來，人比較瘦。

4. 新娘看起來又聰明又漂亮。

5. 這個菜吃起來有點酸，是不是壞了？

練習：請用「V 起來₁」來形容下圖。

Exercise：Please use V 起來 *qǐlái*₁ to describe the pictures below.

話題	V 起來
1. 紅包袋	（看／用） 印度的紅包袋，看起來漂亮，用起來方便
2. 印度大餅	（聞／吃）
3. auto	（看／坐）
4. 紗麗	（看／穿）
5. 新人	（笑⋯好看／看⋯幸福）

三、連⋯都／也⋯　連 *lián*... 都 *dōu*/ 也 *yě* even

說明：「連⋯都／也⋯　」用介詞「連」引出要強調的成分，可以是主語也可
　　　以是賓語。表示強調的都這樣了，其他情況更不用說了。焦點主要在

「連」引出的部分上，如果是正面的意義，強調最好的可能性，如果是負面的意思，則是最差的情形。「連…都／也…」其中「都」和「也」可以互相替換，強調的成分要放在「連」和「都／也」的中間。

Explanation：連 *lián*... 都 *dōu*/ 也 *yě*... uses the preposition 連 *lián* to introduce the element to be emphasized which can be the subject or the object. That is all that is emphasized without commenting on other situations. The focus is mainly on the part led by 連 *lián*. If it is a positive meaning, it highlights the best possibility. If it is a negative meaning, it then emphasizes a worst case. In 連 *lián*... 都 *dōu*/ 也 *yě*..., 都 *dōu* and 也 *yě* are mutually replaceable, and emphasis should be placed on the content in the middle of 連 *lián* and 都 *dōu*/ 也 *yě*.

1. 強調主語。

   It emphasizes the subject.

   如：(1) 連老師都到了，你怎麼還在家裡？

   (2) 這個字連三歲小孩都會寫。

2. 強調賓語，可以是詞或詞組。

   It emphasizes the object, which can be a word or phrase.

   如：(1) 他什麼菜都會做，連法國大餐也沒問題。

   (2) 今天忙著工作，他連一口飯都沒吃。

3. 強調謂語動詞。「連」如果後接動詞，特別是強調動詞重疊的否定句，表示可能生氣或比較不禮貌。

   It emphasizes the predicate verb. If 連 *lián* is followed by a verb, especially in a negative sentence that emphasizes the overlapping of verbs, it carries an angry or impolite connotation.

   如：(1) 妹妹哭了，爸爸連問都沒問，就打了弟弟。

   (2) 李先生送她的禮物，王小姐連看都沒看，就送給朋友了。

4. 如果重點在引出的賓語上，「連 + 強調成分」這個部分，則放在主詞前、後都可以。

   If the emphasis is on the elicited object, the " 連 *lián*... + emphasized component" part can be placed before or after the subject.

如：(1) 他連照片都忘了帶。

　　　(2) 連照片，他都忘了帶。

例句：

1. 這首歌很容易，連小孩都會唱。

2. 他會說英文、中文、印度文，連法文也說得很好。

3. 他已經學了四個多月的中文了，可是連一到十都說不好。

4. 媽媽要送給朋友的蛋糕，弟弟回家連問都沒問就吃了。

5. 他常常上課連課本都不帶，真不是好學生。

6. 連課本，他常常上課都不帶，真不是好學生。

練習：請把下面的句子改寫一遍。

Exercise：Please rewrite the following sentences.

例句：

　　王經理很喜歡旅行，他去過德里（Delhi）、孟買（Mumbai）、加爾各答（Kolkata），瓦拉納西（Varanasi）也都去過。

　　→王經理很喜歡旅行，他去過德里、孟買、加爾各答，連瓦拉納西都去過。

1. 昨天雨下得好大，在高速公路上開車，一公尺前的路都看不見。
　→ _____ 。

2. 他的成績太差了，三次加起來不到一百分。
　→ _____ 。

3. 桑吉的皮包丟了，別說一千塊，現在一塊也沒有。
　→ _____ 。

4. 他會打籃球、棒球、網球…（什麼球都會打），印度板球也打得很好。
　→ _____ 。

5. 他太累了，沒洗澡就睡了。
　→ _____ 。

6. 弟弟太不小心了，出國忘了帶護照（*hùzhào* passport）。

→ _____。（主語＋連＋focus part＋都）

→ _____。（連＋focus part＋主語＋都）

四、越 *yuè* …，越 *yuè* …　　　the more…, the more …

說明：「越…，越… 」是兩種或兩種以上的動作或狀態，第二部分隨著前者的變化而發展、增加或變化，是一種程度上的改變，越來越強或越來越弱均可。

Explanation：越 *yuè* …，越 *yuè* … are used to describe two or more actions or states. The second part develops, increases, or changes with the change of the former. It is a kind of change which becomes stronger and stronger or weaker and weaker.

1. 有多種搭配，A 可以是動作或狀態，B 是一種狀態，B 隨 A 變化。第一部分和第二部分大部分出現在同一個句子中，但有時也會分開，以兩個分句的形式出現。

   There are many collocations, "A" can be an action or a state; if "B" is a state, then "B" changes with "A." The first part and the second part mostly appear in the same sentence, but sometimes they are separated and appear in the form of two clauses.

   如：

(1) 越 V 越 Vs	• 越吃越胖 • 雨越下越大 • 越走越快 • 越想越擔心 • 字越寫越快 • 歌越唱越好
(2) 越 Vs 越 Vs	• 越多越好 • 越快越好 • 越好越貴 • 越辣越香 • 越難越好玩
(3)（兩個分句） 主語一…越 A，（主語二）…越 B	• 你越不會，越應該多練習 • 酒放得越久，味道越香 • 客人越多，氣氛越熱鬧

2. 複習「越來越」：是用來比較人或事物的數量或程度隨著時間不斷發展或變化，是同一事物不同時期或不同條件的發展，後面不能用其他的程度副詞，如：很、非常…等。句尾常用「了」表示改變了。Review of 越 *yuè* 來 *lái* 越 *yuè*…: This sentence pattern which literally means "more and more...", is used to compare the number of people or degree of a certain state that develops continuously or changes over time. It refers to the development of the same event in different periods or under different conditions. Other degree adverbs, such as 很 *hěn* and 非常 *fēicháng*, cannot be used after it. The 了 *le* at the end of the sentence indicates change.

　如：(1) 學中文的人越來越多了。

　　　(2) *學中文的人越來越很多了。

例句：

1. 他的中文越說越好了。　　　　　　　　　　（越 V 越 Vs）
2. 印度人覺得印度菜越辣越好吃。　　　　　　（越 Vs 越 Vs）
3. 你們最近關係越不好，越應該多聊聊。　　　（…越 A，…越 B）
4. 按照習俗，關係越近，婚禮的紅包送得越大。（…越 A，…越 B）
5. 地點離市中心越近，房子越貴。　　　　　　（…越 A，…越 B）

練習：請用下列括弧裡的動詞或形容詞，完成越…越…的句子。

Exercise：Please use the following verbs or adjectives in the brackets to complete 越 *yuè*…，越 *yuè*… sentences.

1. 這麼晚了她還沒回家，媽媽＿＿＿＿＿＿＿。（想，怕）
2. 這種甜點真好吃，一吃就停不下來，＿＿＿＿＿＿。（吃，停）
3. 雨＿＿＿＿＿＿，開車得小心一點。（下，大）
4. 他這兩年生意＿＿＿＿＿＿，現在非常有錢。（做，好）
5. 有些人覺得咖啡＿＿＿＿＿＿。（苦，好喝）
6. 東西＿＿＿＿＿＿，當然賣得＿＿＿＿＿＿。（好，貴）

Lesson 5

跨文化延伸 Cross-Cultural Extension

The Wedding Ceremony

The Chinese wedding ceremony is associated with many unique cultural elements. For example, weddings were originally called "dusk ceremony;" "bridal chamber," "throwing a fan," and "crossing the fire," are each also meaningful in their own way.

In ancient times, there was no formal wedding ceremony. If the bridegroom fancied a girl, he would just take the girl and ran away during dusk. Then they would hide in a cave to become a husband and wife. When the bride's family finished working the fields, only then would they find out that their daughter was taken. When the daughter was found, it would already be on the second day, so they had to agree to the wedding. Because at dusk the groom's family gained a daughter, it was changed to the "wedding."[1] Similarly, because the first night of the marriage was consummated in a cave, the bridal chamber thus was called the "cave room."

In addition, the custom of the bride's "throwing a fan," apart from the pronunciation of "fan" (*shàn*) and "to separate" (*sàn*) sounding similar, parents also hope that as soon as their daughter marries out, she would lose any bad habits. The ceremony of "crossing over a hot stove" is a way of praying to the fire god to get rid of any bad luck and bring "prosperity," represented by the fire's roaring flame (in the character of 旺 *wàng)* into the husband's house.

---

[1] 「女」+「昏」=「婚」

India also attaches great importance to weddings. The bride and groom must walk seven laps around the fire, asking the god of fire to bless them with peace, health, love forever, and the ability to revitalize the family. This is like the meaning of our country's proverbs "bearing a precious son early" and "a hundred years of harmony." Although Taiwan and India have different languages, they have similar cultures. Isn't it interesting?

「扇 shàn」和「散 sàn」

火神的祝福
Blessing of the fire god

跨火爐
Crossing a hot stove

語言任務 Language Tasks

一、任務：兩個人一組

(1) 將下面的五張圖按照婚禮習俗，由 1 至 5 依序編號。

(2) 各組按照圖片跟同學說說臺灣婚禮的情形，每組兩分鐘。

1. Task：Groups of two

   (1) Number the following five pictures in order from 1 to 5 in accordance with the wedding customs.

   (2) According to the pictures, each group will tell each other about weddings in Taiwan. Each group will have two minutes.

Lesson 5

圖一　　　　　圖二　　　　　圖三　　　　　圖四　　　　　圖五

二、角色扮演：介紹一個你參加過或看過的婚禮。

學生四人一組，一人當主持人，訪問三位朋友。請用下面表格做訪問，每人用本課學過的語法或生詞，回答 3-4 個問題。

Role play: Introduce a wedding ceremony you have attended or seen.

Divide students into groups of four students, with one student as the host, interviewing three friends. Please use the form below for the interviews. Each person should use the grammar or new words learned in this lesson to answer 3-4 questions.

問題	回答
1. 誰結婚？	我表哥結婚。
2. 跟誰一起去參加的？	
3. 婚禮是在哪裡舉行的？	
4. 新郎、新娘穿什麼禮服？	
5. 客人穿什麼？	
6. 你包紅包了嗎？怎麼包的？為什麼？	
7. 貴國包禮金有什麼習俗？	
8. 你在婚禮中還看到什麼風俗或文化？	
9. 臺灣和印度婚禮有什麼不同？	
10. 你想要一個什麼樣的婚禮？為什麼？	
11. 自由提問	
12. 自由提問	

第六課　古蹟的故事
Lesson 6　Stories of Ancient Monuments

課程目標：

Topic：古蹟巡禮

    1. 能概略介紹泰姬瑪哈陵。

    2. 能簡單說明印度陵寢的設計文化。

    3. 能概略介紹兵馬俑。

    4. 能對古蹟維護表示感謝

Lesson Objectives：

Topic：A Tour of Ancient Monuments

    1. Students can briefly introduce the Taj Mahal.

    2. Students can explain the design and culture associated with Indian mausoleums.

    3. Students can introduce the Terracotta Army.

    4. Students can learn to be thankful for the preservation of such ancient sites.

Taj Mahal

對話 Dialogue 🎧

【桑吉陪著周經理和王祕書，一起到泰姬瑪哈陵參觀，周經理看著這座陵寢的牆。】

周經理：四百年前的建築就知道用白色大理石和珠寶，真不可思議。

桑　　吉：不過偉大的建築，沒有浪漫的故事，就不夠吸引人。

周經理：你是說泰姬瑪哈陵又是古蹟，又有故事？

王祕書：我知道，這座陵寢是沙迦罕王為了王后蓋的。

桑　　吉：對！「泰姬瑪哈」是結婚時，他給王后取的名字，「陵」是…

王祕書：「陵」是陵寢，它會因為日夜光線的變化，有紅、藍不同
　　　　的顏色。

周經理：我聽說國王後來被關在對面的阿格拉堡？

桑　　吉：沒錯，沙迦罕王每天從阿格拉堡看著陵寢流淚，想著王后。

王祕書：他花了太多錢蓋泰姬陵，所以兒子把他關了起來！

周經理：真可憐！不過只要來參觀的人，就會說起他們的愛情故事。

桑　　吉：要是有興趣，明天再去古達明納塔看另外一個偉大的故事，

怎麼樣？

王祕書：好啊！可惜現在古達明納塔已經不能爬上去了。

桑　吉：對，為了保護古蹟，也怕危險。

王祕書：胡馬雍陵也該去看看，泰姬陵就是參考它蓋的。

周經理：桑吉，謝謝您帶我們認識印度文化。

課文漢語拼音 Text in Hanyu Pinyin

[Sāngjí péizhe Zhōu jīnglǐ hàn Wáng mìshū, yìqǐ dào Tàijīmǎhā Líng cānguān, Zhōu jīnglǐ kànzhe zhè zuò língqǐn de qiáng.]

Zhōu jīnglǐ : Sìbǎi nián qián de jiànzhú jiù zhīdào yòng báisè dàlǐshí hàn zhūbǎo, zhēn bùkě sīyì.

Sāngjí : Búguò wěidà de jiànzhú, méiyǒu làngmàn de gùshì, jiù búgòu xīyǐn rén.

Zhōu jīnglǐ : Nǐ shì shuō Tàijīmǎhā Líng yòu shì gǔjī, yòu yǒu gùshì?

Wáng mìshū : Wǒ zhīdào, zhè zuò língqǐn shì Shājiāhǎn Wáng wèile wánghòu gài de.

Sāngjí : Duì! "Tàijīmǎhā" shì jiéhūn shí, tā gěi wánghòu qǔ de míngzi, "líng" shì…

Wáng mìshū : "Líng" shì língqǐn, tā huì yīnwèi rìyè guāngxiàn de biànhuà, yǒu hóng, lán bùtóng de yánsè.

Zhōu jīnglǐ : Wǒ tīngshuō guówáng hòulái bèi guān zài duìmiàn de Āgélā bǎo?

Sāngjí : Méicuò, Shājiāhǎn Wáng měitiān cóng Āgélā bǎo kànzhe língqǐn liúlèi, xiǎngzhe wánghòu.

Wáng mìshū : Tā huāle tài duō qián gài Tàijī Líng, suǒyǐ érzi bǎ tā guānle qǐlái!

Lesson 6

Zhōu jīnglǐ : Zhēn kělián! Búguò zhǐyào lái cānguān de rén, jiù huì shuōqǐ tāmen de àiqíng gùshì.

Sāngjí : Yàoshi yǒu xìngqù, míngtiān zài qù Gǔdámíngnà Tǎ kàn lìngwài yí ge wěidà de gùshi, zěnmeyàng?

Wáng mìshū : Hǎo a! Kěxí xiànzài Gǔdámíngnà Tǎ yǐjīng bùnéng pá shàngqù le.

Sāngjí : Duì, wèile bǎohù gǔjī, yě pà wéixiǎn.

Wáng mìshū : Húmǎyōng Líng yě gāi qù kànkan, Tàijī Líng jiùshì cānkǎo tā gài de.

Zhōu jīnglǐ : Sāngjí, xièxie nín dài wǒmen rènshì Yìndù wénhuà.

課文英譯 Text in English

Dialogue

[Sanji is accompanying Manager Zhou and Secretary Wang to visit the Taj Mahal. Manager Zhou is looking at the mausoleum wall.]

Manager Zhou : Four hundred years ago, the builders already knew how to use white marble stones and jewelry. It's unbelievable.

Sanji : But great architecture, without romantic stories, is not attractive enough.

Manager Zhou : You mean the Taj Mahal is a monument that has a story?

Secretary Wang : I know that this mausoleum was built by King Shah Jahan for his Queen.

Sanji : That's right! "Taj Mahal" is the name the King bestowed upon his Queen when they got married. The word "tomb" was...

Secretary Wang : The word "tomb" meant mausoleum. Because of changes in the light during the day and night, the mausoleum reflects different shades of red and blue.

Manager Zhou : I heard that the King was later locked up in Agra Fort opposite the mausoleum. Is that right?

Sanji : Yes, King Sharjah looked at the mausoleum from Agra Fort every day and wept, thinking of the Queen.

Secretary Wang : He spent too much money on the construction of the Taj Mahal, so his son locked him up!

Manager Zhou : How very sad! But as long as people come to see it, their love story will always be told.

Sanji : If you are interested, how about going to Qutub Mina tomorrow to see another great story?

Secretary Wang : OK! Unfortunately, you can't climb up the Qutub Mina anymore now.

Sanji : Yes, it is done to protect the monuments and because they are afraid of danger.

Secretary Wang : We should also go to see Humayun's Tomb. The Taj Mahal was built using it as a reference.

Manager Zhou : Sanji, thank you for taking us around to learn about Indian culture.

Lesson 6

生詞一 Vocabulary I 🎧

編號	生詞	漢語拼音	詞性	英文翻譯
1.	古蹟	gǔjī	N	ancient monuments
2.	故事	gùshì	N	story
3.	陵寢	língqǐn	N	mausoleum
4.	建築	jiànzhú	N	architecture
5.	大理石	dàlǐshí	N	marble
6.	偉大	wěidà	Vs	great
7.	浪漫	làngmàn	Vs	romantic
8.	吸引	xīyǐn	Vst	to attract
9.	王后	wánghòu	N	queen
10.	蓋	gài	V	to construct
11.	光線	guāngxiàn	N	light
12.	變化	biànhuà	N	changes
13.	關	guān	V	to close
14.	流淚	liúlèi	V-sep	to shed tears
15.	可憐	kělián	Vs	pitiful
16.	愛情	àiqíng	N	love
17.	另外	lìngwài	Det	another
18.	可惜	kěxí	Vs	regrettable
19.	爬	pá	V	to climb
20.	保護	bǎohù	V	to protect
21.	危險	wéixiǎn	Vs	dangerous
22.	參考	cānkǎo	V	to use as a reference

第六課　古蹟的故事 Stories of Ancient Monuments

專有名詞 Proper Nouns

編號	生詞	漢語拼音	英文翻譯
1.	泰姬瑪哈陵	Tàijīmǎhā Líng	Taj Mahal mausoleum
2.	沙迦罕王	Shājiāhǎn Wáng	King Shah Jahan
3.	阿格拉堡	Āgélā Bǎo	Agra Fort
4.	古達明納塔	Gǔdámíngnà Tǎ	Qutub Minar
5.	胡馬雍陵	Húmǎyōng Líng	Humayun's Tomb

短語 Phrases

編號	生詞	漢語拼音	英文翻譯
1.	不可思議	bùkě sīyì	unbelievable, incredible
2.	取名字	qǔ míngzi	to give someone a name
3.	說起	shuōqǐ	to speak of something

短文 Reading 🎧

皇家陵寢

　　中國秦始皇陵和印度泰姬瑪哈陵都是皇家的陵寢，也都是世界遺產。從泰姬瑪哈陵可以看到波斯和伊斯蘭教的文化；而秦始皇陵的兵馬俑對研究秦朝文化，也有很大的幫助。

　　「俑」是古代用土做的人或動物，放進陵寢去陪葬的東西，「兵馬俑」是用土做的軍隊來陪葬。剛開始皇家陪葬是用真人，後來才改用土做的「俑」。

　　「兵馬俑」被發現，最早是在 1932 年，西安附近挖出了一個跪著的俑，跟真人非常像。可是那時候，他們不知道是陵寢，還有人覺得俑是不吉祥的東西，就把它打壞丟了。到 1974 年挖井，才

挖出這個古蹟來。「俑」本來有顏色，可惜因為離現在的時間太久了，所以從地下挖出來才十幾秒，很多俑的顏色就開始變了，後來也慢慢掉了，就是我們現在看到的樣子。

在今天，我們能看著一支秦朝軍隊，多不可思議啊！除了激動，怎麼能不感謝研究文化和保護古蹟的人呢？

課文漢語拼音 Text in Hanyu Pinyin

Huángjiā Língqǐn

Zhōngguó Qínshǐhuáng Líng hàn Yìndù Tàijīmǎhā Líng dōu shì huángjiā de língqǐn, yě dōu shì shìjiè yíchǎn. Cóng Tàijīmǎhā Líng kěyǐ kàn dào Bōsī hàn Yīsīlán jiào de wénhuà; ér Qínshǐhuáng Líng de Bīngmǎ Yǒng duì yánjiù Qíncháo wénhuà, yěyǒu hěn dà de bāngzhù.

"Yǒng" shì gǔdài yòng tǔ zuò de rén huò dòngwù, fàng jìn língqǐn qù péizàng de dōngxi, "Bīngmǎ Yǒng" shì yòng tǔ zuò de jūnduì lái péizàng. Gāng kāishǐ huángjiā péizàng shì yòng zhēnrén, hòulái cái gǎi yòng tǔ zuò de "yǒng".

"Bīngmǎ Yǒng" bèi Fāxiàn, zuìzǎo shì zài yījiǔsān'èr nián, Xī'ān fùjìn wā chūle yí ge guìzhe de yǒng, gēn zhēnrén fēicháng xiàng. Kěshì nà shíhòu, tāmen bù zhīdào shì língqǐn, hái yǒu rén juéde yǒng shì bù jíxiáng de dōngxi, jiù bǎ tā dǎ huài diūle. Dào yījiǔqīsì nián wā jǐng, cái wāchū zhège gǔjī lái. "Yǒng" běnlái yǒu yánsè, kěxí yīnwèi lí xiànzài de shíjiān tài jiǔ le, suǒyǐ cóng dìxià wā chūlái cái shí jǐ miǎo, hěnduō yǒng de yánsè jiù kāishǐ biànle, hòulái yě mànmàn diàole, jiùshì wǒmen xiànzài kàndào de yàngzi.

Zài jīntiān, wǒmen néng kànzhe yì zhī Qíncháo jūnduì, duō bùkě sīyì a! Chúle jīdòng, zěnme néng bù gǎnxiè yánjiù wénhuà hàn bǎohù gǔjī de rén ne?

課文英譯 Text in English

Imperial Tombs

China's first Emperor Qin Shihuang's Mausoleum and India's Taj Mahal mausoleum are royal tombs and World Heritage sites. Persian and Islamic cultures can be seen from the design of the Taj Mahal, and the Terracotta Warriors of Qin Shihuang's mausoleum were of great help to the study of Qin Dynasty culture.

"Yongs" are ancient earth-made persons or animals, placed into the mausoleum to be buried together with the dead. "Terracotta Warriors" are made of earth to accompany the emperor in the burial. At first, the royal burial was accompanied by real people, but then it was changed to earth-made "yongs."

The Terracotta Warriors were first discovered in 1932, near Xi'an, when a kneeling terracotta warrior, much like a real person, was dug up. But at that time, people did not know it was a mausoleum, and some felt that the "Yongs" were bad omens. So, they broke and lost them. It was not until 1974 when a well was dug, that the monument was excavated. "Yongs" originally had colors. Unfortunately, it was too long ago when they were dug out from the ground. After only ten seconds or more, the colors of the "Yongs" would begin to change until they slowly faded away. It is what we see now.

Today, we can still look at a Qin Dynasty army. How incredible! Apart from being moved by them, how can you not thank the people who study culture and protect the monuments?

Lesson 6

生詞二 Vocabulary II 🎧

編號	生詞	漢語拼音	詞性	英文翻譯
1.	皇家	huángjiā	N	imperial family
2.	研究	yánjiù	V	to research
3.	俑	yǒng	N	clay figures buried with the dead
4.	動物	dòngwù	N	animals
5.	陪葬	péizàng	Vi	to be buried together with the dead
6.	軍隊	jūnduì	N	army
7.	真人	zhēn rén	N	real people
8.	挖	wā	V	to dig
9.	跪	guì	Vi	to kneel
10.	井	jǐng	N	water well
11.	本來	běnlái	Adv	originally
12.	秒	miǎo	M	second
13.	激動	jīdòng	Vs	moved, touched, thrilled

專有名詞 Proper Nouns

編號	生詞	漢語拼音	英文翻譯
1.	秦始皇陵	Qínshǐhuáng Líng	Tomb of the first Emperor Qin
2.	波斯	Bōsī	Persia
3.	兵馬俑	Bīngmǎ Yǒng	Terracotta Army
4.	秦朝	Qíncháo	Qin dynasty

第六課　古蹟的故事 Stories of Ancient Monuments

短語 Phrases

編號	生詞	漢語拼音	英文翻譯
1.	世界遺產	shìjiè yíchǎn	World Heritage

語法 Grammar 🎧

一、只要 *zhǐyào* …，就 *jiù* …　　*As long as ...,*

說明：「只要…，就…」是一個條件複句，前後分句有條件關係，當「只要」
　　　子句所限定的條件滿足了，「就」接著引出後面的結果。這個句式是指
　　　一種比較容易達成的條件關係。

Explanation：只要 *zhǐyào* …，就 *jiù* … is a conditional complex sentence. When
the conditions set out in the 只要 *zhǐyào* clause are met, 就 *jiù* leads to the
subsequent results. This sentence pattern refers to a conditional relationship
that is easier to achieve.

1. 「只要」是連接詞，放在主語前或後都可以。對象明確時，主語可省
　　略。

　　只要 *zhǐyào* is a conjunction. It can be placed before or after the subject.
　　When the person one is talking to is understood implicitly, the subject
　　can be omitted.

　　如：(1) 只要你喜歡，就拿去吧。

　　　　　　你只要喜歡，就拿去吧。

　　　　(2) 只要多喝水、多休息，病就會好得比較快。

2. 如果主語相同，兩個分句其中一個分句的主語可省略，通常省略後
　　主語。

　　If the subjects of both causes are the same, the subject of either one can
　　be omitted.

　　如：(1) 大家只要來泰姬瑪哈陵，就會談起沙加罕王的愛情。

　　　　(2) 只要來泰姬瑪哈陵，大家就會談起沙加罕王的愛情。

3. 如果主語不同，主語要放在「就」之前。

If the subjects of both causes are different, the subject should be placed before 就 *jiù*.

如：只要不下雨，我就去。

例句：

1. 只要有空，我們就可以去參觀皇家陵寢。
2. 中文不難學，你只要多練習，就能說得好。
3. 只要早點去，就一定有位子。

練習：請用「只要…，就…」完成下面對話。

Exercise：Please use 只要 *zhǐyào* …，就 *jiù* … to finish the following conversations.

---

1. A：醫生，我怎麼樣才能更健康？

   B：很容易，你＿＿＿＿＿＿＿，＿＿＿＿＿＿＿。（運動；健康）

2. A：我們明天想去胡馬雍陵參觀，那裡好找嗎？

   B：胡馬雍陵是很高大的建築，＿＿＿＿＿＿＿，＿＿＿＿＿＿＿。（開車經過；看見）

3. A：我的腳不舒服，請問哪裡可以買到冰塊？

   B：＿＿＿＿＿＿＿，＿＿＿＿＿＿＿。（便利商店；買到）

4. A：聽說你想去英國念書，是不是＿＿＿＿＿＿＿，＿＿＿＿＿＿＿？

   B：是啊，不過我父母還有一點捨不得我去那麼遠。（同意；去）

5. A：跟印度的珠寶設計合作，談好了嗎？

   B：快了，＿＿＿＿＿＿＿，＿＿＿＿＿＿＿。（對方同意；簽合約）

二、V 起　V + Verb Particle 起 *qǐ*　to touch upon

說明：「起」放在動作動詞後，表示動作開始關涉到某事物，像想起、說起、問起、談起、聊起等，賓語則是從前面未言明的狀態產生。

第六課 古蹟的故事 Stories of Ancient Monuments

Explanation：V 起 *qǐ* is placed after an action verb, to indicate that the action begins to relate to something, such as remembering, talking, asking, talking, chatting, etc., and the object is generated from the previously unspoken state.

如：很多人到了這裡，都會談起跟這個古蹟有關的愛情故事。

例句：

1. 說起昨晚的籃球比賽，年輕人都好激動。
2. 一年沒回國了，她一想起家人就很難過。
3. 我忘了我們是怎麼聊起在印度參加婚禮的經驗。

練習：請用「說起、問起、聊起」重寫句子。

Exercise：Please use 說起 *shuōqǐ*, 問起 *wènqǐ,* and 聊起 *liáoqǐ* to rewrite the sentences.

1. 他一聊波斯的建築，就聊個不停。
   → _____。
2. 多年不見的朋友在一起的時候，別問薪水的事。
   → _____。
3. 他一說上次在網路上買東西的經驗，就很生氣。
   → _____。
4. 他是個印度通，一聊印度文化就忘了時間。
   → _____。
5. 媽媽一問怎麼還不結婚的事，她就覺得很煩。
   → _____。
6. 男生一說以前在軍隊的事，就很激動。
   → _____。

三、趨向動詞＋來／去　　Directional Verbs ＋ 來 *lái* / 去 *qù*

說明：「趨向動詞」表示移動的動作，「來」和「去」是表示方向性，以說話者為基準，越來越靠近說話者用「來」，離說話者越來越遠用「去」。主要有兩種結構類型，第一種是方向動詞＋來／去，如：上來，下去；第二種是移動動詞＋方向動詞＋來／去，如：走進來，跑出去。

A "directional verb" means verbs involving directions. The directions of 來 *lái* and 去 *qù* are based on the point of view of the speaker. When someone or something is "moving" closer to the speaker, 來 *lái* is used by the speaker. When it is "going" farther and farther away from the speaker, 去 *qù* is used by the speaker. There are two main types of structure; the first is the verb + 來 *lái* / 去 *qù*, such as "come up"（上來）, "go down"（下去）, and the second is a verb of movement + directional verb + 來 *lái* / 去 *qù*, such as "come in"（進來）, "go out"（出去）.

1. V_1V_2：Directional verbs + 來 *lái* / 去 *qù*

direction / reference	上	下	進	出	回	過
來 toward the speaker	上來	下來	進來	出來	回來	過來
去 away from the speaker	上去	下去	進去	出去	回去	過去

如：(1) 我家在二樓，請你上來。

　　(2) 那裡人太多了，別過去。

　　(3) 十點多了爸爸還沒回來。

2. $V_1V_2V_3$：Movement verbs + directional verbs + 來 *lái* / 去 *qù*

第六課　古蹟的故事 Stories of Ancient Monuments

V1	走	跑	爬	站	坐	拿	追	帶	開	放

＋

V2	上		下		進		出		回		過	
來/去	來	去	來	去	來	去	來	去	來	去	來	去

如：(1) 請你走進來。

(2) 這是古蹟，不能爬上去照相。

(3) 東西用了以後，要放回去。

3. 如果移動結構有一個目的地，必須把目的地放在「方向動詞」和「來」、「去」的中間。

If the movement structure has a destination, the destination must be placed in the middle of the directional verb and the 來 *lái* or 去 *qù*.

如：(1) 她慢慢地走進教室來。

(2) 我好像付錢的時候忘了一包菜，只好跑回超市去找。

(3) 錢丟了，我沒錢買票，只好走回家去。

4. 移動結構常跟「把」搭配使用，而被移動的事、物必須是定指。

Movement structures are often used in conjunction with 把 *bǎ*, and things that are moved must be definite.

如：(1) 對不起，您不能把吃的東西帶進圖書館來。

(2) 古代常把俑放進陵寢去陪葬。

(3) 這個是學校的東西，您不能把它帶回家去。

例句：

1. 太熱了，別站在外面，請進來聊吧。

2. 婚禮快開始了，大家都走進去。

3. 鞭炮不可以帶進學校去。

4. 秦朝開始把俑放進陵寢去陪葬。

Lesson 6

練習：請看看這些情形，你會怎麼說？請用下面的 $V_1V_2V_3$ 完成句子。

Exercise：Please look at the following situations in the pictures. How would you describe them? Please use the following directional verbs to complete the sentences.

（帶出去、爬上去、拿進（房間）去、跑下去、拿出去、收進來、走下去、停（不）進去）

停車位太小，我_____。	快下雨了，快把外面的東西_____。	天氣很好，快把衣服_____，比較容易乾。	小狗想出去玩了，快把牠_____。
要是你在樓上，火很大的時候，不能_____，怎麼辦？	古達明納塔不可以_____。	媽媽說不可以把牛肉麵_____吃，只能在飯廳吃。	真的泰姬瑪哈陵在地下一樓，參觀的人不可以_____。

第六課　古蹟的故事 Stories of Ancient Monuments

四、才₁ *cái*₁　　merely, only

說明：

1. 「才₁」是副詞。「才」＋ 數量詞，表示 merely/only（有），數量少，程度低。

   才₁ *cái*₁ is an adverb. The word 才₁ *cái*₁ plus quantity indicates merely/only (yes), a small number, or a low degree.

   如：(1) 這支手機才兩千塊，真便宜。

   　　(2) 我才學了四個多月的中文。

   　　(3) 假期太多，我們才上了兩課。

   　　(4) 我今天很忙，才喝了一杯牛奶。

2. 「才₂」是副詞。事情開始或完成得比預期晚，或歷時較長，時間詞放在「才」的前面。

   才₂ *cái*₂ is an adverb. Things start or finish later than expected or take longer, and the word 才₂ *cái*₂ precedes them.

   如：(1) 三點十分的飛機，他兩點半才到機場。

   　　(2) 九點半開會，他十點多才來。

   　　(3) 剛開始皇家陪葬是用真人，後來才改成俑。

例句：

1. 這本書我才看了一點兒。（只 only/merely）
2. 從這裡到捷運站，走路才五分鐘。（只 only/merely）
3. 才十幾秒，俑的顏色開始不一樣了。（只 only/merely）
4. 昨晚我兩點多才睡覺，現在好累。（晚 longer/later than expected）
5. 他們是到臺灣才認識的。（晚 longer/later than expected）
6. 到 1974 年才挖出這個古蹟來。（晚 longer/later than expected）

練習：請用「才 only」或「才 late」完成句子

Exercise：Please use 才₁ *cái*₁ and 才₂ *cái*₂ to complete the sentences.

1. 這本書不貴，_____。
2. 我家離學校很近，走路_____。
3. 古達明納塔我_____，很想再去。
4. 你不是喜歡吃甜點，今天怎麼_____？
5. 他週末不上課，常常_____起床。
6. 他一下班就去喝酒，_____回家。
7. 這個建築蓋了很久，上個月_____。
8. 工作不好找，他找了半年_____。

文化延伸 Cross-Cultural Extension

The Science of Monuments

Although China and India are ancient countries, they all have monuments built using science. There are Qin Shihuang's Mausoleum's Terracotta Warriors and Great Towers in Xi'an. Structures such as India's Qutub Minar Tower's iron columns, Humayun's Tomb, and inverted pyramid-shaped moon ladders are all representative of such monuments.

In India, the manufacturing technology of India's Qutub Minar iron columns enables them to stand without rusting for 1600 years. The Humayun's Tomb was an early Persian and Islamic cultural building in India with outdoor pools and indoor designs providing warmth and cool in the winter and summer. The inverted moon-shaped ladder is near the desert, and it had long been used as a prototype for reservoirs. Residents could walk down the 3,500-level steps to the well to fetch water regardless of drought, rain, or the water level.

第六課　古蹟的故事 Stories of Ancient Monuments

Taiwan has more mountains than rivers. Furthermore, rivers are short. Therefore, the construction of modern reservoirs utilizes the same concept for water storage. In addition, just as the technology of Qin Shihuang's mausoleum allowed the Terracotta Warriors to be preserved, the Dayan Tower was said to have been built at the request of Xuanxuan after he took the preserved Buddhist scriptures back to China. It was used to protect the Buddhist scriptures. In the absence of ladder technology, a 64.1-meter tower was built. To this day, scientists still cannot solve the mystery of how the tower was built. We cannot but admire the wisdom of the ancestors of these ancient civilizations.

古達明納塔旁的鐵柱
Qutub Minar Tower's iron columns

泰姬瑪哈陵原型—胡馬雍陵
Original Shape of Taj Mahal — Humayun's Tomb

月亮梯井到處可見類月亮梯井的設計（印度齋蒲爾）
The design of the inverted moon ladders is commonly seen (India, Jaipur)

Lesson 6

語言任務 Language Tasks

一、找找風景區。

Find the scenic spots.

任務：1. 學生兩人一組，每組抽一張印度風景區卡片。同組學生合作查完相
關資料後，寫在表格裡，貼上黑板。

2. 老師將教室地板當作印度地圖，學生依資訊選擇喜歡的地點，站在
正確的地方，並報告自己選這裡的理由。

Task 1：Divide students into groups of two and let every group choose a card
containing relevant information on an Indian scenic spot. After students in
the group collaborate and look up relevant information on the net, write the
information in the form, and then put it on the blackboard.

Task 2：The teacher should use the classroom floor as a map of India, and students
should choose their chosen place according to the information. Once found,
students should stand in the right place on the floor and then report their
reasons for choosing it.

你抽到哪裡？	印度風景區名稱
1. 在印度哪裡？	在印度的…部
2. 這個風景區有什麼好玩和特別的地方？	
3. 選擇來這裡玩的理由是什麼？	
4. 以前來過嗎？跟誰來的？怎麼來的？	
5. 去那裡要注意什麼？	

二、請給來印度旅遊的朋友一個建議，包括下列資料。請至少使用 10 個本課的生詞和句型，完成後向全班同學報告，然後全班票選最想去的地方，並說明為什麼想去。（可參考本課文化延伸及本書第一課景點。）

Please give a friend who comes to India to travel a suggestion, including the following information. Please use at least ten new words and sentence patterns in this lesson to describe the place, and then report them to the class when you finish. Then the whole class votes for where they want to go most and explains why they want to go to these places. (You can refer to the cultural extension of this lesson and the attractions in the first lesson of this book.)

a. 到哪裡玩？是古蹟嗎？
b. 怎麼去？在那裡參觀要多久？
c. 到這裡一定不能不看什麼？
d. 這個古蹟有什麼故事？是浪漫的愛情故事嗎？
e. 這個地方是用什麼科學方法建的？

例如：

　　印度的泰姬瑪哈陵是一座古蹟，是用白色大理石蓋的，建築早上和晚上因為光線的變化，會有不同的顏色。開車去很方便，可以在那裡住一個晚上。只要來這裡參觀的人就都會談起沙迦罕王浪漫的愛情故事。泰姬瑪哈陵是世界遺產，印度人門票才幾十塊，但外國人得付幾百塊。雖然很貴，但是一定要去看。因為要維護古蹟，真的陵寢放在地下一樓，所以參觀的旅客不能走下去。

第七課　逛逛市集
Lesson 7　Going to the Market

課程目標：

Topic：民俗文化

    1. 能說明印度市集的概況。

    2. 能了解市集是印度人民的重要經濟活動。

    3. 能比較印度市集與臺灣夜市的異同。

Lesson Objectives：

Topic：Folk Culture

    1. Students can explain an overview of an Indian market.

    2. Students can gain an understanding of going to the market being an important economic activity for the people of India.

    3. Students can compare the similarities and differences between Indian bazaars and night markets in Taiwan.

a corner of an Indian market

對話 Dialogue 🎧

【桑吉陪周經理和王祕書，逛印度傳統市集。】

周經理：東西好多啊，連樹上都掛著東西呢。

王祕書：對啊，有衣服、鞋子、飾品，還有傳統香料和紗麗什麼的。

桑　吉：這裡人擠人，巷子又多，小心點，別只看東西，走丟了。

周經理：好的。天氣真熱，那裡有鮮果汁和小吃，我們買一點吧？

王祕書：不行，一邊逛一邊吃路邊的東西，小心拉肚子。

桑　吉：外國人剛來，還不習慣，真的得小心一點。

【在路上賣飾品的小妹妹，把一個手環很快地戴在周經理手上。】

周經理：小妹妹為什麼把手環戴在我的手上？桑吉，你在跟她說什麼？

桑　吉：我跟小妹妹說您戴起來很漂亮，可惜太貴了。所以她賣我三個五十五塊。

王祕書：經理，您戴起來真的不錯。桑吉，還你五十五塊。

桑　吉：開玩笑，才五十幾塊，要是給我，就不是我的朋友了。

周經理：桑吉，你幫我們殺價，等一下我請大家到店裡喝印度奶茶。

王祕書：太好了！前面那個人好厲害，頭上放了好多衣服。

桑　吉：市集人多巷子又窄，貨這麼多，沒有一點頂上功夫是不行的。

王祕書：雖然市集有點亂，不過看到印度人為生活這麼認真工作，很感動。

周經理：沒錯，市集保存了傳統，也刺激了觀光，真了不起。

課文漢語拼音 Text in Hanyu Pinyin

[Sāngjí péi Zhōu jīnglǐ hàn Wáng mìshū, guàng Yìndù chuántǒng shìjí.]

Zhōu jīnglǐ : Dōngxi hǎo duō a, lián shù shàng dōu guàzhe dōngxi ne.

Wáng mìshū : Duì a, yǒu yīfú, xiézi, shìpǐn, hái yǒu chuántǒng xiāngliào hàn shālì shénme de.

Sāngjí : Zhèlǐ rén jǐ rén, xiàngzi yòu duō, xiǎoxīn diǎn, bié zhǐ kàn dōngxi, zǒu diūle.

Zhōu jīnglǐ : Hǎo de. Tiānqì zhēn rè, nàlǐ yǒu xiān guǒzhī hàn xiǎochī, wǒmen mǎi yìdiǎn ba?

Wáng mìshū : Bùxíng, yìbiān guàng yìbiān chī lù biān de dōngxi, xiǎoxīn lā dùzi.

Sāngjí : Wàiguó rén gāng lái, hái bù xíguàn, zhēnde děi xiǎoxīn yìdiǎn.

[Zài lù shàng mài shìpǐn de xiǎo mèimei, bǎ yí ge shǒuhuán hěn kuài de dài zài Zhōu jīnglǐ shǒu shàng.]

Zhōu jīnglǐ : Xiǎo mèimei wèishénme bǎ shǒuhuán dài zài wǒ de shǒu shàng? Sāngjí, nǐ zài gēn tā shuō shénme?

Sāngjí : Wǒ gēn xiǎo mèimei shuō nín dài qǐlái hěn piàoliàng, kěxí tài guì le. Suǒyǐ tā mài wǒ sān ge wǔshíwǔ kuài.

Wáng mìshū : Jīnglǐ, nín dài qǐlái zhēnde búcuò. Sāngjí, huán nǐ wǔshíwǔ kuài.

Sāngjí : Kāi wánxiào, cái wǔshí jǐ kuài, yàoshi gěi wǒ, jiù búshì wǒ de péngyǒu le.

Zhōu jīnglǐ : Sāngjí, nǐ bāng wǒmen shājià, děng yíxià wǒ qǐng dàjiā dào diàn lǐ hē Yìndù nǎichá.

Wáng mìshū : Tài hǎo le! Qiánmiàn nà ge rén hǎo lìhài, tóu shàng fàngle hǎo duō yīfú.

Sāngjí : Shìjí rén duō xiàngzi yòu zhǎi, huò zhème duō, méiyǒu yìdiǎn dǐngshàng gōngfū shì bùxíng de.

Wáng mìshū : Suīrán shìjí yǒudiǎn luàn, búguò kàndào Yìndù rén wèi shēnghuó zhème rènzhēn gōngzuò, hěn gǎndòng.

Zhōu jīnglǐ : Méicuò, shìjí bǎocúnle chuántǒng, yě cìjīle guānguāng, zhēn liǎobuqǐ.

課文英譯 Text in English

Dialogue

[Sanji accompanies Manager Zhou and Secretary Wang to visit the traditional Indian market.]

Manager Zhou : There are so many things. Things are even hanging off trees.

Secretary Wang : Yes, there are clothes, shoes, accessories, and traditional spices, and saris, etc.

Sanji : It is very crowded with people here. There are many alleys. Be careful; don't just look at things. You might get lost.

Manager Zhou : OK. It's really hot; there are fresh juices and snacks over there. Shall we buy some?

Secretary Wang : No, don't eat from the street stalls while shopping. Be careful; you might get diarrhea.

Sanji : When foreigners have just arrived, they are not used to the condition here, so they really must be careful.

[A little girl selling jewelry on the road puts a bracelet on the manager's arm quickly.]

Manager Zhou : Why is this little girl putting a bangle on my arm? Sanji, what did you say to her?

Sanji : I told the girl that it looked beautiful on you. Unfortunately, it was too expensive. So, she sold three to me for fifty-five rupees.

Secretary Wang : Manager Zhou, they look good on you. Sanji, here is your fifty-five rupees back.

Sanji : It's a joke; it's only fifty some rupees. If you insist on giving it to me, then you are not my friend.

Manager Zhou : Sanji, you help us bargain the price down, so I'll invite you to the shop to drink Indian milk tea later.

Secretary Wang : That's great! Wow, the man in front of us is tremendous, carrying a lot of clothes on his head.

Sanji : The market has many narrow alleys and lanes, and they are always crowded with people and goods. Without a bit of technique of carrying things on your head, it would be impossible.

Secretary Wang : Although the market is a bit chaotic, seeing Indians work so hard, I am very moved.

Manager Zhou : Yes, the markets not only preserve tradition, but they also stimulate sightseeing. It is amazing.

生詞一 Vocabulary I 🎧

編號	生詞	漢語拼音	詞性	英文翻譯
1.	市集	shìjí	N	market
2.	飾品	shìpǐn	N	accessory
3.	香料	xiāngliào	N	spices
4.	巷子	xiàngzi	N	lane
5.	鮮	xiān	Vs-attr	fresh
6.	手環	shǒuhuán	N	bangles
7.	戴	dài	V	to wear on hand
8.	厲害	lìhài	Vs	amazing
9.	窄	zhǎi	Vs	narrow
10.	貨	huò	N	goods
11.	亂	luàn	Vs	chaotic
12.	生活	shēnghuó	N	life
13.	認真	rènzhēn	Vs	seriously
14.	感動	gǎndòng	Vs	to be moved
15.	保存	bǎocún	V	to keep

編號	生詞	漢語拼音	詞性	英文翻譯
16.	刺激	cìjī	V	to stimulate, to excite
17.	觀光	guānguāng	N	sightseeing
18.	了不起	liǎobuqǐ	Vs	amazing, terrific, marvelous

短語 Phrases

編號	生詞	漢語拼音	英文翻譯
1.	人擠人	rén jǐ rén	people upon people
2	走丟	zǒudiū	to be lost
3.	拉肚子	lā dùzi	have diarrhea
4.	開玩笑	kāi wánxiào	to make a joke
5.	頂上功夫	dǐngshàng gōngfū	top-notch kungfu, lit. "the technique of carrying things on one's head"

短文 Reading 🎧

逛夜市

晚上去哪裡玩？「夜市」一定是臺灣人第一個想到的地方。

臺灣小吃，種類多，味道好，是最能代表臺灣人生活的飲食文化。逛夜市吃個蚵仔煎、大餅包小餅、大腸麵線、甜不辣、肉圓、滷肉飯什麼的，然後喝杯珍珠奶茶，多痛快！小吃攤，一攤連著一攤，什麼都有，便宜又好吃，還能從「吃」發現當地的文化特色。而賣東西的人常很有創意地大聲叫著「走過，路過，不能錯過」，也非常有趣。夜市還有一些好玩的遊戲，像撈金魚、射氣球、電動遊戲都很常見，還可以做腳底按摩。有時候外國朋友也會來擺攤子，賣些家鄉食物，非常熱鬧。

臺灣從南到北差不多每天都有夜市，跟西方國家只有在假日或節日才有市集不一樣，跟印度市集比較像，不過夜市一定在晚上。約幾個好朋友去逛夜市，開開心心地一邊吃一邊玩，真的是很快樂的事。

一攤連著一攤的夜市
snack stalls one after another

印度市集
an Indian market

課文漢語拼音 Text in Hanyu Pinyin

Guàng Yèshì

Wǎnshàng qù nǎlǐ wán? "Yèshì" yídìng shì Táiwān rén dì-yī ge xiǎngdào de dìfāng.

Táiwān xiǎochī, zhǒnglèi duō, wèidào hǎo, shì zuì néng dàibiǎo Táiwān rén shēnghuó de yǐnshí wénhuà. Guàng yèshì chī ge ézǐjiān, dàbǐng bāo xiǎobǐng, dàcháng miànxiàn, tiánbúlà, ròuyuán, lǔròufàn shénme de, ránhòu hē bēi zhēnzhū nǎichá, duō tòngkuài! Xiǎochī tān, yì tān liánzhe yì tān, shénme dōu yǒu, piányí yòu hǎochī, hái néng cóng "chī" fāxiàn dāngdì de wénhuà tèsè. Ér mài dōngxi de rén cháng hěn yǒu chuàngyì de dàshēng jiàozhe " zǒuguò, lùguò, bùnéng cuòguò", yě fēicháng yǒuqù. Yèshì hái yǒu yìxiē hǎowán de yóuxì, xiàng lāo jīnyú, shè qìqiú, diàndòng yóuxì dōu hěn chángjiàn, hái kěyǐ zuò jiǎodǐ ànmó. Yǒu shíhòu wàiguó péngyǒu yě huì lái bǎi tānzi, mài xiē jiāxiāng shíwù, fēicháng rènào.

Táiwān cóng nán dào běi chàbuduō měitiān dōu yǒu yèshì, gēn xīfāng guójiā zhǐyǒu zài jiàrì huò jiérì cái yǒu shìjí bù yíyàng, gēn Yìndù shìjí bǐjiào xiàng, búguò yèshì yídìng zài wǎnshàng. Yuē jǐ ge hǎo péngyǒu qù guàng yèshì, kāikāi-xīnxīn de yìbiān chī yìbiān wán, zhēnde shì hěn kuàilè de shì.

課文英譯 Text in English

Going to the Night Market

Where to have some fun in the evening? The "night market" must be the first place Taiwanese think of.

A wide variety of tasty Taiwanese snacks is perhaps the most representative of Taiwanese cuisine in their daily lives. When you go to the night market, you can eat pancakes, big and small biscuits, intestine vermicelli, Taiwanese tempura, meat balls, stewed meat, rice, etc. Then after eating, you may drink a glass of pearl milk tea. How delightful it would feel! Snack stalls one after another, with everything cheap and delicious. Eating this way would also allow one to discover the characteristics of local culture. It is also interesting that the sellers would often come up with creative slogans such as "Walk past (us), (but) don't miss us." There are also some fun games, such as goldfish catching, balloon shooting, and video games at the night markets. There are also foot massages to be had.

Sometimes, foreign friends will come to put up stalls to sell their hometown food. The night market is extremely lively.

There are night markets, from the south to the north of Taiwan, almost every day. This phenomenon is different from the markets that are open only on holidays in Western countries. Such night markets are very similar to Indian markets, except night markets must be at night. To gather a few good friends to go to the night market to eat and have fun happily is really a very enjoyable thing to do.

生詞二 Vocabulary II 🎧

編號	生詞	漢語拼音	詞性	英文翻譯
1.	種類	zhǒnglèi	N	category
2.	蚵仔煎	ézǐjiān	N	fried oyster
3.	甜不辣	tiánbúlà	N	tempura (Taiwanese style)
4.	肉圓	ròuyuán	N	meat ball
5.	滷肉飯	lǔròufàn	N	stewed meat with rice
6.	然後	ránhòu	Conj	then
7.	痛快	tòngkuài	Vs	joyful
8.	攤	tān	M	stall, stand or booth in a market
9.	連著	liánzhe	V	attached
10.	創意	chuàngyì	N	originality
11.	路過	lùguò	V	to pass by (a place)
12.	錯過	cuòguò	Vpt	to miss something
13.	約	yuē	V	to make a date with people

短語 Phrases

編號	生詞	漢語拼音	英文翻譯
1.	大腸麵線	dàcháng miànxiàn	intestine vermicelli
2.	撈金魚	lāo jīnyú	goldfish catching
3.	射氣球	shè qìqiú	balloon shooting
4.	電動遊戲	diàndòng yóuxì	video games
5.	腳底按摩	jiǎodǐ ànmó	foot massage
6.	擺攤子	bǎi tānzi	to set up a stall at a market

語法 Grammar 🎧

一、什麼的 *shénmede*　　things like (that), etc.

說明：「什麼的」用在列舉一連串事物之後，因項目太多，故僅以數項作為代表，並表示至此停止舉例，像英文的「and so on」或「etc.」。「什麼的」一般用在口語，和「等（等）」用於書面不同。

Explanation：什麼的 *shénmede* is used to list a series of items. Because there are too many items, only a few are taken as representative, like in English "and so on" or "etc." 什麼的 *shénmede* is generally used in spoken language, and 等等 *děngděng* is used in writing.

1.「什麼的」放在所列舉的兩個或兩個以上並列詞語項目後。

　　什麼的 *shénmede* is placed after two or more items listed.

　　如：(1) 他很喜歡吃蚵仔煎、滷肉飯什麼的。

　　　　(2) 泰姬瑪哈陵、胡馬雍陵、古達明納塔什麼的，都是印度有名的古蹟。

例句：

　　1. 你如果想買香料、紗麗、飾品什麼的，印度市集都有。

　　2. 德里有 auto、地鐵、火車什麼的，到哪裡都很方便。

Lesson 7

3. 甜不辣、肉圓、珍珠奶茶什麼的，都是能代表臺灣文化的小吃。

練習：請用「什麼的」改寫下面的句子。

Exercise：Please rewrite the following sentences with 什麼的 *shénmede*.

---

1. 棒球、籃球、桌球、網球…，都是臺灣人很喜歡的運動。

   →＿＿＿＿＿＿＿＿＿＿＿＿＿＿＿＿＿＿＿＿＿＿＿＿＿＿＿。

2. 她從小就在市集幫媽媽賣東西，手環、衣服、鞋子…，差不多都賣過。

   →她從小就在市集幫媽媽賣東西，＿＿＿＿＿＿＿＿＿＿＿＿＿。

3. 逛夜市的時候，蚵仔煎、大腸麵線、肉圓、滷肉飯…，都是大家常吃的東西。

   →逛夜市的時候，＿＿＿＿＿＿＿＿＿＿＿＿＿＿＿＿＿＿＿。

4. 臺北附近好玩的地方真多，像淡水、九份、十分…，都很有意思。

   →臺北附近好玩的地方真多，＿＿＿＿＿＿＿＿＿＿＿＿＿＿。

5. 臺灣拍了不少有名的電影，像小城故事、喜宴、Life of Pi…，我都看過。

   →臺灣拍了不少有名的電影，＿＿＿＿＿＿＿＿＿＿＿＿＿＿。

二、一邊……，一邊…　　two Simultaneous Actions with 一邊 *yìbiān*… 一邊 *yìbiān*

說明：「一邊…，一邊…」是指兩個動作，在同一時間進行。主要是強調動作、行為正在進行的動態表現，如跑、叫、爬、打、看…等。

Explanation：一邊 *yìbiān*... 一邊 *yìbiān* refers to two actions that are performed at the same time. This pattern mainly emphasizes the ongoing dynamic performance of actions and behaviors, such as running, barking, climbing, hitting, watching, etc.

1. 用來連結兩個同時進行的動作。

   It is used to link two simultaneous actions.

   如：(1) 他喜歡一邊開車，一邊聽新聞。

(2) 弟弟常一邊吃飯，一邊看電視。

(3) 那個人一邊跑，一邊叫，不知道是什麼事。

2. 非動態表現的持續性狀態如「坐」、「站」等動詞不可使用這個句型。
Non-dynamic verbs such as " 坐 *zuò*" and " 站 *zhàn*" which are in a continuous state, cannot be used in this sentence pattern.

如：(1) *他習慣一邊站，一邊吃飯。→他習慣站著吃飯。

(2) *學生一邊坐，一邊上課。→學生坐著上課。

例句：

1. 他喜歡一邊逛夜市，一邊吃東西。

2. 週末我常跟朋友一邊喝咖啡，一邊聊天。

3. 媽媽說別一邊看書，一邊聽歌。

練習：請說說他 / 她 / 他們喜歡同時做什麼？哪些事一起做，是不好的習慣？

Exercise：Please say what things he/she/they are doing at the same time. Doing which actions together is considered a bad habit?

1.	
2.	
3.	

| 4. | |
| 5. | |

三、幾 *jǐ* a few, several

說明：「幾」是表示一個概數，不是一個精確的數字。

Explanation：幾 *jǐ* means several, an estimate, not an exact number.

1. 「幾」非疑問詞的時候，為十以下的數字，表示少量的一個概數。

When 幾 *jǐ* is not a question word, this number denotes that it is below ten and indicates a small number like in English "a few" or "several").

如：(1) 我只有幾本書。

(2) 我昨晚拉了好幾次肚子。

2. 「數字＋幾」表示必須是十以上，一百以下的「十位數」，然後再多幾個，如十幾、二十幾、三十幾…。

Numbers + 幾 *jǐ* mean that there must be more than ten but less than one hundred. The figure must only be in the range of "two digits," such as ten and over, twenty and over, or thirty and over.

如：(1) 他十幾歲的時候就離開老家了。（10～19，年紀小）

(2) 才二十幾塊錢，不必客氣。（20～29，數量少）

(3) 你是二十多歲的大學生了，怎麼還像個小孩子？（20～29）

3. 「幾＋數字」，代表十、百、千、萬、億…的倍數。

When 幾 *jǐ* occurs followed by a number such as ten, it represents multiples of ten; when the number is a hundred, then it represents multiples of a hundred; when the number is a thousand or ten thousand or a billion, it represents multiples of a thousand or ten thousand or a billion.

如：(1) 她很有錢，買一輛車子就花了幾千萬。（千萬的倍數）

(2) 才幾十塊錢，不必客氣。（十的倍數）

(3) 出國幾十年，臺灣好多地方我都不認識了。（十的倍數）

例句：

1. 他先念書，三十幾歲才開始工作。

2. 市集的飾品不太貴，有時候十幾塊一個。

3. 有的印度菜會放十幾種香料。

練習：請用「數字＋幾」完成下面的句子。

Exercise：Please use Number + 幾 *jǐ* to finish the following sentences.

1. 他沒去念小學，才_____，就在市集幫父母賣東西。

2. 這個手環才_____，真便宜。

3. 他真厲害，才_____分鐘就會唱這首中文歌了。

4. 這裡的房子真貴，連只有一間房間的小套房常常都要_____。

5. 沒想到他已經喝了_____杯酒了，還能自己走回家去。

四、然後 *ránhòu*　　"then"

說明：「然後」是副詞，表示兩件事情發生的先後次序關係，一定是在整句後面的子句部分，可以用在過去或未來。與「先…再…」的搭配方式一樣。

Explanation：然後 *ránhòu* is an adverb that indicates the order in which two things occur and must be in the clause after the whole sentence. It can be used for the past or future.

1.「先…然後…」可以和「先…再…」互相替換使用，但後者不可使

用在過去的事情。

先 *xiān*... 然後 *ránhòu*... and 先 *xiān*..., 再 *zài*… can replace each other,
but the latter pattern cannot be used in the past.

如：(1) 上了一天課好累，我想先睡一下，然後起來念書。

(2) 上了一天課好累，我想先睡一下，再起來念書。

2.「先……然後……」和「先…再…」也可以在同一個句子中使用，如：
「先、然後、再、然後再、最後」等，以交替使用的方式來完成一
個小段落，比較有變化。

先 *xiān*... 然後 *ránhòu*... and 先 *xiān*... 再 *zài*... can also be used in the
same sentence, such as 先 *xiān*, 然後 *ránhòu*, 再 *zài*, 然後再 *ránhòu zài*,
最後 *zuìhòu* and so on, as an alternate way to complete a short discourse.

如：我打算先念大學，然後工作，有了工作，再結婚。

例句：

1. 吃中國菜的時候，先吃飯，然後喝湯。
2. 今天我們打算先去印度門，然後去月光市集逛逛。
3. 週末我打算先寫功課，再去打球，然後再跟女朋友去看電影。

練習：請用「然後」或「先…然後…」，完成下面的句子。

Exercise：Please use 然後 *ránhòu* or 先 *xiān*... 然後 *ránhòu*… to complete the
following sentences.

---

1. A：這次三天兩夜的旅行，你的計畫是什麼？

   B：我打算＿＿＿＿＿＿＿＿＿＿＿＿＿＿＿＿＿。

2. A：你知道做印度香料奶茶 (Indian Masala Chai）的時候，牛奶和茶，哪個
   先放？

   B：你得先＿＿＿＿＿＿，＿＿＿＿＿。

3. A：媽媽，我打了一下午球，現在肚子好餓。

   B：桌上有幾塊蛋糕，你先＿＿＿＿＿，＿＿＿＿＿。

---

4. A：我的錢不夠，不能買房子，真不知道怎麼結婚？

　　B：別想那麼多，很多人也都是先＿＿＿＿＿＿，＿＿＿＿＿＿。

5. A：撈金魚、射氣球好多遊戲，你想先玩哪個？

　　B：我要＿＿＿＿＿＿，＿＿＿＿＿＿。

五、雙音節狀態動詞重疊（AABB 式）　Reduplication of Disyllabic Adjectives (AABB)

說明：「雙音節狀態動詞重疊」一般表示程度的加強以及強調生動的形式，狀態動詞的結構形式從 AB 變為 AABB。

Explanation："Reduplication of Disyllabic Adjectives" generally expresses a degree of strengthening and emphasis on vivid forms, with the structure of state verbs changing from AB to AABB.

如：開心→開開心心 / 高興→高高興興

1.「雙音節狀態動詞重疊 AABB」修飾名詞要 +「的」

　　With "Reduplication of Disyllabic Adjectives (AABB)," nouns need to have 的 *de* added in front of the noun.

　　如：(1) 他是一個客客氣氣的人，所以誰都喜歡他。

　　　　(2) 漂漂亮亮的東西，大家都喜歡。

2.「雙音節狀態動詞重疊 AABB」修飾動詞 + 地。

　　With "Reduplication of Disyllabic Adjectives (AABB)," verbs need to have 地 *di* added in front of the verb.

　　如：(1) 忙了一個多月，我現在只想舒舒服服地睡一覺。

　　　　(2) 好久不見，我們找個地方輕輕鬆鬆地聊一聊吧。

3.「雙音節狀態動詞重疊 AABB」作為補語，「的」可以省略。

　　When "Reduplication of Disyllabic Adjectives (AABB)" is used as a complement, 的 *de* can be omitted.

　　如：(1) 他們買了一棟大房子，全家住得舒舒服服（的）。

　　　　(2) 他們在夜市玩遊戲，玩得高高興興（的）。

4.「雙音節狀態動詞重疊 AABB」作為謂語時，後面接「的」。

When "Reduplication of Disyllabic Adjectives (AABB)" is used as a predicate, it is followed by 的 *de*.

如：(1) 他們一家人每天都開開心心的。

　　(2) 他的習慣很好，做了飯，廚房還是乾乾淨淨的。

5.「雙音節狀態動詞重疊 AABB」不可與程度副詞「很、非常、相當、極⋯」等並用。

"Reduplication of Disyllabic Adjectives (AABB)" cannot be associated with the degree adverbs " 很 *hěn*, 非常 *fēicháng*, 相當 *xiāngdāng*, 極 *jí*" and so on.

如：(1) *他們非常開開心心地給媽媽過生日。

　　(2) *我們教室每天都很乾乾淨淨的。

6. 非所有雙音節狀態動詞均可重疊為「AABB」形式。像：便宜、傳統、好看、方便、麻煩、討厭、可怕、便利⋯等等都不可使用。

Not all disyllabic adjectives can be reduplicated in the form of "AABB." Adjectives such as 便宜 *piányí*, 傳統 *chuántǒng*, 好看 *hǎokàn*, 方便 *fāngbiàn*, 麻煩 *máfán*, 討厭 *tǎoyàn*, 可怕 *kěpà*, 便利 *biànlì* cannot be used in the form of "AABB."

如：(1) *這條路便便利利的。

　　(2) *她每天都穿得好好看看的。

例句：

1. 有快快樂樂的老師，才有快快樂樂的學生。
2. 那位老闆是一個客客氣氣的人，所以生意很好。
3. 那家餐廳，現在不擠，我們去那裡舒舒服服地吃飯吧。
4. 天氣很好，我們可以去公園開開心心地騎腳踏車。
5. 去參加婚禮，大家都穿得漂漂亮亮（的）。
6. 這張照片裡的每個人都笑得開開心心（的）。
7. 這裡的窗戶都乾乾淨淨的。
8. 老師來了，孩子們馬上都安安靜靜的。

練習：請用（開心、漂亮、乾淨、舒服、快樂）完成下面的句子。

Exercise：Please complete the following sentences with (開心 *kāixīn*, 漂亮 *piàoliàng*, 乾淨 *gānjìng*, 舒服 *shūfú*, 快樂 *kuàilè*).

1. 弟弟剛上小學，每天都＿＿＿＿＿＿去上課。
2. 父母都希望孩子＿＿＿＿＿＿長大。
3. 工作了一天，真想快點回家洗個＿＿＿＿＿＿澡。
4. 這個學生真好，把每個字都寫得＿＿＿＿＿＿。
5. 他很餓，把菜吃得＿＿＿＿＿＿，一點都沒了。
6. 這家飯店的房間都＿＿＿＿＿＿，真舒服！

跨文化延伸 Cross-Cultural Extension

The Vegetarian Cultures of Taiwan and India

Vegetarianism is a common phenomenon in Taiwan and is very convenient because there are vegetarian restaurants everywhere. Except for a few people who eat vegetarian food to lose weight, most are vegetarian for religious reasons or to protect animals. Some people would eat vegetarian food on the first and fifteenth of the month. Some people eat vegetarian food every day, and some only eat vegetarian food during early morning fasting. As to how vegetarian food should be eaten, this can be done according to their own ideas.

Some people in Taiwan are "total vegetarians," and some people can eat "milk and egg with vegetarian food." But these two types of vegetarians cannot eat spicy food, onions, garlic cloves, and leeks. In addition, there is a very special vegetarian cooking in which the dishes can contain meat, but the vegetarian eater can only eat the vegetables. It is known as '鍋邊素 *guōbiānsù*.'

As one of the world's biggest vegetarian countries, India has many varieties of spices. When eating vegetarian food, Hindus can put spices, onions, and garlic into the food, but it must be totally without meat. However, for some Indian men, even if they are meat-eaters, they would choose to be vegetarian every week on the day when the God of their faith is in charge. For instance, if someone believes that the monkey god symbolizes power, he would choose to be vegetarian every Tuesday. In fact, no matter what way vegetarian food is consumed, "nutritional balance" and "sincerity" are most important because sincerity is spiritual, and "nutritional balance" is healthy!

臺灣素食大餐
a Taiwanese vegetarian meal

印度南部喀拉拉邦的素食香蕉葉拼盤
a Sadhya/Sadya in Kerala, India

語言任務 Language Tasks

一、猜猜看 Guess what?

任務：學生每人用「雙音節狀態動詞重疊」(AABB)，寫下兩個句子，放進盒子裡，作為指令。然後每個學生依序隨機抽出，把情境表演出來，其他

學生猜猜看，是什麼句子。

Task：Each student uses the pattern "Reduplication of Disyllabic Adjectives (AABB)" to write down two sentences, puts them in a box, and acts according to the instructions. Each student then randomly pulls one out, acts out the situation, and the other students guess what the sentence is.

例句：我開開心心地吃大餐。

二、句子接龍 Sentence solitaire

學生用「先、然後、再、然後再、最後」、「什麼的」和「一邊…，一邊… 」，大家一起討論「逛臺灣夜市、逛印度市集、學中文、做甜點、泡印度奶茶／中國茶、旅行」等話題。

Students should use 先 *xiān*, 然後 *ránhòu*, 再 *zài*, 然後再 *ránhòu zài*, 最後 *zuìhòu*, 什麼的 *shénmede*, and 一邊 *yìbiān* …, 一邊 *yìbiān* … to discuss topics such as "Going to a Taiwan Night Market; Visiting an Indian Market; Learning Chinese; Making Desserts; Making Indian Milk Tea/Chinese Tea; Traveling" and so on.

例如：A：我們這次旅行，先坐高鐵去臺中玩一天……

　　　B：然後到臺南去逛夜市吃小吃，……

　　　C：臺南的蚵仔煎、甜不辣、大腸麵線什麼的都好吃極了，……

　　　D：然後再一邊吃小吃，一邊玩遊戲……

　　　E：像撈金魚、射氣球什麼的……

　　　F：……

　　　G：最後……

第八課　養生的方法
Lesson 8　Ways of Keeping Healthy

課程目標：

Topic：健康養生

　　1. 能了解印度傳統的養生方法。

　　2. 能比較兩種人或事物的異同。

　　3. 能了解中醫與阿育吠陀的共同點。

Lesson Objectives：

Topic：Health and Wellness

　　1. Students can learn about traditional Indian health methods.

　　2. Students can compare the similarities and differences between two kinds of people or things.

　　3. Students can understand what Chinese medicine and Ayurveda have in common.

Lesson 8

洛迪公園「草地瑜珈」
Lodhi Park's "Meadow Yoga"

對話 Dialogue 🎧

王祕書：經理，您這幾天看起來有一點累！

周經理：是啊！我們每天都有活動，還得準備合作資料。

王祕書：我建議您早上去新德里的洛迪公園慢跑。

周經理：我不太喜歡慢跑、健走這些運動。

王祕書：那瑜珈呢？洛迪公園的「草地瑜珈」非常有名。

周經理：瑜珈！我不但有興趣，而且也常常練習。

王祕書：太好了！我們現在就去報名明天的草地瑜珈課吧！

【第二天，在洛迪公園草地瑜珈課後，有一位對印度養生頗有研究的人，跟周經理聊印度的瑜珈和養生。】

印度人：印度瑜珈種類很多。現在大家比較常做運動瑜珈。

周經理：我們今天早上練習的就是吧？

印度人：是的，在草地上跟大自然溝通，讓我們身心健康。

第八課　養生的方法 Ways of Keeping Healthy

周經理：您對這方面真有研究。

印度人：哪裡，哪裡。

王秘書：我聽說印度的阿育吠陀養生方法很有名。

印度人：對！我們會用瑜珈、按摩、食物和草藥來養生。

王秘書：這跟傳統的中醫很像。

周經理：不早了，我們有事得先走，希望有機會再聊。

課文漢語拼音 Text in Hanyu Pinyin

Wáng mìshū : Jīnglǐ, nín zhè jǐ tiān kàn qǐlái yǒu yìdiǎn lèi!

Zhōu jīnglǐ : Shì a! Wǒmen měi tiān dōu yǒu huódòng, hái děi zhǔnbèi hézuò zīliào.

Wáng mìshū : Wǒ jiànyì nín zǎoshàng qù Xīndélǐ de Luòdí Gōngyuán mànpǎo.

Zhōu jīnglǐ : Wǒ bú tài xǐhuān mànpǎo, jiànzǒu zhèxiē yùndòng.

Wáng mìshū : Nà yújiā ne? Luòdí Gōngyuán de "cǎodì yújiā" fēicháng yǒumíng.

Zhōu jīnglǐ : Yújiā! Wǒ búdàn yǒu xìngqù, érqiě yě chángcháng liànxí.

Wáng mìshū : Tài hǎo le! Wǒmen xiànzài jiù qù bàomíng míngtiān de cǎodì yújiā kè ba!

[Dì-èr tiān, zài Luòdí Gōngyuán cǎodì yújiā kè hòu, yǒu yí wèi duì Yìndù yǎngshēng pǒ yǒu yánjiù de rén, gēn Zhōu jīnglǐ liáo Yìndù de yújiā hàn yǎngshēng.]

Yìndù rén : Yìndù yújiā zhǒnglèi hěn duō. Xiànzài dàjiā bǐjiào cháng zuò yùndòng yújiā.

Zhōu jīnglǐ : Wǒmen jīntiān zǎoshàng liànxí de jiùshì ba?

Yìndù rén : Shì de, zài cǎodì shàng gēn dàzìrán gōutōng, ràng wǒmen shēnxīn jiànkāng.

Zhōu jīnglǐ :	Nín duì zhè fāngmiàn zhēn yǒu yánjiù.
Yìndù rén :	Nǎlǐ, nǎlǐ.
Wáng mìshū :	Wǒ tīngshuō Yìndù de Āyùfèituó yǎngshēng fāngfǎ hěn yǒumíng.
Yìndù rén :	Duì! Wǒmen huì yòng yújiā, ànmó, shíwù hàn cǎoyào lái yǎngshēng.
Wáng mìshū :	Zhè gēn chuántǒng de zhōngyī hěn xiàng.
Zhōu jīnglǐ :	Bù zǎo le, wǒmen yǒu shì děi xiān zǒu, xīwàng yǒu jīhuì zài liáo.

課文英譯 Text in English

Dialogue

Secretary Wang :	Manager Zhou, you look a little tired these days!
Manager Zhou :	Yes! We are packed with activities every day, and we have to prepare collaboration materials.
Secretary Wang :	I suggest you go jogging in Lodhi Garden in New Delhi in the morning.
Manager Zhou :	I don't like sports such as jogging or brisk walking.
Secretary Wang :	What about yoga? "Meadow Yoga" in Lodhi Garden is very famous.
Manager Zhou :	Yoga! Not only am I interested, but I also practice it a lot.
Secretary Wang :	That's great! Let's go and sign up for tomorrow's meadow yoga class now!

第八課　養生的方法 Ways of Keeping Healthy

[The next day, after the yoga class in Lodhi Garden, a man who had studied Indian health talks to Manager Zhou about yoga and wellness in India.]

Indians : There are many kinds of yoga in India. Nowadays, we often do sports yoga.

Manager Zhou : Wasn't that what we practiced this morning?

Indian : Yes, communing with nature on the grass makes us healthy.

Manager Zhou : You really have made a study of this.

Indian : You are welcome.

Secretary Wang : I heard that India's Ayurvedic method of health is very famous.

Indian : That's right! We use yoga, massage, food, and herbs to recuperate.

Secretary Wang : This is very similar to traditional Chinese medicine.

Manager Zhou : It's a bit late now. We have something to attend to so we have to go. We hope to have a chance to talk again.

生詞一 Vocabulary I 🎧

編號	生詞	漢語拼音	詞性	英文翻譯
1.	養生	yǎngshēng	Vi/Vs/N	health; to keep one's body healthy
2.	方法	fāngfǎ	N	method
3.	活動	huódòng	N	activity
4.	資料	zīliào	N	material, data, information
5.	慢跑	mànpǎo	Vi/N	to jog; jogging
6.	健走	jiànzǒu	Vi/N	to walk briskly; brisk walking

編號	生詞	漢語拼音	詞性	英文翻譯
7.	瑜珈	yújiā	N	yoga
8.	草地	cǎodì	N	lawn
9.	而且	érqiě	Conj	and, moreover
10.	報名	bàomíng	V	to register
11.	大自然	dàzìrán	N	nature
12.	溝通	gōutōng	V	to communicate
13.	身心	shēnxīn	N	body and mind
14.	研究	yánjiù	N	research, study
15.	按摩	ànmó	N	massage
16.	食物	shíwù	N	food
17.	草藥	cǎoyào	N	herbs
18.	中醫	zhōngyī	N	Chinese medicine
19.	聊	liáo	V	to chat

專有名詞 Proper Nouns

編號	生詞	漢語拼音	英文翻譯
1.	阿育吠陀	Āyùfèituó	Ayurveda
2.	洛迪公園	Luòdí Gōngyuán	Lodhi Garden

短文 Reading 🎧

食療

　　從以前到現在，每一個人都希望健康，沒有人想生病，所以養生很重要。

　　中國人認為：「食物是最好的藥物」。只要吃對的食物，就會

對身體有幫助，也不容易生病。知道吃什麼對身體好，就是食療養生。

　　中國傳統的食療養生，是按照不同的年齡、體質、疾病和季節，吃一些讓身體健康，或是能治療疾病的食物。跟一般的食物比起來，這些食物比較養生，所以現在吃的人就多起來了。

　　印度的阿育吠陀跟中醫一樣也有食療養生。按照不同的體質，吃不同的食物。但是阿育吠陀比中醫更注意「季節飲食」，一年分春天、夏天、雨季、秋天、冬前和冬天六個季節，每個季節有兩個月，每一季有不同的食療方法。但是現在很多人是按照個人喜好或是家庭的狀況，決定吃什麼。

中醫食療養生
Chinese medicine dietary regimens

阿育吠陀養生料理
Ayurvedic regimen cuisine

課文漢語拼音 Text in Hanyu Pinyin

Shíliáo

　　Cóng yǐqián dào xiànzài, měi yí ge rén dōu xīwàng jiànkāng, méi yǒu rén xiǎng shēngbìng, suǒyǐ yǎngshēng hěn zhòngyào.

　　Zhōngguó rén rènwéi: "Shíwù shì zuì hǎo de yàowù." Zhǐyào chī duì de shíwù, jiù huì duì shēntǐ yǒu bāngzhù, yě bù róngyì shēngbìng. Zhīdào chī shénme duì shēntǐ hǎo, jiùshì shíliáo yǎngshēng.

　　Zhōngguó chuántǒng de shíliáo yǎngshēng, shì ànzhào bùtóng de niánlíng, tǐzhí, jíbìng hàn jìjié, chī yìxiē ràng shēntǐ jiànkāng, huò shì néng zhìliáo jíbìng de shíwù. Gēn yìbān de shíwù bǐ qǐlái, zhèxiē shíwù bǐjiào yǎngshēng, suǒyǐ xiànzài chī de rén jiù duō qǐlái le.

Yìndù de Āyùfèituó gēn zhōngyī yíyàng yěyǒu shíliáo yǎngshēng. Ànzhào bùtóng de tǐzhí, chī bùtóng de shíwù. Dànshì Āyùfèituó bǐ zhōngyī gèng zhùyì "jìjié yǐnshí", yì nián fēn chūntiān, xiàtiān, yǔjì, qiūtiān, dōngqián hàn dōngtiān liù ge jìjié, měi ge jìjié yǒu liǎng ge yuè, měi yí jì yǒu bùtóng de shíliáo fāngfǎ. Dànshì xiànzài hěn duō rén shì ànzhào gèrén xǐhào huò shì jiātíng de zhuàngkuàng, juédìng chī shénme.

課文英譯 Text in English

Food Therapy

From the beginning of time until now, everyone wants to be healthy. No one wants to get sick. Therefore, health is very important.

For the Chinese: Food is the best medicine. Eating the right food can help your body and make you less likely to get sick. Knowing what is good for your health is staying healthy through diet.

The traditional Chinese way to stay healthy through diet is to eat foods that are healthy or can treat diseases according to age, physique, diseases, and season. Compared with average food, such foods are healthier. Therefore, more people are starting to eat healthier now.

India's Ayurveda medicine, like traditional Chinese medicine, also has a diet regimen. One is to eat different foods according to your physique. However, compared with Chinese medicine, Ayurveda pays more attention to seasonal diets. A year is divided into six seasons, including Spring, Summer, rainy season, Autumn, before Winter, and Winter. There are two months in each season, and there is a different diet regimen within each season. But now many people use their personal preferences or family situation to decide what to eat.

生詞二 Vocabulary II 🎧

編號	生詞	漢語拼音	詞性	英文翻譯
1.	食療	shíliáo	N	food therapy
2.	認為	rènwéi	V	to think
3.	藥物	yàowù	N	drug
4.	身體	shēntǐ	N	body
5.	幫助	bāngzhù	N	help
6.	不同	bùtóng	Vs	different
7.	年齡	niánlíng	N	age
8.	體質	tǐzhí	N	physique
9.	疾病	jíbìng	N	disease
10.	季節	jìjié	N	season
11.	讓	ràng	V	to let
12.	治療	zhìliáo	V	to treat
13.	一般	yìbān	Vs-attr	normal
14.	飲食	yǐnshí	N	diet, drinks, and food
15.	雨季	yǔjì	N	rainy season
16.	冬前	dōngqián	N	before winter
17.	喜好	xǐhào	N	preference, what a person likes
18.	狀況	zhuàngkuàng	N	situation

短語 Phrases

編號	生詞	漢語拼音	英文翻譯
1.	比起來	bǐqǐlái	compared with, by comparison

語法 Grammar 🎧

一、不但 *búdàn*…，而且 *érqiě*…　　Not only…, but also…

說明：「不但…，而且…」連接兩個分句，表示遞進。

Explanation：不但 *búdàn* …，而且 *érqiě* … connects two sentences to represent an ongoing situation.

1. 兩句主語相同時，主語可放在「不但」前面，後句主語可省略。

   When the subjects of the two sentences are the same, the subject can be placed in front of 不但 *búdàn*, and the subject of the latter sentence can be omitted.

   如：我不但要上班，而且要上課。

2. 如果主語不同，主語要放在「不但」和「而且」之後。

   If the subjects are different, the subjects should be placed after 不但 *búdàn* and 而且 *érqiě* ….

   如：臺東，不但風景漂亮，而且天氣也很好。

3. 有時候，也可以省略「不但」，後接「而且還／也」。

   Sometimes, you can omit 不但 *búdàn*, followed by 而且還／也 *érqiě hái/ yě* …

   如：他租的房子房租不貴，而且還／也很方便。

例句：

1. 食療不但能養生，而且能治病。
2. 這部電影，不但我喜歡看，而且我同學也喜歡看。
3. 現在的手機都能拍照，而且還／也能上網買東西。

第八課　養生的方法 Ways of Keeping Healthy

練習：請用「不但…，而且…」完成下面句子

Exercise：Please use 不但 *búdàn* …，而且 *érqiě* … to complete the following
sentences.

---

1. 水果不但＿＿＿＿＿＿，而且＿＿＿＿＿＿。（好吃；健康）

2. 臺灣的夏天不但＿＿＿＿＿＿，而且＿＿＿＿＿＿。（熱；溼）

3. 瑜珈不但對＿＿＿＿＿＿，而且＿＿＿＿＿＿。（身體好；養生）

4. 我昨天不但去＿＿＿＿＿，而且還／也去＿＿＿＿＿。（VO；VO）

5. 來臺灣學中文，不但＿＿＿＿＿＿，而且＿＿＿＿＿＿。

二、對 *duì* …有 *yǒu* …　　　towards …

說明：「對」是介詞，常搭配「有」，「有」後面的賓語常是抽象名詞，如：
　　　研究、好處、幫助、經驗…等。

Explanation：對 *duì* … is a preposition, often accompanied by 有 *yǒu*. The object
　　　after 有 *yǒu* is usually an abstract noun such as 研究 *yánjiù*, 好處 *hǎochù*,
　　　幫助 *bāngzhù*, 經驗 *jīngyàn*, 興趣 *xìngqù*, etc.

　　1.「有」前面可加程度副詞。

　　　　Before 有 *yǒu* there can be an adverb.

　　　　如：他對養生很有／沒有研究。

　　2. 名詞前面也可加修飾語。

　　　　Nouns can also be preceded by modifiers.

　　　　如：食療對養生有很大的幫助。

例句：

　　1. 我媽媽對做菜很有研究。

　　2. 多吃青菜、水果，對身體有很大的好處。

　　3. 有些人對運動沒有興趣。

練習：請用「對…有研究／有好處／有幫助／有經驗／有興趣」的句型回答問

題

Exercise：Please answer questions with 對 *duì*... 有研究 *yǒu yánjiù*, 有好處 *yǒu hǎochù*, 有幫助 *yǒu bāngzhù*, 有經驗 *yǒu jīngyàn*, and 有興趣 *yǒu xìngqù*.

---

1. A：你每天走半小時的路去上班，不累嗎？

   B：有一點累，可是我覺得_____。

2. A：我們明天去看電影，好嗎？

   B：我不想去，我_____。

3. A：李老師懂很多食療養生的方法。

   B：是啊，他_____。

4. A：我不知道怎麼去臺灣學中文。

   B：我可以告訴你，我_____。

5. A：你為什麼下班以後還去學瑜珈？

   B：因為_____。

三、A 跟 *gēn* B 比起來 *bǐqǐlái*　　A compared with B

說明：「比起來」是短語。說話者比較兩個事物之後，做出評論、選擇或偏好。不用否定式。

Explanation：比起來 *bǐqǐlái* is a phrase. After the speaker compares two things, make a comment, choice, or preference. It cannot be used in negative sentences.

1. 「比」是主要動詞，常與介詞「跟」或連詞「和」搭配使用。

   "比 *bǐ*" is the main verb and is often used in conjunction with the preposition 跟 *gēn* or the conjunction 和 *hé/hàn*.

   如：(1) 我跟妹妹比起來，我比較矮。

   　　(2) 茶和咖啡比起來，我比較常喝咖啡。

2. 兩者比較後的結果，常用程度副詞或補語。如：比較、一點、多了。

In the second clause, where the results of the comparison are stated, there is often an adverb or complement such as 比較 *bǐjiào*, 一點 *yìdiǎn*, 多了 *duōle.*

如：(1) 臺灣北部的冬天和南部比起來，北部冷一點。

　　(2) 美國的東西跟臺灣比起來，美國貴多了。

3. 如果前後兩句主語相同，前句主語可以省略。

If the first two subjects are the same, the subject of the previous sentence can be omitted.

如：（我們學校）跟你們學校比起來，我們學校遠多了。

4. 如果後句省略主語，所省略的是指前句的第一個主語。

如：這家餐廳跟那家餐廳比起來，貴多了。(「這家餐廳」貴多了。)

例句：

1. 打籃球跟踢足球比起來，哪個比較好學？

2. 他跟他哥哥比起來，他哥哥高一點兒。

3. （這家餐廳）跟那家餐廳比起來，這家餐廳比較便宜。

4. 我覺得傳統的春節跟現代的春節比起來，熱鬧多了。（「傳統的春節」熱鬧多了。）

練習：請用你學過的生詞，用「比起來」回答問題及完成句子。

（有意思、快、慢、有興趣、貴、便宜、喜歡、好玩、漂亮、舒服…）

Exercise：Please use the new words you have learned and answer questions and complete sentences with 比起來 *bǐqǐlái*.

（有意思 *yǒu yìsi*、快 *kuài*、慢 *màn*、有興趣 *yǒu xìngqù*、貴 *guì*、便宜 *piányi*、喜歡 *xǐhuān*、好玩 *hǎo wán*、漂亮 *piàoliang*、舒服 *shūfú*）

例句：

A：週末你要去打球還是去看電影？為什麼？

B：我要去看電影。我覺得看電影比較有意思 / 有意思多了。

1. 火車跟高鐵 / 快　　　　　（比起來、比較）

2. 夏天和春天 / 熱　　　　　（比起來、比較）

3. 日本菜跟泰國菜 / 酸、辣　　　　　（比起來、比較）

4. 日文和法文 / 難學　　　　　　　　（比起來、一點）

5. 城市跟鄉下 / 好玩　　　　　　　　（比起來、多了）

四、Ｖ起來 *qǐlái₂*　　Inchoative Meaning with Ｖ起來 *qǐlái₂*

說明：「Ｖ起來₂」的「起來」是補語。表示動作或狀態的開始。

Explanation：The 起來 *qǐlái* of Ｖ *qǐlái₂* is a complement. It represents the beginning of an action or state.

1. Ｖ可以是動作動詞或是狀態動詞。「了」可出現在動詞之後或起來之後。

V can be an action verb or a stative verb. 了 *le* may appear after the verb or after 起來 *qǐlái*.

如：(1) 同學一進教室，就聊（了）起來了。（Ｖ）

　　　(2) 過年快到了，菜都貴（了）起來了。（Vs）

2. 如果動詞有受詞（VO 結構），受詞放在「起」和「來」之間。

If a verb has an object (VO structure), the object is placed between 起 *qǐ* and 來 *lái.*

如：他最近學起中文來了。

例句：

1. 一到週末，出去玩的人就多了起來。　（Vs 起來）

2. 小孩沒看到媽媽，就哭起來了。　　　（Ｖ起來）

3. 我一出門，就下起雨來了。　　　　　（Ｖ起（Ｏ）來）

練習：請選用下列的動詞或形容詞，及「Ｖ起（Ｏ）來」完成句子。

Exercise：Use the following verbs or adjectives and Ｖ起 (Ｏ來) to complete the sentences.

（吃 *chī*、笑 *xiào*、胖 *pàng*、熱 *rè*、喝茶 *hēchá*、唱歌 *chànggē*）

1. 我太餓了，一回家就＿＿＿＿＿＿＿。
2. 夏天到了，天氣也＿＿＿＿＿＿＿。
3. 我最近吃太多甜點，覺得＿＿＿＿＿＿＿。
4. 他一高興，就＿＿＿＿＿＿＿。（V 起（O）來）
5. 小孩一看到媽媽，就＿＿＿＿＿＿＿。
6. 你不是不喜歡茶嗎？怎麼今天＿＿＿＿＿＿＿。

跨文化延伸 Cross-Cultural Extension

Traditional Chinese Medicine and Ayurveda

Traditional Chinese medicine and Ayurvedic medicine in India are two ancient traditional medicines and have much in common.

Ayurveda means the science of life. It is not only a medicinal practice but also a healthy way of life. This medical treatment pays attention to human characteristics, such as physical fitness, age, living environment, social and cultural background. Diagnosis includes touch, check-up and conversations, and the use of herbs, massage, and yoga to restore organ function.

The diagnostic method of Chinese medicine includes four steps: look, smell, ask and check. The doctor first observes the patient's appearance, listens to the sound made by the patient, then smells the breath emitted by the patient, then asks about the illness, the medical history, and finally checks the patient's pulse. Common treatments are traditional Chinese medicine, acupuncture, Chinese massage, and injury treatment. Chinese medicine is very popular in Taiwan. Even Western medical centers have Chinese medicine clinics in them. Chinese herbal medicine is often added

Lesson 8

into daily family dishes to improve people's physical health from its very foundation.

Both medical methods attach importance to the treatment of illness by treating the foundational property of the body. Furthermore, the maintenance of a correct balanced diet promotes physical and mental health. They all contribute a lot to medicine and are much integrated into people's lives.

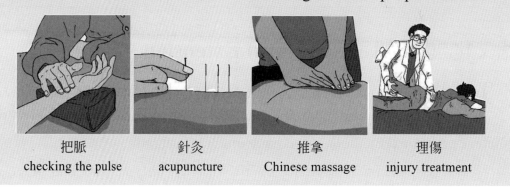

把脈
checking the pulse

針灸
acupuncture

推拿
Chinese massage

理傷
injury treatment

語言任務 Language Tasks

一、學生兩個人一組，互相訪問，並寫在表格上。

任務：A 問對方：為什麼對…有（研究、好處、幫助、經驗、興趣）？

B 回答：因為…，不但…，而且…。

1. Form groups of two students, interview each other, and write the information on the form.

Task：A asks the other person: 為什麼對…有（研究 *yánjiù*, 好處 *hǎochù*, 幫助 *bāngzhù*, 經驗 *jīngyàn*, 興趣 *xìngqù*）？

B answers: 因為 yīnwèi …，不但 *búdàn* …，而且 *érqiě*.

對看中文電影有興趣	因為看中文電影，不但可以學中文，而且可以了解中國文化。
1.	
2.	
3.	
4.	

二、學生兩個人一組，針對臺灣與印度的交通、食物、天氣進行討論。並使用課本提供的句型，向全班同學報告同伴的說法。

Divide students into groups of two to discuss transportation, food, and weather in Taiwan and India. Then use the sentence patterns provided in the textbook to tell your classmates what your opinions are.

例句：他說他覺得印度的食物比較好吃。因為印度的食物跟臺灣比起來，_____的食物比較_____，而且_____。雖然臺灣的食物_____，但是他還是喜歡吃印度的食物。

印度交通狀況
transport in India

印度食物
Indian food

臺灣食物
Taiwanese food

第九課　伴手禮
Lesson 9　Souvenirs

課程目標：

Topic：文化禮俗

    1. 能知道印度特產及如何挑選適合的伴手禮。

    2. 能了解印度的珠寶文化和中國的玉文化。

    3. 能了解伴手禮所代表的意義及其效應。

Lesson Objectives：

Topic：Cultural Etiquette

    1. Students can know about Indian local specialties and choose the right souvenirs.

    2. Students can gain information about India's jewelry culture and China's jade culture.

    3. Students can understand the meaning and effect of souvenirs.

souvenirs

對話 Dialogue 🎧

【印度珠寶公司韋經理、周經理和王祕書談去新德里市集買伴手禮。】

韋經理：時間過得真快！不久你們就要回臺灣了。

周經理：是啊！回國以前，想買一些這裡有特色的東西。

韋經理：對！來印度一定要帶我們的特產回臺灣當伴手禮。

王祕書：經理，我帶您去逛新德里有名的市集跟商場，順便買些禮物。

韋經理：王祕書是印度通，在這方面更有經驗吧！

王祕書：我認為逛市集，除了能買到當地的特產以外，還能看到不同的文化。

韋經理：說得好！阿薩姆紅茶、香料、手工鞋、首飾…，都有我們的文化。

王祕書：我建議買草本的喜馬拉雅產品，更有特色。

周經理：好建議。這次我不但要買伴手禮，而且想欣賞欣賞印度的珠寶設計。

韋經理：沒問題。明天我陪您去參觀我的珠寶公司。

【韋經理帶周經理去參觀珠寶公司，談到黃金。】

韋經理：這些是黃金首飾，這些是黃金加上不同寶石的流行設計。

周經理：又美又有創意！而且都是一套一套的，有耳環、項鍊、手鐲。

韋經理：這是我們的傳統風格。現在也流行白金和純銀的首飾。

一套珠寶
A set of jewelry

周經理：不過，看起來還是黃金首飾比較多。

韋經理：沒錯。因為在印度人心中，金色是最高貴的顏色。

周經理：聽您這麼說，我決定買一套黃金首飾了。

課文漢語拼音 Text in Hanyu Pinyin

[Yìndù zhūbǎo gōngsī Wéi jīnglǐ, Zhōu jīnglǐ hàn Wáng mìshū tán qù Xīn Délǐ shíjí mǎi bànshǒulǐ.]

Wéi jīnglǐ : Shíjiān guò de zhēn kuài! Bùjiǔ nǐmen jiù yào huí Táiwān le.

Zhōu jīnglǐ : Shì a! Huí guó yǐqián, xiǎng mǎi yìxiē zhèlǐ yǒu tèsè de dōngxi.

Wéi jīnglǐ : Duì! Lái Yìndù yídìng yào dài wǒmen de tèchǎn huí Táiwān dāng bànshǒulǐ.

Wáng mìshū : Jīnglǐ, wǒ dài nín qù guàng Xīn Délǐ yǒumíng de shíjí gēn shāngchǎng, shùnbiàn mǎi xiē lǐwù.

Wéi jīnglǐ : Wáng mìshū shì Yìndù tōng, zài zhè fāngmiàn gèng yǒu jīngyàn ba!

Wáng mìshū : Wǒ rènwéi guàng shìjí, chúle néng mǎidào dāngdì de tèchǎn yǐwài, hái néng kàndào bù tóng de wénhuà.

Wéi jīnglǐ : Shuō de hǎo! Āsàmǔ hóngchá, xiāngliào, shǒugōng xié, shǒushì…, dōu yǒu wǒmen de wénhuà.

Wáng mìshū : Wǒ jiànyì mǎi cǎoběn de Xǐmǎlāyǎ chǎnpǐn, gèng yǒu tèsè.

Zhōu jīnglǐ : Hǎo jiànyì. Zhè cì wǒ búdàn yào mǎi bànshǒulǐ, érqiě xiǎng xīnshǎng xīnshǎng Yìndù de zhūbǎo shèjì.

Wéi jīnglǐ : Méi wèntí. Míngtiān wǒ péi nín qù cānguān wǒ de zhūbǎo gōngsī.

[Wéi jīnglǐ dài Zhōu jīnglǐ qù cānguān zhūbǎo gōngsī, tándào huángjīn.]

Wéi jīnglǐ : Zhèxiē shì huángjīn shǒushì, zhèxiē shì huángjīn jiāshàng bù tóng bǎoshí de liúxíng shèjì.

Zhōu jīnglǐ : Yòu měi yòu yǒu chuàngyì! Érqiě dōu shì yí tào yí tào de, yǒu ěrhuán, xiàngliàn, shǒuzhuó.

Wéi jīnglǐ : Zhè shì wǒmen de chuántǒng fēnggé. Xiànzài yě liúxíng báijīn hàn chúnyín de shǒushì.

Zhōu jīnglǐ : Búguò, kàn qǐlái háishì huángjīn shǒushì bǐjiào duō.

Wéi jīnglǐ : Méicuò. Yīnwèi zài Yìndù rén xīn zhōng, jīnsè shì zuì gāoguì de yánsè.

Zhōu jīnglǐ : Tīng nín zhème shuō, wǒ juédìng mǎi yí tào huángjīn shǒushì le.

課文英譯 Text in English

Dialogue

[Indian Jewelry Company's Manager Wei, Manager Zhou, and Secretary Wang talk about going to the New Dehli Market to buy souvenirs.]

Manager Wei : Time goes by so fast! Soon you'll be back in Taiwan.

Manager Zhou : Yes! Before returning home, I want to buy something special from here.

Manager Wei : Yes! If you come to India, you must bring our specialties back to Taiwan as souvenirs.

Secretary Wang : Manager Zhou, I'll show you around New Delhi's famous markets and shopping malls and buy some presents on the way.

Manager Wei : Secretary Wang is an India expert. He must have a lot of experience in this area.

Secretary Wang : I think we can shop at the market. In addition to buying local specialties, we can also see different aspects of Indian culture.

Manager Wei : That's a good point! Assam black tea, spices, handmade shoes, jewelry, everything has our culture in them.

Secretary Wang : I suggest that we buy some unique herbal Himalayan products.

Manager Zhou : Good advice. This time, not only do I want to buy some souvenirs, but I also want to appreciate Indian jewelry design.

Manager Wei : No problem. I'll take you to visit my jewelry company tomorrow.

[Manager Wei takes Manager Zhou to visit his jewelry company the next day, and they talk about gold jewelry design.]

Manager Wei : This is gold jewelry. These are popular designs for gold jewelry with different gemstones.

Manager Zhou : Such beauty and creativity! And all in a set, with earrings, necklaces, and bracelets.

Manager Wei : This is our traditional style. Platinum and sterling silver jewelry are also popular now.

Manager Zhou : However, it looks as though most of the jewelry is gold jewelry.

Manager Wei : That's right. It's because gold is seen as the noblest color in the hearts of Indians.

Manager Zhou : After listening to you, I've decided to buy a set of gold jewelry.

生詞一 Vocabulary I 🎧

編號	生詞	漢語拼音	詞性	英文翻譯
1.	伴手禮	bànshǒulǐ	N	souvenir
2.	不久	bù jiǔ	Adv	soon
3.	特産	tèchǎn	N	specialty
4.	當	dāng	V	as
5.	商場	shāngchǎng	N	shopping mall
6.	順便	shùnbiàn	Adv	on the way, in passing, without much extra effort
7.	方面	fāngmiàn	N	aspect

編號	生詞	漢語拼音	詞性	英文翻譯
8.	首飾	shǒushì	N	jewelry
9.	草本	cǎoběn	N	herb
10.	產品	chǎnpǐn	N	product
11.	欣賞	xīnshǎng	V	to appreciate, to admire
12.	黃金	huángjīn	N	gold
13.	寶石	bǎoshí	N	gemstone
14.	套	tào	M	a set of
15.	耳環	ěrhuán	N	earrings
16.	項鍊	xiàngliàn	N	necklace
17.	手鐲	shǒuzhuó	N	bracelet
18.	風格	fēnggé	N	style
19.	白金	báijīn	N	platinum
20.	純銀	chúnyín	N	pure silver
21.	高貴	gāoguì	Vs	noble

專有名詞 Proper Nouns

編號	生詞	漢語拼音	英文翻譯
1.	阿薩姆紅茶	Āsàmǔ hóngchá	Assam Black Tea
2.	喜馬拉雅	Xǐmǎlāyǎ	Himalaya

短語 Phrases

編號	生詞	漢語拼音	英文翻譯
1.	手工鞋	shǒugōng xié	handmade shoes

短文 Reading 🎧

伴手禮的意義

當臺灣人旅行或是回家鄉的時候，總是想買一些旅遊地或是居住地方的特產送給親戚朋友，這些東西就叫伴手禮。臺灣人覺得只有這樣做，才能表達對朋友的心意，所以伴手禮也代表華人社會濃厚的人情味。

來印度，臺灣人帶臺灣特產烏龍茶、鳳梨酥；回臺灣，當然帶印度的特產阿薩姆紅茶、香料、喜馬拉雅產品，還有文化特色的手工鞋、耳環、項鍊、手鐲等。臺灣人常說：「禮輕情意重」，意思是雖然送的禮物不貴，但是它表示臺灣人對朋友的心意。

除了心意以外，伴手禮還能代表當地特色，也能給商家帶來財富，又能對國家經濟有幫助，所以各地都積極發展一些有代表性的產品，讓觀光客開開心心地逛完景點以後，也高高興興地大採購。

印度阿薩姆紅茶
Indian Assam Black Tea

印度喜馬拉雅產品
Indian "Himalaya" products

臺灣鳳梨酥
Taiwanese pineapple cakes

課文漢語拼音 Text in Hanyu Pinyin

Bànshǒulǐ de yìyì

Dāng Táiwān rén lǚxíng huòshì huí jiāxiāng de shíhòu, zǒngshì xiǎng mǎi yìxiē lǚyóudì huòshì jūzhù dìfāng de tèchǎn sòng gěi qīnqī péngyǒu, zhèxiē dōngxi jiù jiào bànshǒulǐ. Táiwān rén juéde zhǐyǒu zhèyàng zuò, cái néng biǎodá duì péngyǒu de xīnyì, suǒyǐ bànshǒulǐ yě dàibiǎo huárén shèhuì nónghòu de rénqíngwèi.

Lái Yìndù, Táiwān rén dài Táiwān tèchǎn wūlóngchá, fènglísū; huí Táiwān, dāngrán dài Yìndù de tèchǎn Āsàmǔ hóngchá, xiāngliào, Xǐmǎlāyǎ chǎnpǐn, háiyǒu wénhuà tèsè de shǒugōng xié, ěrhuán, xiàngliàn, shǒuzhuó děng. Táiwān rén cháng shuō: "lǐ qīng qíngyì zhòng", yìsi shì suīrán sòng de lǐwù bú guì, dànshì tā biǎoshì Táiwān rén duì péngyǒu de xīnyì.

Chúle xīnyì yǐwài, bànshǒulǐ hái néng dàibiǎo dāngdì tèsè, yě néng gěi shāngjiā dàilái cáifù, yòu néng duì guójiā jīngjì yǒu bāngzhù, suǒyǐ gèdì dōu jījí fāzhǎn yìxiē yǒu dàibiǎoxìng de chǎnpǐn, ràng guānguāngkè kāikāi-xīnxīn de guàngwán jǐngdiǎn yǐhòu, yě gāogāo-xìngxìng de dà cǎigòu.

課文英譯 Text in English

The Meaning of Souvenirs

When Taiwanese travel or return to their hometowns, they always want to buy some specialties from tourist destinations or places the visitors went to give to relatives and friends. These things are called souvenirs. Taiwanese feel that only by doing so can they express their warm feelings to their friends. Therefore, souvenirs also represent a strong human touch of Chinese society.

When going to India, Taiwanese bring Taiwanese specialties Oolong tea and pineapple cakes. When going back to Taiwan, they will, of course, bring back Indian specialties such as Assam black tea, spices, "Himalaya" products, handmade shoes full of cultural significance, earrings, necklaces, bracelets, etc. Taiwanese often say: "It's the thought that counts." It means that although the gifts are not expensive, they indicate Taiwanese's affection for friends.

In addition to a token of kindness, souvenirs can also represent local characteristics. Not only do they bring wealth to businesses, they also are helpful to the national economy. Therefore, people actively design representative products in various places. This allows tourists to have a shopping spree after happily enjoying nearby attractions.

生詞二 Vocabulary II 🎧

編號	生詞	漢語拼音	詞性	英文翻譯
1.	意義	yìyì	N	significance
2.	居住	jūzhù	V	to reside
3.	親戚	qīnqī	N	relative
4.	表達	biǎodá	V	to express
5.	心意	xīnyì	N	kindly feelings
6.	代表	dàibiǎo	V	to represent
7.	濃厚	nónghòu	Vs	strong, thick
8.	人情味	rénqíngwèi	N	human kindness
9.	鳳梨酥	fènglísū	N	pineapple cakes
10.	商家	shāngjiā	N	business
11.	積極	jījí	Vs	aggressive, active
12.	代表性	dàibiǎoxìng	N	representativeness
13.	觀光客	guānguāngkè	N	tourist
14.	景點	jǐngdiǎn	N	scenic attraction

短語 Phrases

編號	生詞	漢語拼音	英文翻譯
1.	華人社會	huárén shèhuì	Chinese society
2.	禮輕情意重	lǐ qīng qíngyì zhòng	It is the thought that counts.
3.	大採購	dà cǎigòu	shopping spree

語法 Grammar 🎧

一、除了 chúle …（外 wài／以外 yǐwài／之外 zhīwài），還 hái／也 yě …　in addition to …, besides …

說明：「除了」是介詞，後可接「外」、「以外」或「之外」。「除了…，還…」句型表示補充，意為：除此之外，還有別的。

Explanation：除了 chúle is a preposition, which can be followed by 外 wài, 以外 yǐwài or 之外 zhīwài. The sentence pattern 除了 chúle …, 還 hái… expresses the addition of supplementary information, which means in addition to the elements after 除了 chúle, there are other elements as well.

1. 「除了」後面的短語，可以是名詞組、動詞組和小句，「還」進一步補充「除了」所指的內容。

   The phrase following 除了 chúle can be a noun phrase, verb phrase, or clause. 還 hái further supplements what is mentioned by 除了 chúle.

   如：(1) 我喜歡的水果，除了香蕉以外，還有芒果。

   　　(2) 朋友結婚，除了參加婚禮外，還要包紅包。

2. 此句型的「還」，可以用「也」取代，意思相同。

   The 還 hái of this sentence pattern can be replaced with 也 yě with the meaning remaining the same.

   如：(1) 排燈節的活動，除了點油燈以外，也放鞭炮。

   　　(2) 周經理除了要買伴手禮外，也要參觀珠寶公司。

例句：

    1. 阿育吠陀養生方法，除了瑜珈外，還有食療。

    2. 我不舒服，除了不想吃東西以外，也不想看書。

    3. 你今天除了上課之外，是不是還有別的活動？

練習：請用「除了⋯外／以外／之外，還／也⋯」回答下面的問題

Exercise：Please use 除了 *chúle* ⋯外 *wài* ／以外 *yǐwài* ／之外 *zhīwài*, 還 *hái* ／也 *yě* to answer the questions below.

---

1. A：除了印度外，你還去過哪些國家？

   B：_____。

2. A：臺灣的婚禮，新人除了敬酒外，還要做什麼？

   B：_____。

3. A：臺灣的小吃，除了種類多外，還有什麼特色？

   B：_____。

4. A：你為什麼常常出國？

   B：我常出國，_____。（旅遊、做生意）

5. A：你覺得印度的伴手禮怎麼樣？

   B：我覺得_____。（不貴、有特色）

二、雙音節動詞重疊（ABAB 式）Tentative Action with Reduplicated Disyllabic Verbs ABAB

說明：雙音節動詞重疊（ABAB 式）與單音節動詞重疊相同，產生「量性」的變化，都具有弱化或減量的作用。

Explanation：Reduplicated disyllabic verbs ABAB achieve the same aims as reduplicated monosyllabic verbs, resulting in "quantitative" changes. Both have the effect of weakening or reducing changes.

1. 表示動作持續的時間短、進行的次數少或強度弱。

   Using this pattern indicates a short time, few times, or that the intensity is weak.

   如：(1) 今天教的課有一點難，我得練習練習。

   　　(2) 快大考了，我要準備準備。

2. 動詞重疊後，不能再跟也是具有減量意思的「一點」或「一下」一起使用。

   When verbs are reduplicated, they can no longer be used with 一點 *yìdiǎn* or 一下 *yíxià* to further reduce intensity.

   如：(1) * 我要參加足球比賽，我得練習練習一下。（練習一下）

   　　(2) * 媽媽生病了，我應該關心關心她一點。（關心她一點）

例句：

1. 明天要開會，我得整理整理要用的資料。
2. 出國旅行的事，我們要先計畫計畫。
3. 新年的時候，我常去拜訪拜訪親戚朋友。

練習：請用動詞重疊（ABAB 式），重寫下面的句子

Exercise：Rewrite the following sentences with the "Tentative Action with Reduplicated Disyllabic Verbs ABAB" form.

---

1. 媽媽的生日到了，我們要好好地慶祝。

   →＿＿＿＿＿＿＿＿＿＿＿＿＿＿＿＿＿＿。

2. 這個週末，我想去看古蹟，參觀博物院。

   →＿＿＿＿＿＿＿＿＿＿＿＿＿＿＿＿＿＿。

3. 朋友要結婚了，我們應該祝福他們。

   →＿＿＿＿＿＿＿＿＿＿＿＿＿＿＿＿＿＿。

4. 這是我的建議，你可以參考一下。

   →＿＿＿＿＿＿＿＿＿＿＿＿＿＿＿＿＿＿。

---

5. 我想多認識印度朋友。

→ _____ 。

三、只有 *zhǐyǒu* …，才₃ *cái*₃ …　　　cannot…, unless…

說明：「只有」為連接詞。是唯一有效的條件，其他的不行。「只有…才₃…」
表示「才」後面的結果不容易達成。

Explanation：只有 *zhǐyǒu* is a conjunction. It indicates that what comes after 只
有 *zhǐyǒu* is the only condition which must be met. No other conditions will
suffice. 只有 *zhǐyǒu* …，才 *cái* … expresses that the result following 才
cái cannot easily be achieved.

如：(1) 我只有週末，才有空跟妳出去吃飯。

(2) 她認為只有按照食譜做菜，才能做得好吃。

「只有…，才…」與「只要…，就…」相較，兩者都是表示必要的條件。
但是前者表示唯一有效條件，不易達成；後者表示只要滿足某一條件即可，聽
起來比較容易達成。兩者語義不同。比較如下：

Both 只有 *zhǐyǒu* …，才 *cái* … and 只要 *zhǐyào* …，就 *jiù* … require the
necessary conditions to be met. However, the former means that the condition is
the only one that must be met, and meeting that condition is not easily achievable.
The latter means that if one of the conditions can be met, the action after 就 *jiù* is
more achievable. The condition in this sentence can be achieved more easily. The
two sentences are semantically different. The comparisons are provided below:

如：(1) 只有本校的外國學生，才能拿到這項獎學金。（The condition is
difficult to meet.）

(2) 只要是本校外國學生，就能拿到這項獎學金。（The condition is
easy to meet.）

例句：

1. 感冒只有吃藥多休息，才好得快。

2. 你是不是只有要考試了，才看書？

3. 很多人認為只有不吃速食，身體才健康。（速食 *sùshí* "fast food"）

練習：請適當選用「只有…，才…」、「只要…，就…」，完成下面的句子。

Exercises：Please choose 只有 *zhǐyǒu* …，才 *cái* … and 只要 *zhǐyào* …，就 *jiù* … to complete the following sentences.

---

1. A：逛市集買東西一定要「殺價」嗎？

　B：我覺得逛市集，_____殺價，_____買得到便宜的東西。

2. A：外國人也能教中文嗎？

　B：外國人_____中文說得很好，_____。

3. A：什麼樣的人，中文才學得下去？

　B：我認為_____對_____的人，_____。（對…有興趣）

4. A：上網買東西很麻煩嗎？

　B：不麻煩。_____有_____，_____。（網路）

5. A：怎麼在寺廟點光明燈？

　B：很容易，_____，寫好姓名、生日和地址，_____。（付錢）

四、V 完 *wán*　Completion of an Action with V + 完 *wán*

說明：「完」是一個表示結果的後綴（resultative suffix）。「V 完」是指該動作的完成。

Explanation：完 *wán* is a suffix that expresses the finished result (resultative suffix). V 完 *wán* means the action is complete.

1.「V 完」的後面可接賓語。

　V 完 *wán* can be followed by an object.

　如：(1) 我已經寫完功課了。

　　　(2) 我看完這一課書了。

2.「V 完」後面的賓語常前置當作話題，或用把字句將賓語放在動詞前

面。

The object after V 完 *wán* can often be brought to the front and made into a topic, or one can use a 把 *bǎ* sentence to place the object in front of the verb.

如：(1) 這些水果，我吃完了。

(2) 我把這些水果吃完了。

3. 如果是離合詞（separable verbs），「完」要放在中間。

If the verb is a separable verb, V 完 *wán* is placed in the middle.

如：(1) 考完試後，我要跟同學去看電影。

(2) 他吃完飯，常出去運動。

例句：

1. 他一游完泳，就去學校上課。

2. 我沒把工作做完，所以不能休息。

3. 觀光客逛完景點以後，常買當地的特產當伴手禮。

練習：請選用下列合適的動詞，用「V 完」表示動作完成。

Exercise：Use the appropriate verbs below to indicate that an action is complete with V 完 *wán*.（吃、做、賣、喝、用、逛、念、說、考）

1. 明天就要考試了，書我還沒_____，怎麼辦？

2. 這個故事，我還沒_____呢。

3. 這家店的麵包太好吃了，所以很快就_____了。

4. 這個月媽媽給我的錢，我還沒_____。

5. _____試以後，我一定要快快樂樂地玩一玩。

6. A：你不是要去夜市嗎？

B：是啊，我已經_____夜市回家了。

跨文化延伸 Cross-Cultural Extension

Chinese Jade Culture

Chinese people value jade as much as Indians love gold. Jade is one of the essential parts of traditional Chinese culture that profoundly influences ancient Chinese ideology.

Jade is a beautiful mineral, usually indicating jadeite and nephrite. Commonly seen types of nephrite are white jade, yellow jade, green jade, dark greed jade, etc. The hard jade is the familiar jadeite. Jade, in Chinese culture, is thought to ward off evil. In ancient times, it was often used as a decoration that signifies one's identity and status. The Chinese emperor's seal was carved out of jade. In modern times, apart from using it as a decoration, it is also often worn as a talisman to keep one safe.

Jade's cultural connotations are extremely rich. The most distinguishable characteristic is the concept of "using Jade to make a comparison with one's virtue." There are many words and idioms with jade in them in the Chinese language. Most of the meanings of these words express beauty, honor and nobility, and elegance. There are words such as jade hand, jade appearance, jade body, using jade to express a life of luxury. Jade is also often used in a person's name, such as 玉玲 *Yùlíng*, 清玉 *Qīngyù*.

In sum, there is still a cultural tradition of love and respect for jade from ancient times to the present in Chinese society.

翡翠 jadeite

語言任務 Language Tasks

一、看圖說故事。

任務：學生分五組，第一組依照 1 號圖片，結合「V 完」、「只有…，才…」說故事。其餘四組類推。每題的 AB 問答可作參考。

　如：昨天晚上媽媽看到我在看電視，就大聲說：「又在看電視了！快去寫功課。」我笑著回答：「媽媽，我已經<u>寫完</u>功課了。我<u>只有</u>寫完功課以後，<u>才</u>看電視。」放心吧。

1. Look at the picture and tell the story.

Task：Students are divided into five groups, the first group using V 完 *wán* combined with 只有 *zhǐyǒu* …，才 *cái* … to tell the story indicated in picture 1.

　The remaining four sets will be done similarly. Each question can be answered in the form of A and B. The examples in each picture can be used as a reference.

1.	A：你怎麼不寫功課，在看電視？ B：我已經_____功課了。我_____寫完功課以後，_____看電視。
2.	A：你的錢，都_____了！不要再買衣服了。（V 完） B：我_____喜歡的衣服，_____買。
3.	A：不要玩_____了，跟我聊天。 B：我不是在玩手機。_____重要的郵件，我_____。（看）這些郵件很重要，我得____。（V 完）

4.	A：別＿＿＿＿＿＿了，我們去踢足球。 B：我不想去。我＿＿＿＿＿＿週末，＿＿＿＿＿＿能上網跟朋友聊天。我們還沒＿＿＿＿＿＿呢。（V 完）
5.	A：聽說你常去爬山？ B：沒有啊。我＿＿＿＿＿＿的時候，＿＿＿＿＿＿。不過，我真的很喜歡爬山，我希望能＿＿＿＿＿＿每座山。（V 完）

二、請學生課後，參考下列提示或自創提問，訪問三位同學，再用「除了…還／也…」完成語句。第二天上臺報告。

Please ask students after class to refer to the following tips or self-created questions to interview three students. They need to use 除了 *chúle* …還 *hái* / 也 *yě* … to complete the statements. Students also need to report back to class the next day.

提示：打工、學過、去過、吃過、喝過、逛過、用過、會…在餐廳上班…

例句：(1) 我同學除了打過工，還學過太極拳。

　　　(2) 他除了學過日文，也學過中文。

第十課　歡送會
Lesson 10 Farewell Dinner

課程目標：

Topic：惜別

　　1. 能明白惜別會的意義。

　　2. 能聊惜別會中的相關話題。

　　3. 能知道珠寶展覽會怎麼宣傳。

　　4. 能了解臺灣、印度不同的商務談判方式。

Lesson Objectives：

Topic：Saying Goodbye

　　1. Students can understand the meaning of a farewell dinner.

　　2. Students can chat about relevant topics at the farewell party.

　　3. Students can understand how jewelry is advertised at the jewelry fair.

　　4. Students can learn about the different ways of negotiating business in Taiwan and India.

惜別餐會 Farewell Party

對話 Dialogue 🎧

【印度珠寶公司韋經理為周經理和王祕書舉辦歡送晚會。】

周經理：韋經理，謝謝您特地為我們舉辦這個歡送晚會。

韋經理：應該的。除了歡送你們，也讓你們體會一下印度人的熱情。

王祕書：體會到了。晚會不但有印度美食，還有印度歌舞。

周經理：是啊，道地的口味，華麗的歌舞，這趟印度行真值得。

韋經理：周經理，您覺得我們的咖哩，味道怎麼樣？

周經理：很特別，我喜歡上你們的咖哩羊肉了。小王，你呢？

王祕書：除了咖哩，我也愛上印度歌舞了。

第十課　歡送會 Farewell Dinner

【晚會結束以前，周經理邀請他們來臺灣參加珠寶展覽。】

周經理：韋經理，很高興，我們的珠寶設計第
　　　　一次合作就成功了。

韋經理：這要謝謝你們準備了這麼好的合作方
　　　　案。

周經理：明年十一月，臺北世貿要舉辦「臺灣
　　　　珠寶首飾展覽會」。

韋經理：我知道，規模很大，聽說會有很多頂
　　　　級的珠寶參加展覽。

周經理：你們公司的珠寶設計很有特色，想邀
　　　　請您參加。

韋經理：我對這個展覽很有興趣，但是得好好
　　　　地計畫計畫。

王祕書：歡迎歡迎。我們一邊吃一邊聊吧，菜都涼了。

韋經理：真捨不得你們離開，什麼時候回臺灣？

周經理：後天。謝謝您今晚的安排，明年臺北見！

課文漢語拼音 Text in Hanyu Pinyin

[Yìndù zhūbǎo gōngsī Wéi jīnglǐ wèi Zhōu jīnglǐ hàn Wáng mìshū jǔbàn huānsòng wǎnhuì.]

Zhōu jīnglǐ : Wéi jīnglǐ, xièxie nín tèdì wèi wǒmen jǔbàn zhège huānsòng wǎnhuì.

Wéi jīnglǐ : Yīnggāide. Chúle huānsòng nǐmen, yě ràng nǐmen tǐhuì yí xià Yìndù rén de rèqíng.

Wáng mìshū : Tǐhuì dào le. Wǎnhuì búdàn yǒu Yìndù měishí, hái yǒu Yìndù gēwǔ.

Zhōu jīnglǐ : Shì a, dàodì de kǒuwèi, huálì de gēwǔ, zhè tàng Yìndù xíng zhēn zhíde.

Wéi jīnglǐ : Zhōu jīnglǐ, nín juéde wǒmen de kālǐ, wèidào zěnmeyàng?

Zhōu jīnglǐ : Hěn tèbié, wǒ xǐhuān shàng nǐmen de kālǐ yángròu le. Xiǎo Wáng, nǐ ne?

Wáng mìshū : Chúle kālǐ, wǒ yě àishàng Yìndù gēwǔ le.

[Wǎnhuì jiéshù yǐqián, Zhōu jīnglǐ yāoqǐng tāmen lái Táiwān cānjiā zhūbǎo zhǎnlǎn.]

Zhōu jīnglǐ : Wéi jīnglǐ, hěn gāoxìng, wǒmen de zhūbǎo shèjì dì-yī cì hézuò jiù chénggōng le.

Wéi jīnglǐ : Zhè yào xièxie nǐmen zhǔnbèile zhème hǎo de hézuò fāng'àn.

Zhōu jīnglǐ : Míngnián shíyī yuè, Táiběi shìmào yào jǔbàn "Táiwān Zhūbǎo Shǒushì zhǎnlǎnhuì".

Wéi jīnglǐ : Wǒ zhīdào, guīmó hěn dà, tīngshuō huì yǒu hěnduō dǐngjí de zhūbǎo cānjiā zhǎnlǎn.

Zhōu jīnglǐ : Nǐmen gōngsī de zhūbǎo shèjì hěn yǒu tèsè, xiǎng yāoqǐng nín cānjiā.

Wéi jīnglǐ : Wǒ duì zhège zhǎnlǎn hěn yǒu xìngqù, dànshì děi hǎohǎo de jìhuà jìhuà.

Wáng mìshū : Huānyíng huānyíng. Wǒmen yìbiān chī yìbiān liáo ba, cài dōu liáng le.

Wéi jīnglǐ : Zhēn shěbùde nǐmen líkāi, shénme shíhòu huí Táiwān?

Zhōu jīnglǐ : Hòutiān. Xièxie nín jīn wǎn de ānpái, míng nián Táiběi jiàn!

課文英譯 Text in English

Dialogue

[Manager Wei of the Indian Jewelry Company holds a farewell party for Mr. Zhou and Secretary Wang.]

Manager Zhou : Mr. Wei, thank you for hosting the farewell party for us.

Manager Wei : That's how it should be. In addition to sending you off, let's experience the hospitality of Indian people.

Secretary Wang : Yes, I can feel it. The party includes not only Indian cuisine but also Indian song and dance.

Manager Zhou : Yes, the taste of authentic food and gorgeous song and dance. This trip to India was really worth it.

Manager Wei : Manager Zhou, what do you think of our curry?

Manager Zhou : Very special. I like your curry lamb. Xiao Wang, what about you?

Secretary Wang : In addition to curry, I also fell in love with Indian song and dance.

[Before the end of the party, Manager Zhou invites them to come to Taiwan to participate in the jewelry exhibition.]

Manager Zhou : Manager Wei, I'm glad that our jewelry design was successful the first time we worked together.

Manager Wei : Thank you for preparing such a good plan for cooperation.

Manager Zhou : In November next year, the Taipei World Trade Organization will hold the Taiwan Jewelry Exhibition.

Manager Wei : I know the scale is significant, and I hear there will be a lot of top-grade jewelry on display.

Manager Zhou : Your company's jewelry design is very distinctive, and I would like to invite you to participate.

Manager Wei : I'm interested in the exhibition, but I must plan it well.

Secretary Wang : Welcome. Let's eat and chat; otherwise, the dishes will be cold.

Manager Wei : I can't bear the thought of you leaving. When will you go back to Taiwan?

Manager Zhou : The day after. Thank you for your arrangements tonight. See you in Taipei next year!

生詞一 Vocabulary I 🎧

編號	生詞	漢語拼音	詞性	英文翻譯
1.	歡送	huānsòng	V/N	to see someone off, to bid farewell to; seeing-off, send-off
2.	晚會	wǎnhuì	N	evening party, evening reception
3.	特地	tèdì	Adv	specially
4.	體會	tǐhuì	V	to experience
5.	熱情	rèqíng	N	hospitality, enthusiasm
6.	歌舞	gēwǔ	N	singing and dancing
7.	華麗	huálì	Vs	gorgeous, splendid
8.	趟	tàng	M	measure word for a trip
9.	值得	zhíde	Vs	worthy of, to be worth
10.	展覽	zhǎnlǎn	N	exhibition
11.	規模	guīmó	N	scale

編號	生詞	漢語拼音	詞性	英文翻譯
12.	頂級	dǐngjí	Vs-attr	top-grade, first-rate
13.	涼	liáng	Vs	cool

專有名詞 Proper Nouns

編號	生詞	漢語拼音	英文翻譯
1.	臺北世貿 （臺北世界貿易中心）	Táiběi Shìmào (Táiběi Shìjiè Màoyì Zhōngxīn)	Taipei World Trade Center
2.	臺灣珠寶首飾展覽會	Táiwān Zhūbǎo Shǒushì Zhǎnlǎnhuì	Taiwan Jewelry & Gem Fair

短語 Phrases

編號	生詞	漢語拼音	英文翻譯
1.	應該的	yīnggāide	Sure, my pleasure.
2.	印度行	Yìndù xíng	India trip

短文 Reading 🎧

珠寶展覽會怎麼宣傳

　　珠寶廠商舉辦展覽會的目的，當然是希望商品能大賣，而想賣得好，得先讓人有興趣買，所以商家怎麼宣傳才能吸引客人，是展覽會最重要的準備工作。

　　現在是網路時代，一切透過網站宣傳。在主要的網頁上，一定要有幾張有特色又能吸引人的珠寶照片，讓從來不買珠寶或是對珠寶從來沒興趣的人，都想去看看！這些照片同時也可以當作宣傳海報。

主要網頁上要有和展覽資訊有關的連結，如：展覽會簡介、參加展覽和參觀展覽的聯絡方式、參展的資料，比方説為什麼要參展、參展費用什麼的。另外，展覽哪些系列的珠寶、展覽會的影片、宣傳的新聞稿、交通、簽證和旅遊應該注意的事情。

網頁上和展覽會場上，最重要的是都要有清楚的展區圖示，讓參觀的人很容易就能找到自己需要的商品，這樣才不會浪費他們的時間。

課文漢語拼音 Text in Hanyu Pinyin

Zhūbǎo zhǎnlǎnhuì zěnme xuānchuán

Zhūbǎo chǎngshāng jǔbàn zhǎnlǎnhuì de mùdì, dāngrán shì xīwàng shāngpǐn néng dà mài, ér xiǎng mài de hǎo, děi xiān ràng rén yǒu xìngqù mǎi, suǒyǐ shāngjiā zěnme xuānchuán cái néng xīyǐn kèrén, shì zhǎnlǎnhuì zuì zhòngyào de zhǔnbèi gōngzuò.

Xiànzài shì wǎnglù shídài, yíqiè tòuguò wǎngzhàn xuānchuán. Zài zhǔyào de wǎngyè shàng, yídìng yào yǒu jǐ zhāng yǒu tèsè yòu néng xīyǐn rén de zhūbǎo zhàopiàn, ràng cónglái bù mǎi zhūbǎo huòshì duì zhūbǎo cónglái méi xìngqù de rén, dōu xiǎng qù kànkan! Zhèxiē zhàopiàn tóngshí yě kěyǐ dàngzuò xuānchuán hǎibào.

Zhǔyào wǎngyè shàng yào yǒu hàn zhǎnlǎn zīxùn yǒuguān de liánjié, rú: zhǎnlǎnhuì jiǎnjiè, cānjiā zhǎnlǎn hàn cānguān zhǎnlǎn de liánluò fāngshì, cānzhǎn de zīliào, bǐfāng shuō wèishénme yào cānzhǎn, cānzhǎn fèiyòng shénme de. Lìngwài, zhǎnlǎn nǎxiē xìliè de zhūbǎo, zhǎnlǎnhuì de yǐngpiàn, xuānchuán de xīnwéngǎo, jiāotōng, qiānzhèng hàn lǚyóu yīnggāi zhùyì de shìqíng.

Wǎngyè shàng hàn zhǎnlǎn huìchǎng shàng, zuì zhòngyào de shì dōu yào yǒu qīngchǔ de zhǎnqū túshì, ràng cānguān de rén hěn róngyì jiù néng zhǎodào zìjǐ xūyào de shāngpǐn, zhèyàng cái bú huì làngfèi tāmen de shíjiān.

課文英譯 Text in English

Promotion at a Jewelry Fair

The purpose of jewelry manufacturers holding exhibitions is, of course, to hope that the goods can be sold in great quantity and can sell well. If a company wants their goods to sell well, first, people need to be interested in buying. Therefore, how to promote the business to attract customers is the most important work for an exhibition to prepare for.

Today in the Internet age, everything is publicized through websites. On the main web page, be sure to have a few unique and attractive photos of jewelry to attract customers. In this way, people who have never bought jewelry or have never been interested in jewelry will want to visit the webpage to take a look! These photos can also be used as publicity posters.

The main web page should have links and information related to the exhibition, such as a simple introduction to the exhibition, contact information for participating in the exhibition and for visiting the exhibition, information on exhibits. For example, why companies should participate in the exhibition and the cost of exhibiting a company's products, etc. In addition, what series of jewelry to exhibit, exhibition films, promotional press releases, transportation, visas, and things to be aware of when traveling to the exhibition should also be included.

The most important thing on the web and the exhibition floor is to have a clear map of the exhibition floor so that visitors can easily find the goods they need. This way, no time would be wasted on their part.

生詞二 Vocabulary II 🎧

編號	生詞	漢語拼音	詞性	英文翻譯
1.	宣傳	xuānchuán	V	to publicize
2.	廠商	chǎngshāng	N	manufacturer
3.	目的	mùdì	N	purpose, aim
4.	商品	shāngpǐn	N	goods, merchandise
5.	網路	wǎnglù	N	internet
6.	時代	shídài	N	era, age
7.	透過	tòuguò	Prep	through
8.	網站	wǎngzhàn	N	websites
9.	網頁	wǎngyè	N	web page
10.	當作	dàngzuò	V	to treat as, to take as
11.	海報	hǎibào	N	posters
12.	資訊	zīxùn	N	information
13.	連結	liánjié	N	link
14.	新聞稿	xīnwéngǎo	N	press release

編號	生詞	漢語拼音	詞性	英文翻譯
15.	簽證	qiānzhèng	N	visa
16.	事情	shìqíng	N	thing, matter
17.	展區	zhǎnqū	N	exhibition area
18.	圖示	túshì	N	icon
19.	浪費	làngfèi	V	to waste

短語 Phrases

編號	生詞	漢語拼音	英文翻譯
1.	大賣	dà mài	to sell a lot, sell well

語法 Grammar 🎧

一、不但 *bùdàn* …，還 *hái* ／也 *yě* …　　not only..., but also ...

說明：「不但」是連接詞，「還／也」是副詞。這個句型連接兩個分句，屬於遞進複句，後句有遞進的意思。

Explanation：不但 *bùdàn* ... is a conjunction, and 還 *hái* ／也 *yě* ... is an adverb. This sentence pattern connects two phrases that describe the progressive aspects of the same action. The first clause is about the effect of an action, and the second clause progressively increases the effect of that activity.

1. 同一主題，「不但」、「還／也」放在主語的後面。

If the topic is the same, 不但 *bùdàn* …, 還 *hái* ／也 *yě* … is placed after the subject.

如：(1) 做瑜珈不但能運動，還能養生。

　　(2) 這個學生不但聰明，也很用功。

2. 同一主題，兩個主語時，第一個主語可以在「不但」的前面或後面。「還／也」放在第二個主語的後面。

If the topic is the same, when two subjects are spoken, the first subject can be before or after 不但 *búdàn*. 還 *hái* / 也 *yě* … is placed after the second subject in a complex sentence.

如：(1) 這個地方，環境不但好，風景也很漂亮。　　　（主語在前）

　　(2) 我媽媽做的菜，不但味道很香，顏色還很好看。（主語在後）

3. 如果「不但」後面有「而且」，那麼，「還／也」可以省略。

If after 不但 *búdàn* …, there is 而且 *érqiě*, then 還 *hái* / 也 *yě* … can be omitted.

如：(1) 這件衣服不但好看，而且（也）不貴。

　　(2) 伴手禮不但給商家帶來財富，而且（還）對國家經濟有幫助。

4. 有時候「不但」可以省略。

Sometimes 不但 *búdàn* can be omitted.

如：她昨天買的那件衣服（不但）很便宜，也很好看。

例句：

1. A：為什麼那麼多人愛逛夜市？

　B：因為夜市的東西不但好吃，還很便宜。

2. A：昨天的晚會，真讓人忘不了！

　B：是啊，不但菜好吃，還有好看的歌舞。

3. A：在華人世界，包禮金要注意什麼？

　B：不但要注意袋子的顏色，而且（也）要注意禮金的數字。

4. A：你昨天去吃的那家餐廳怎麼樣？

　B：那家餐廳的菜（不但）好吃，價錢也很便宜。

練習：請用「不但…，還／也…」回答下面的問題。

Exercise：Please use 不但 *búdàn* …, 還 *hái* / 也 *yě* …　to answer the following questions.

1. A：你昨天跟老師聊了什麼？

   B：＿＿＿＿＿＿＿＿＿＿＿＿＿＿＿＿＿＿＿＿＿。

2. A：你為什麼愛上印度了？

   B：因為＿＿＿＿＿＿＿＿＿＿＿＿＿＿＿＿＿＿。

3. A：你跟家人上個週末去哪裡玩？

   B：＿＿＿＿＿＿＿＿＿＿＿＿＿＿＿＿＿＿＿＿＿。

4. A：聽說你最近很忙。

   B：是啊，＿＿＿＿＿＿＿＿＿＿＿＿＿＿＿＿＿。

5. A：排燈節好熱鬧啊！

   B：＿＿＿＿＿＿＿＿＿＿＿＿＿＿＿＿＿＿＿＿＿。

二、V 上 *shàng*　　Verb particle *shàng*

說明：「上」是動助詞（verb particle）。動助詞是用來說明動詞對主語或賓語所產生的作用。「上」原本是具有客觀空間移動意義的動詞，語意經過延伸之後，產生了跟原本語意相關卻虛化的意思，表示該動作發生之後的結果，可視為結果補語，說明兩個事物接觸後的結果。

Explanation：上 *shàng* is a verb particle. The verb particle 上 *shàng* is used to explain the influence of the action verb on the subject or object. The 上 *shàng* originally is a verb which describes movement in an objective space. Through semantic extension, the original meaning of this word has become abstract to express the result of that action. It can be seen as a resultative complement indicating the result of contact between two events.

1.「上」所搭配的動詞，本身必須具有「接觸」的語義。如：穿、戴、寫、簽、換、加、看、愛、搭、送、連、喜歡…等。後接所接觸的目標。

Verbs that can pair with 上 *shàng* must possess the meaning of 'contact.' For example, 穿 *chuān*, 戴 *dài*, 寫 *xiě*, 簽 *qiān*, 換 *huàn*, 加 *jiā*, 看 *kàn*,

愛 *ài*, 搭 *dā*, 送 *sòng*, 連 *lián*, 喜歡 *xǐhuān* and so on. The target of contact should be a noun.

如：(1) 外面風大，出門戴上帽子吧。

　　(2) 考試的時候，我常忘了寫上名字。

2. 「V 上」的補語結構，可分為是否具潛在能力的（potential form）和表示事實的（actual form）兩種形式。但是有的動詞不能使用表示可能性的形式。請參考下表：

The complement structure of V 上 *shàng* can be divided into potential and actual forms. However, some verbs cannot be used to express the potential form. Please refer to the following table:

V	Actual （＿，沒）	Potential （得 / 不）
穿	✓	✓
戴	✓	✓
寫	✓	✓
換	✓	✕
加	✓	✓
看	✓	✓
愛	✓	✕
搭	✓	✓
送	✓	✕
連	✓	✓
簽	✓	✓
喜歡	✓	✕

如：(1) 王祕書喜歡上了印度歌舞。

　　(2) 這幾件衣服雖然很貴，但是她都看不上。

　　(3) * 我買的禮物都送得上嗎？

例句：

　　1. 請在這裡簽上你的名字。

　　2. 她穿上印度的紗麗，看起來美極了。

　　3. 只要連上網路，就能上網了。

　　4. 我搭不上這班公車，因為人太多了。

練習：請用「V 上」或「V ＋ 得 / 不 ＋ 上」回答下面的問題。

Exercise：Please answer the questions below with V 上 *shàng* or「V ＋ 得 *de* / 不 *bu* ＋ 上 *shàng*」．

---

1. A：為什麼李小姐想跟男朋友分手？

　 B：因為她＿＿＿＿＿＿＿＿＿。　　　　　　（愛）

2. A：這些首飾真漂亮！

　 B：是啊，這些是＿＿＿＿＿＿＿的流行設計。（黃金 / 加 / 不同寶石）

3. A：我們去打球，好嗎？

　 B：好的，等我＿＿＿＿運動鞋，就跟你去。（換）

4. A：這麼多的伴手禮，你選哪一個？

　 B：雖然很多也不貴，可是我都＿＿＿＿。　（看）

5. A：外面越來越冷了。

　 B：是啊，出門要＿＿＿＿＿＿＿。　（穿 / 外套）

三、才₃ *cái₃*

說明：「才」是副詞，此課的「才₃」和第六課的「才₁、才₂」語法意義不同。

Explanation：才₃ *cái₃* is an adverb. The grammatical meaning of 才 *cái₃* in this lesson is different from 才 *cái₁* and 才 *cái₂* in Lesson 6.

　　1.「才₁」：表示只（有）merely / only，數量少於期待、程度低。

　　　　才 *cái₁* indicates merely/only, less than expected in numbers and less than expected in degree.

　　如：(1) 印度，我才去過一次。

　　　　(2) 我才學了兩個月的中文，所以聽不懂。

2.「才₂」：表示 longer / later than expected，事情開始或完成得比預期晚或歷時長。

才 *cái*₂ indicates things take longer/later than expected. It means things start or finish later than expected or take longer.

　　如：(1) 我昨天半夜兩點才睡覺，所以現在很累。

　　　　(2) 剛開始皇家陪葬是用真人，後來才改成俑。

3.「才₃」：表示條件，用於後句。意思是：前一句的情況必須完成，也就是條件須做到，才可能發生後一句的情況。前句常與「只有、得、必須、要、因為、為了」配合。

才 *cái*₃ represents a condition that can be used in the subsequent clause. The meaning is that the situation of the preceding clause must be completed, i.e., the condition must be fulfilled; only then can the situation in the latter clause happen. The preceding clause often is paired with 只有 *zhǐyǒu*, 得 *děi*, 必須 *bìxū*, 要 *yào*, 因為 *yīnwèi*, 為了 *wèile*.

　　如：(1) 為了身體健康，我才注意食療養生。

　　　　(2) 只有週末，我才有時間看電影。

例句：

　　1. 我得用功，才能拿到獎學金。

　　2. 感冒要多喝水、多休息，才好得快。

　　3. 是不是要天天看書，中文才學得好？

　　4. 觀光客必須先買票，才能參觀泰姬瑪哈陵。

　　5. 我只有沒空做飯的時候，才去便利商店買吃的。

　　6. 他因為腳踏車被偷了，才坐公車去學校。

練習：請用「才₃」表示條件的意思，完成句子及回答問題。

Exercise：Please use 才 *cái*₃ to express conditions, then complete the sentences and answer the questions.

1. 天氣冷的時候，要多穿衣服，＿＿＿＿＿＿＿＿。
2. 你要把中文學好，＿＿＿＿＿＿＿＿＿＿＿。
3. 週末去餐廳吃飯，一定要先＿＿＿＿＿，才＿＿＿＿＿。（訂位、位子）
4. A：聽說王大年考上有名的大學？
   B：是啊，他＿＿＿＿＿＿＿，＿＿＿＿＿＿。
5. A：在你們國家，誰都能去臺灣學中文嗎？
   B：在我們國家，＿＿＿＿＿＿，＿＿＿＿＿。

四、從來 *cónglái* + 不 *bù* / 沒 *méi* Never

說明：「從來」是副詞，表示從過去到現在都是如此。多用於否定句：「從來＋不 / 沒」。

Explanation：從來 *cónglái* is an adverb. It expresses that something is the same from the past to the present. 從來 *cónglái* + 不 *bù* / 沒 *méi* are mostly used in negative sentences.

1.「從來＋不」：用於一般情形。表示某種情況通常不會發生，後面一般接動作動詞（action verb）和狀態動詞（state verb），不接變化動詞（process verb）。

從來 *cóng lái* + 不 *bù* is used in general situations and usually expresses that certain situations will not happen. It is generally followed by action verbs and state verbs and cannot be used with process verbs.

如：(1) 他去夜市或市集買東西，從來不殺價。
     (2) 這裡的夏天從來不熱，好舒服。
     (3) * 以前的事，我從來不忘記。（忘記 process verb）

2.「從來＋沒」：用於過去。表示某種情況沒有發生過，可接動作動詞（action verb）和變化動詞（process verb），一般不接狀態動詞（state verb）。動詞後面通常要帶「過」。

從來 *cónglái* ＋ 沒 *méi*: is used in the past. It expresses that a certain situation has not happened in the past. It can be joined with action verbs and process verbs; but it cannot be connected to state verbs. Verbs are usually followed by 過 *guò*.

如：(1) 我從來沒吃過道地的印度咖哩。

(2) 他天天運動身體很健康，從來沒感冒過。

(3) * 我從來沒討厭逛街。（討厭 state verb）

例句：

1. 很多外國學生從來不吃臭豆腐。

2. 我媽媽從來不覺得咖啡好喝。

3. 我從來沒買過這麼貴的衣服。

4. 他住臺北，可是從來沒參觀過故宮博物院。

練習：請用「從來不 V」或「從來沒 V 過」，回答下面的問題。

Exercise：Please use 從來 *cónglái* ＋ 不 *bù* V or 從來 *cónglái* ＋ 沒 *méi* V 過 *guò* to reply to the following questions.

1. A：你高中的時候，有打工的經驗嗎？

   B：＿＿＿＿＿＿＿＿＿＿＿＿＿＿＿＿＿＿＿。

2. A：這種酒好喝嗎？

   B：不知道，＿＿＿＿＿＿＿＿＿＿＿＿＿＿。

3. A：聽說你開車開得很快？

   B：你聽誰說的？＿＿＿＿＿＿＿＿＿＿＿。

4. A：今年過年你考不考慮出國旅行？

   B：＿＿＿＿＿＿＿＿＿＿＿＿＿＿＿＿＿＿＿。

5. A：我們週末去逛逛百貨公司，怎麼樣？

   B：＿＿＿＿＿＿＿＿＿＿＿＿＿＿＿＿＿＿＿。

Lesson 10

第十課　歡送會 Farewell Dinner

跨文化延伸 Cross-Cultural Extension

Different Ways of Business Negotiation Between Taiwan and India

The cultures of Taiwan and India are different. The Taiwanese culture is influenced by Chinese culture, and India is a country composed of a unique social system, history, and religion. Different cultures and market environments affect the ways and techniques used in doing business.

In general, Indians in business negotiations or shopping will certainly be engaged in bargaining. It is the instinct that has been honed by experiences in the domestic market. The Indian market is highly competitive, with dozens of importers often importing the same product. Of course, the last resort is price negotiations.

The gentle and polite thinking of Taiwanese has created a culture of saying "sorry." However, in response to bargaining, room to move should be in the first quote. In the face of an excessive counteroffer, attitudes would turn tough. Then they would often use the Chinese method of playing Tai Chi. If the customer says that because there will be a lot of orders in the future, therefore he is hoping that the price should be a little cheaper, the Taiwanese side would then say in turn: "The price cannot be changed this time because there is already cost involved. However, if you buy from us again next time, the price will certainly be lower than this time."

In other words, there is no right or wrong in negotiation techniques. The goal is to arrive at a win-win situation.

Lesson 10

討論 discussions

討價還價 bargaining

成交 sealingthe deal

語言任務 Language Tasks

一、將學生分成兩組，各自敘述自己喜歡或忘不了的人／地／事
　　／物，要說出重點和原因。敘述時，必須用到「不但…，還
　　／也…」和「才₃」兩個語法點。

　　　　First, divide the students into two groups; everyone in the group should describe whom they like or what people/place/events/things they found unforgettable. They need to list the main points and reasons for their choices. When making their presentation, they must use the two grammar points 不但 *búdàn* …, 還 *hái* / 也 *yě* … and 才 *cái*₃.

例如：A：你假日最常做什麼事？
　　　B：找臺灣同學聊天啊！
　　　A：不會無聊嗎？
　　　B：怎麼會！跟他們聊天不但能練習中文語法，還能學到課本上學不到
　　　　　的東西。這樣才能更了解臺灣的文化。

二、「彎彎你的手指頭」玩「從來不 V」或「從來沒 V 過」的遊戲。
做法：1. 學生先在練習單上寫出「我從來不 V」和「我從來沒 V 過」各五句。
　　　　（功課）
　　　2. 學生圍坐，每個人都張開十根手指頭。學生輪流說出「我從來不

V…」或「我從來沒 V 過…」，如果你聽到的句子和自己寫的一樣，就彎一根手指頭（說的人不能彎），最早彎完的人勝出。

"Bend your fingers" to play the "I have never V" or "Never have I ever V" game.

Instruction：1. Students first write five sentences on an exercise sheet: "I have never V" or "Never have I ever V" game. (Homework).

2. Students sit in a circle, each with ten fingers open. Students take turns to say, "I have never been to V..." or "I have never had a V..." and if you hear a sentence that is the same as what you have written yourself, bend a finger (the person who says the sentence cannot bend their fingers). The first person who has all their fingers bent wins.

附錄一 生詞索引 中—英
Vocabulary Index (Chinese-English)

漢語拼音	繁體	簡體	課別
A			
Āgélā bǎo	阿格拉堡	阿格拉堡	6A
àiqíng	愛情	爱情	6A
ànmó	按摩	按摩	8A
ānpái	安排	安排	2A
ànzhào	按照	按照	2A
Āsàmǔ hóngchá	阿薩姆紅茶	阿萨姆红茶	9A
Āyùfèituó	阿育吠陀	阿育吠陀	8A
B			
bǎi tānzi	擺攤子	摆摊子	7B
bàifǎng	拜訪	拜访	4A
báijīn	白金	白金	9A
bāncì	班次	班次	3A
bāngzhù	幫助	帮助	8B
bànshǒulǐ	伴手禮	伴手礼	9A
bó	薄	薄	1A
bǎo	飽	饱	2A
bǎocún	保存	保存	7A
bǎohù	保護	保护	6A
bàomíng	報名	报名	8A

漢語拼音	繁體	簡體	課別
bǎoshí	寶石	宝石	9A
běnlái	本來	本来	6B
biànhuà	變化	变化	6A
biānpào	鞭炮	鞭炮	4A
biǎodá	表達	表达	9B
biǎoshì	表示	表示	2B
bié jí	別急	别急	3A
bīngmǎ yǒng	兵馬俑	兵马俑	6B
bǐqǐlái	比起來	比起来	8B
bó'àizuò	博愛座	博爱座	3B
Bōsī	波斯	波斯	6B
bùjiǔ	不久	不久	9A
bùkěsīyì	不可思議	不可思议	6A
bùtóng	不同	不同	8B
C			
cáifù	財富	财富	4B
cānjiā	參加	参加	5A
cānkǎo	參考	参考	6A
cǎoběn	草本	草本	9A
cǎodì	草地	草地	8A

附錄一　生詞索引 中—英 Vocabulary Index (Chinese-English)

漢語拼音	繁體	簡體	課別
cǎoyào	草藥	草药	8A
cháng	嘗	尝	2A
chǎng shāng	廠商	厂商	10B
chǎnpǐn	產品	产品	9A
chātóu	插頭	插头	1A
cháyè	茶葉	茶叶	1B
chāzi	叉子	叉子	2B
chèn	趁	趁	3A
chéng gōng	成功	成功	2A
chéngshì	城市	城市	3B
chēxiāng	車廂	车厢	3A
chuàngyì	創意	创意	7B
chún yín	純銀	纯银	9A
chūnjié	春節	春节	4A
chūyī	初一	初一	4B
cìjī	刺激	刺激	7A
cuòguò	錯過	错过	7B
D			
dàcǎigòu	大採購	大采购	9B
dàcháng miànxiàn	大腸麵線	大肠面线	7B
dài	戴	戴	7A

漢語拼音	繁體	簡體	課別
dàibiǎo	代表	代表	9B
dàibiǎo xìng	代表性	代表性	9B
dàjiē xiǎoxiàng	大街小巷	大街小巷	3B
dàlǐshí	大理石	大理石	6A
dàmài	大賣	大卖	10B
dāng	當	当	9A
dāngdì	當地	当地	1B
dàngzuò	當作	当作	10B
dànián chū'èr	大年初二	大年初二	4A
dàodì	道地	道地	2A
dàzìrán	大自然	大自然	8A
diǎn yóudēng	點油燈	点油灯	4A
diànyā	電壓	电压	1A
diàndòng yóuxì	電動遊戲	电动游戏	7B
dǐngjí	頂級	顶级	10A
dǐngshàng gōngfū	頂上功夫	顶上功夫	7A
dìtiě	地鐵	地铁	3A
dìtiě zhàn	地鐵站	地铁站	3A

漢語拼音	繁體	簡體	課別
dìzhǐ	地址	地址	4B
dōngqián	冬前	冬前	8B
dòngwù	動物	动物	6B
dōu	都	都	5A
duìfāng	對方	对方	1B
E			
ér	而	而	4B
ěrhuán	耳環	耳环	9A
érqiě	而且	而且	8A
ézǐjiān	蚵仔煎	蚵仔煎	7B
F			
fā	發	发	5A
fàncài	飯菜	饭菜	2A
fàng biānpào	放鞭炮	放鞭炮	4A
fāngfǎ	方法	方法	8A
fāngmiàn	方面	方面	9A
fàngxīn	放心	放心	3A
fāxiàn	發現	发现	3A
fāzhǎn	發展	发展	3B
fēnggé	風格	风格	9A
fènglísū	鳳梨酥	凤梨酥	9B
fēngsú	風俗	风俗	1B
fójīng	佛經	佛经	4B

漢語拼音	繁體	簡體	課別
fútè	伏特	伏特	1A
G			
gài	蓋	盖	6A
gānbēi	乾杯	干杯	2A
gǎndòng	感動	感动	7A
gāoguì	高貴	高贵	9A
gāoxìng	高興	高兴	4A
gèdì	各地	各地	1B
gèwèi	各位	各位	2A
gēwǔ	歌舞	歌舞	10A
gōngjù	工具	工具	3B
gōutōng	溝通	沟通	8A
guà	掛	挂	3A
guàn	罐	罐	1A
guān	關	关	6A
guāng míng	光明	光明	4B
guāngmíng dēng	光明燈	光明灯	4B
guān guāng	觀光	观光	7A
guān guāngkè	觀光客	观光客	9B
guāng xiàn	光線	光线	6A

漢語拼音	繁體	簡體	課別
guānxì	關係	关系	1A
Gǔdá míng nà Tǎ	古達明納塔	古达明纳塔	6A
guì	跪	跪	6B
guìbīn	貴賓	贵宾	2A
guīju	規矩	规矩	2A
guīmó	規模	规模	10A
gǔjī	古蹟	古迹	6A
gùshì	故事	故事	6A
H			
hǎibào	海報	海报	10B
héshì	合適	合适	1B
héyuē	合約	合约	1A
hézuòàn	合作案	合作案	1B
hóngbāo	紅包	红包	5A
hóngbāo dài	紅包袋	红包袋	5A
huálì	華麗	华丽	10A
huàn	換	换	5A
huángjiā	皇家	皇家	6B
huángjīn	黃金	黄金	9A
huānsòng	歡送	欢送	10A

漢語拼音	繁體	簡體	課別
huárén shèhuì	華人社會	华人社会	9B
huí niángjiā	回娘家	回娘家	4A
Húmǎ yōng Líng	胡馬雍陵	胡马雍陵	6A
hūnlǐ	婚禮	婚礼	5A
huò	貨	货	7A
huódòng	活動	活动	8A
J			
jǐ	擠	挤	3A
jiā	加	加	5A
jiànyì	建議	建议	1B
jiànzhú	建築	建筑	6A
jiànzǒu	健走	健走	8A
jiǎodǐ ànmó	腳底按摩	脚底按摩	7B
jiāotōng	交通	交通	3B
jiàqián	價錢	价钱	3A
jiāxiāng	家鄉	家乡	4A
jiāyùn	家運	家运	5A
jíbìng	疾病	疾病	8B
jīchē pùbù	機車瀑布	机车瀑布	3B
jīchē zú	機車族	机车族	3B

漢語拼音	繁體	簡體	課別
jīdòng	激動	激动	6B
jié	節	节	3A
jiēfēng	接風	接风	2A
jiéhūn	結婚	结婚	5B
jiérì	節日	节日	4A
jìhuà	計畫	计划	1B
jījí	積極	积极	9B
jìjié	季節	季节	8B
jíle	極了	极了	5A
jílì	吉利	吉利	5A
jǐng	井	井	6B
jǐngdiǎn	景點	景点	9B
jìngjiǔ	敬酒	敬酒	5B
jīnglǐ	經理	经理	1A
jīngyàn	經驗	经验	1B
jīnsè	金色	金色	5A
jīnshì	金飾	金饰	5A
jiǔlèi	酒類	酒类	1A
jíxiáng	吉祥	吉祥	5B
jǔbàn	舉辦	举办	4B
jǔbēi	舉杯	举杯	2A
jūnduì	軍隊	军队	6B
jǔxíng	舉行	举行	5B
jūzhù	居住	居住	9B

漢語拼音	繁體	簡體	課別
K			
kāi wánxiào	開玩笑	开玩笑	7A
kālǐ	咖哩	咖哩	2B
kànqǐlái	看起來	看起来	5A
kǎobǐng	烤餅	烤饼	2B
kěkǒu	可口	可口	2A
kělián	可憐	可怜	6A
kèrén	客人	客人	2B
kěxí	可惜	可惜	6A
kǒng	孔	孔	1A
kōngqì	空氣	空气	3A
kǒuwèi	口味	口味	4A
kuà huǒlú	跨火爐	跨火炉	5B
L			
lā dùzi	拉肚子	拉肚子	7A
làngfèi	浪費	浪费	10B
làngmàn	浪漫	浪漫	6A
lāo jīnyú	撈金魚	捞金鱼	7B
lǐ qīng qíngyì zhòng	禮輕情意重	礼轻情意重	9B
líang	涼	凉	10A
liánjié	連結	连结	10B

漢語拼音	繁體	簡體	課別
liánzhe	連著	连着	7B
liáo	聊	聊	8A
liǎobuqǐ	了不起	了不起	7A
liǎojiě	了解	了解	1B
lǐfú	禮服	礼服	5A
lìhài	厲害	厉害	7A
lǐhé	禮盒	礼盒	1B
lǐjié	禮節	礼节	2A
líkāi	離開	离开	5B
lǐmào	禮貌	礼貌	2B
língqǐn	陵寢	陵寝	6A
lìngwài	另外	另外	6A
liú	留	留	3A
liúlèi	流淚	流泪	6A
liúxíng	流行	流行	3B
luàn	亂	乱	7A
lúbǐ	盧比	卢比	5A
lùguò	路過	路过	7B
Luòdí Gōng yuán	洛迪公園	洛迪公园	8A
lǔròufàn	滷肉飯	卤肉饭	7B
M			
máfán	麻煩	麻烦	3A

漢語拼音	繁體	簡體	課別
mànpǎo	慢跑	慢跑	8A
miǎo	秒	秒	6B
mǐfàn	米飯	米饭	2B
mìshū	祕書	祕书	1A
mùdì	目的	目的	10B
N			
nǎiyóu kālǐjī	奶油咖哩雞	奶油咖哩鸡	2A
Nǎlǐ, nǎlǐ	哪裡，哪裡	哪里，哪里	2A
nián	黏	黏	5A
niàn jīng	念經	念经	4B
niánlíng	年齡	年龄	8B
níngméng shuǐ	檸檬水	柠檬水	2B
nónghòu	濃厚	浓厚	9B
P			
pá	爬	爬	6A
páidēngjié	排燈節	排灯节	4A
péizàng	陪葬	陪葬	6B
pílèi	皮類	皮类	1A
piàn	騙	骗	3A
píng'ān	平安	平安	4B
píngmín	平民	平民	3A

漢語拼音	繁體	簡體	課別
pútáojiǔ	葡萄酒	葡萄酒	2A
Q			
qiān	簽	签	3A
qiánshuǐ	潛水	潜水	5B
qiān zhèng	簽證	签证	10B
qìfēn	氣氛	气氛	5B
qíguài	奇怪	奇怪	3A
Qíncháo	秦朝	秦朝	6B
qīngsōng	輕鬆	轻松	3A
qìngzhù	慶祝	庆祝	4B
qīnqī	親戚	亲戚	9B
Qínshǐ huáng Líng	秦始皇陵	秦始皇陵	6B
qíqiú	祈求	祈求	4B
qǔ míngzi	取名字	取名字	6A
R			
ràng	讓	让	8B
ràngzuò	讓座	让座	3A
ránhòu	然後	然后	7B
rào huǒduī	繞火堆	绕火堆	5A
rènào	熱鬧	热闹	4A
rénjǐrén	人擠人	人挤人	7A

漢語拼音	繁體	簡體	課別
rén qíngwèi	人情味	人情味	9B
rènwéi	認為	认为	8B
rènzhēn	認真	认真	7A
rèqíng	熱情	热情	2B (Vs)
rèqíng	熱情	热情	10A (N)
ròuyuán	肉圓	肉圆	7B
S			
sāichē	塞車	塞车	3A
sānlún chē	三輪車	三轮车	3A
sāntiě gònggòu	三鐵共構	三铁共构	3B
shājià	殺價	杀价	3A
Shājiāhǎn Wáng	沙迦罕王	沙迦罕王	6A
shālì	紗麗	纱丽	5A
shāng chǎng	商場	商场	9A
shāngjiā	商家	商家	9B
shāngpǐn	商品	商品	10B
shè qìqiú	射氣球	射气球	7B
shěbùdé	捨不得	舍不得	5B
shèjì	設計	设计	1B

附錄一　生詞索引 中—英 Vocabulary Index (Chinese-English)

漢語拼音	繁體	簡體	課別
shēnghuó	生活	生活	7A
shēngyīn	聲音	声音	4A
shēntǐ	身體	身体	8B
shēntǐ jiànkāng	身體健康	身体健康	2A
shēnxīn	身心	身心	8A
shídài	時代	时代	10B
shìjí	市集	市集	7A
shìjiè yíchǎn	世界遺產	世界遗产	6B
shíliáo	食療	食疗	8B
shìpǐn	飾品	饰品	7A
shípǔ	食譜	食谱	4A
shìqíng	事情	事情	10B
shìshì rúyì	事事如意	事事如意	4B
shíwù	食物	食物	8A
shíwǔ	十五	十五	4B
shǒudū	首都	首都	3B
shǒugōng xié	手工鞋	手工鞋	9A
shǒuhuán	手環	手环	7A
shǒushì	首飾	首饰	9A
shǒuzhuó	手鐲	手镯	9A
shùnbiàn	順便	顺便	9A

漢語拼音	繁體	簡體	課別
shuōqǐ	說起	说起	6A
sìmiào	寺廟	寺庙	4B
sòng	送	送	1B
sùjiāo bù	塑膠布	塑胶布	3A
T			
Táiběi Shìmào	臺北世貿／臺北世界貿易中心	台北世贸／台北世界贸易中心	10A
Tàijīmǎhā Líng	泰姬瑪哈陵	泰姬玛哈陵	6A
Táiwān zhūbǎo shǒushì zhǎn lǎnhuì	臺灣珠寶首飾展覽會	台湾珠宝首饰展览会	10A
tán	談	谈	1B
tān	攤	摊	7B
tàng	趟	趟	10A
tào	套	套	9A
tèchǎn	特產	特产	9A
tèdì	特地	特地	10A
tèsè	特色	特色	3B
tiánbúlà	甜不辣	甜不辣	7B
tiándiǎn	甜點	甜点	4A

漢語拼音	繁體	簡體	課別
tiàosǎn	跳傘	跳伞	5B
tiǎozhàn	挑戰	挑战	5B
tǐhuì	體會	体会	10A
tǐzhí	體質	体质	8B
tòngkuài	痛快	痛快	7B
tòuguò	透過	透过	10B
tuǐ	腿	腿	3A
túshì	圖示	图示	10B
W			
wā	挖	挖	6B
wàisòng	外送	外送	3B
wǎnglù	網路	网路	10B
wánghòu	王后	王后	6A
wǎngyè	網頁	网页	10B
wǎngzhàn	網站	网站	10B
wǎnhuì	晚會	晚会	10A
wěidà	偉大	伟大	6A
wèidào	味道	味道	2A
wèilái	未來	未来	5A
wěishù	尾數	尾数	5A
wéixiǎn	危險	危险	6A
wénhuà	文化	文化	1B
wénjiàn	文件	文件	1A
wūrǎn	汙染	污染	3A

漢語拼音	繁體	簡體	課別
X			
xiān	鮮	鲜	7A
xiāng dāng	相當	相当	3B
xiǎngfǎ	想法	想法	4B
xiàngliàn	項鍊	项链	9A
xiāngliào	香料	香料	7A
xiàngzi	巷子	巷子	7A
xiěguǎn	血管	血管	3B
xǐhào	喜好	喜好	8B
xǐjiǔ	喜酒	喜酒	5A
Xǐmǎlāyǎ	喜馬拉雅	喜马拉雅	9A
xìn	信	信	2B
Xīn Délǐ	新德里	新德里	1A
xíngdòng	行動	行动	3B
xìngqù	興趣	兴趣	2B
xíngshì	形式	形式	5B
xīngwàng	興旺	兴旺	5A
xíng zhuàng	形狀	形状	1A
xīnkǔle	辛苦了	辛苦了	1A
xīnláng	新郎	新郎	5A
xīnniáng	新娘	新娘	5A
xīnrén	新人	新人	5B

漢語拼音	繁體	簡體	課別
xīnshǎng	欣賞	欣赏	9A
xīnwéngǎo	新聞稿	新闻稿	10B
xǐyàn	喜宴	喜宴	5A
xìnyǎng	信仰	信仰	1B
xīnyì	心意	心意	9B
xǐshǒu	洗手	洗手	2B
xísú	習俗	习俗	4B
xǐtáng	喜糖	喜糖	5B
xǐyàn	喜宴	喜宴	5B
xīyǐn	吸引	吸引	6A
xuānchuán	宣傳	宣传	10B
Y			
yángròu	羊肉	羊肉	2B
yǎngshēng	養生	养生	8A
yánjiù	研究	研究	6B (V)
yánjiù	研究	研究	8A (N)
yánzhòng	嚴重	严重	3A
yāoqǐng	邀請	邀请	4A
yàowù	藥物	药物	8B
yèwù	業務	业务	1B

漢語拼音	繁體	簡體	課別
yìbān	一般	一般	8B
yìhuǐr	一會兒	一会儿	2A
Yìndìyǔ	印地語	印地语	1B
Yìndùtōng	印度通	印度通	1B
Yìndùxíng	印度行	印度行	10A
Yìndùjiào	印度教	印度教	2B
yíngcáishén	迎財神	迎财神	4A
yīnggāide	應該的	应该的	10A
yǐnshí	飲食	饮食	8B
yìsi	意思	意思	4A
Yīsīlánjiào	伊斯蘭教	伊斯兰教	2B
yìyì	意義	意义	9B
yǒng	俑	俑	6B
yóuxì	遊戲	游戏	5B
yǒuyì	友誼	友谊	2A
yōuyóukǎ	悠遊卡	悠游卡	3B
yǔ	與	与	4B
yuánxíng	圓形	圆形	1A
yuē	約	约	7B
yǔjì	雨季	雨季	8B
yújiā	瑜珈	瑜珈	8A

漢語拼音	繁體	簡體	課別
yúkuài	愉快	愉快	2A
yùnfù	孕婦	孕妇	3B
Z			
zhǎi	窄	窄	7A
zhǎnlǎn	展覽	展览	10A
zhǎnqū	展區	展区	10B
zhāodài	招待	招待	2B
zhěnglǐ	整理	整理	1A
zhèngshì	正式	正式	2B
zhēnrén	真人	真人	6B
zhíde	值得	值得	10A
zhìhuì	智慧	智慧	4B
zhìliáo	治療	治疗	8B
zhǒnglèi	種類	种类	7B
zhòngyào	重要	重要	4B
zhōngyī	中醫	中医	8A
zhuā	抓	抓	2B
zhuàngkuàng	狀況	状况	8B
zhūbǎo	珠寶	珠宝	1B
zhùfú	祝福	祝福	5A
zhǔjiǎo	主角	主角	2B
zhùmíng	著名	着名	4B
zhǔnbèi	準備	准备	2B

漢語拼音	繁體	簡體	課別
zhūròu	豬肉	猪肉	2B
zhǔshí	主食	主食	2B
zhǔyào	主要	主要	3B
zīliào	資料	资料	8A
zīxùn	資訊	资讯	10B
zìyóu xíng	自由行	自由行	3A
zōngjiào	宗教	宗教	1A
zǒu	走	走	4A
zǒudiū	走丟	走丢	7A
zuànlái zuànqù	鑽來鑽去	钻来钻去	3B
zūnzhòng	尊重	尊重	1B
zuòkè	做客	做客	2B
zuòwèi	座位	座位	2A

附錄二　生詞索引 英一中
Vocabulary Index (English-Chinese)

English definition	Traditional Characters	Simplified Characters	Lesson
A			
accessory	飾品	饰品	7A
according to	按照	按照	2A
activity	活動	活动	8A
to add	加	加	5A
address	地址	地址	4B
age	年齡	年龄	8B
aggressive, active	積極	积极	9B
Agra Fort	阿格拉堡	阿格拉堡	6A
air	空氣	空气	3A
already	都	都	5A
amazing	厲害	厉害	7A
amazing, terrific, marvelous	了不起	了不起	7A
ancient monuments	古蹟	古迹	6A
and	與	与	4B
and, and yet, but	而	而	4B
and, moreover	而且	而且	8A
animals	動物	动物	6B
another	另外	另外	6A
to appreciate, to admire	欣賞	欣赏	9A
architecture	建築	建筑	6A
army	軍隊	军队	6B
arrangement; to arrange	安排	安排	2A
as	當	当	9A
a set of	套	套	9A
aspect	方面	方面	9A
Assam Black Tea	阿薩姆紅茶	阿萨姆红茶	9A
atmosphere	氣氛	气氛	5B
attached	連著	连着	7B
to attract	吸引	吸引	6A
auspicious	吉利	吉利	5A

English definition	Traditional Characters	Simplified Characters	Les- son
auspicious- ness, good luck	吉祥	吉祥	5B
authentic, genuine	道地	道地	2A
Ayurveda	阿育吠 陀	阿育吠 陀	8A
B			
balloon shooting	射氣球	射气球	7B
baked flat- bread	烤餅	烤饼	2B
bangles	手環	手环	7A
to bargain	殺價	杀价	3A
to be a guest	做客	做客	2B
to be at ease, not to worry	放心	放心	3A
before win- ter	冬前	冬前	8B
belief, faith	信仰	信仰	1B
to believe	信	信	2B
big streets and small alleyways	大街小 巷	大街小 巷	3B

English definition	Traditional Characters	Simplified Characters	Les- son
blessings; to wish sb. well	祝福	祝福	5A
blood ves- sel	血管	血管	3B
body	身體	身体	8B
body and mind	身心	身心	8A
bracelet	手鐲	手镯	9A
bride	新娘	新娘	5A
bridegroom	新郎	新郎	5A
bright	光明	光明	4B
Buddhist sutras	佛經	佛经	4B
to be bur- ied together with the dead	陪葬	陪葬	6B
business	商家	商家	9B
butter chicken, Murgh Makhani	奶油咖 哩雞	奶油咖 哩鸡	2A
C			
capital	首都	首都	3B
carriage	車廂	车厢	3A
category	種類	种类	7B

English definition	Traditional Characters	Simplified Characters	Lesson
to celebrate	慶祝	庆祝	4B
to change	換	换	5A
to chant Buddhist scripture	念經	念经	4B
to chat	聊	聊	8A
to cheat	騙	骗	3A
Cheers! Bottoms up! Lit. "dry cup"	乾杯	干杯	2A
city	城市	城市	3B
challenge	挑戰	挑战	5B
changes	變化	变化	6A
chaotic	亂	乱	7A
Chinese medicine	中醫	中医	8A
Chinese society	華人社會	华人社会	9B
clay figures buried with the dead	俑	俑	6B
to climb	爬	爬	6A
to close	關	关	6A
to communicate	溝通	沟通	8A

English definition	Traditional Characters	Simplified Characters	Lesson
to construct	蓋	盖	6A
contract	合約	合约	1A
cool	涼	凉	10A
cooperative project	印度通	印度通	1B
to cross a hot stove	跨火爐	跨火炉	5B
crowded	擠	挤	3A
culture	文化	文化	1B
compared with, by comparison	比起來	比起来	8A
to be congested with cars	塞車	塞车	3A
curry	咖哩	咖哩	2B
custom, convention, tradition	習俗	习俗	4B
D			
dangerous	危險	危险	6A
delicious	可口	可口	2A
delivery	外送	外送	3B
design	設計	设计	1B
development	發展	发展	3B

English definition	Traditional Characters	Simplified Characters	Les-son
diet, drinks, and food	飲食	饮食	8B
different	不同	不同	8B
to dig	挖	挖	6B
to discover	發現	发现	3A
to discuss	談	谈	1B
disease	疾病	疾病	8B
dishes, food	飯菜	饭菜	2A
to dive	潛水	潜水	5B
Diwali	排燈節	排灯节	4A
document	文件	文件	1A
do not worry	別急	别急	3A
drug	藥物	药物	8B
E			
earrings	耳環	耳环	9A
Easy Card	悠遊卡	悠游卡	3B
electronic	電動	电动	7B
enthusias-tic	熱情	热情	2B
era, age	時代	时代	10B
etiquette, courtesy	禮節	礼节	2A

English definition	Traditional Characters	Simplified Characters	Les-son
evening party, eve-ning recep-tion	晚會	晚会	10A
everybody	各位	各位	2A
Everything goes as you wish.	事事如意	事事如意	4B
exhibition	展覽	展览	10A
exhibition area	展區	展区	10B
experience	經驗	经验	1B
to experi-ence	體會	体会	10A
to express	表達	表达	9B
expression	表示	表示	2B
extremely	極了	极了	5A
F			
family fortunes	家運	家运	5A
famous	著名	着名	4B
festival	節日	节日	4A
firecrack-ers	鞭炮	鞭炮	4A
fish for goldfish	撈金魚	捞金鱼	7B

English definition	Traditional Characters	Simplified Characters	Lesson
first day of a month	初一	初一	4B
flavor, taste	口味	口味	4A
food	食物	食物	8A
food therapy	食療	食疗	8B
foot massage	腳底按摩	脚底按摩	7B
fork	叉子	叉子	2B
form	形式	形式	5B
formal	正式	正式	2B
formal dress, full dress	禮服	礼服	5A
fresh	鮮	鲜	7A
fried oyster	蚵仔煎	蚵仔煎	7B
friendship	友誼	友谊	2A
to be full in the stomach	飽	饱	2A
future	未來	未来	5A
G			
game	遊戲	游戏	5B
gemstone	寶石	宝石	9A
to get married	結婚	结婚	5B

English definition	Traditional Characters	Simplified Characters	Lesson
gift box	禮盒	礼盒	1B
to give as a present	送	送	1B
to give away a seat	讓座	让座	3A
to give someone a name	取名字	取名字	6A
go around the sacred fire	繞火堆	绕火堆	5A
gold	黃金	黄金	9A
golden color	金色	金色	5A
goldfish catching	撈金魚	捞金鱼	7B
gold jewelry	金飾	金饰	5A
good-for-tune lamp	光明燈	光明灯	4B
Good health	身體健康	身体健康	2A
goods	貨	货	7A
product	商品	商品	10B
gorgeous, splendid	華麗	华丽	10A
to grab	抓	抓	2B

English definition	Traditional Characters	Simplified Characters	Les-son
great	偉大	伟大	6A
guest	客人	客人	2B
H			
handmade shoes	手工鞋	手工鞋	9A
to hang up	掛	挂	3A
happy	高興	高兴	4A
happy, cheerful	愉快	愉快	2A
have diar-rhea	拉肚子	拉肚子	7A
health; to keep one's body healthy	養生	养生	8A
help	幫助	帮助	8B
herb	草本	草本	9A
herbs	草藥	草药	8A
Himalaya	喜馬拉雅	喜马拉雅	9A
Hindi	印地語	印地语	1B
Hinduism	印度教	印度教	2B
to hold a ceremony	舉辦	举办	4B

English definition	Traditional Characters	Simplified Characters	Les-son
to hold (a meeting, conference, etc.)	舉行	举行	5B
to hold a welcome reception	接風	接风	2A
hole	孔	孔	1A
homeland	家鄉	家乡	4A
honored guest, dis-tinguished guest	貴賓	贵宾	2A
hospitality, enthusiasm	熱情	热情	10A
human kindness	人情味	人情味	9B
Humayun's Tomb	胡馬雍陵	胡马雍陵	6A
I			
icon	圖示	图示	10B
imperial family	皇家	皇家	6B
important	重要	重要	4B
in all parts of (a coun-try); vari-ous regions	各地	各地	1B

附錄二　生詞索引 英一中 Vocabulary Index (English-Chinese)

English definition	Traditional Characters	Simplified Characters	Lesson
in a moment	一會兒	一会儿	2A
India trip	印度行	印度行	10A
information	資訊	资讯	10B
to be interested	有興趣	有兴趣	2B
internet	網路	网路	10B
internet site	網站	网站	10B
intestine vermicelli	大腸麵線	大肠面线	7B
to invite	邀請	邀请	4A
Islamism	伊斯蘭教	伊斯兰教	2B
It is the thought that counts.	禮輕情意重	礼轻情意重	9B
J			
jewelry	珠寶	珠宝	1B
jewelry	首飾	首饰	9A
to jog; jogging	慢跑	慢跑	8A
joyful	痛快	痛快	7B
K			
to keep	保存	保存	7A
King Shah Jahan	沙迦罕王	沙迦罕王	6A

English definition	Traditional Characters	Simplified Characters	Lesson
to kneel	跪	跪	6B
L			
lamb	羊肉	羊肉	2B
lane	巷子	巷子	7A
lawn	草地	草地	8A
leather type	皮類	皮类	1A
to leave	走	走	4A
to leave	離開	离开	5B
legs	腿	腿	3A
lemon water	檸檬水	柠檬水	2B
to let	讓	让	8B
to let off firecrackers	放鞭炮	放鞭炮	4A
life	生活	生活	7A
light	光線	光线	6A
to light oil lamps	點油燈	点油灯	4A
link	連結	连结	10B
liquor type	酒類	酒类	1A
lively, bustling with noise and excitement	熱鬧	热闹	4A
local	當地	当地	1B

English definition	Traditional Characters	Simplified Characters	Les-son
Lodhi Garden	洛迪公園	洛迪公园	8A
to look like	看起來	看起来	5A
to be lost	走丟	走丢	7A
love	愛情	爱情	6A
M			
main course in a meal, staple food	主食	主食	2B
mainly	主要	主要	3B
to make a date with people	約	约	7B
to make a joke	開玩笑	开玩笑	7A
to make a toast with wine	敬酒	敬酒	5B
manager	經理	经理	1A
manufacturer	廠商	厂商	10B
marble	大理石	大理石	6A
market	市集	市集	7A

English definition	Traditional Characters	Simplified Characters	Les-son
married women returning to their parents' home	回娘家	回娘家	4A
massage	按摩	按摩	8A
material, data, information	資料	资料	8A
mausoleum	陵寢	陵寝	6A
measure word for a can	罐	罐	1A
measure word for carriages	節	节	3A
meaning	意思	意思	4A
measure word for a trip	趟	趟	10A
meat ball	肉圓	肉圆	7B
method	方法	方法	8A
metro station, subway station	地鐵站	地铁站	3A
metro, subway station	地鐵	地铁	3A

附錄二 生詞索引 英一中 Vocabulary Index (English-Chinese)

English definition	Traditional Characters	Simplified Characters	Les-son
to miss something	錯過	错过	7B
money wrapped in red as a gift, lit. "red enve-lope"	紅包	红包	5A
motorcycle generation	機車族	机车族	3B
motorcycle waterfall	機車瀑布	机车瀑布	3B
to be moved	感動	感动	7A
moved, touched, thrilled	激動	激动	6B
movement	行動	行动	3B
N			
narrow	窄	窄	7A
nature	大自然	大自然	8A
necklace	項鍊	項鍊	9A
New Delhi	新德里	新德里	1A
newly-wed	新人	新人	5B
noble	高貴	高贵	9A
normal	一般	一般	8B

English definition	Traditional Characters	Simplified Characters	Les-son
the number of runs of scheduled buses, trains, flights	班次	班次	3A
O			
on the way, in passing, without much extra effort	順便	顺便	9A
ordinary people	平民	平民	3A
originality	創意	创意	7B
originally	本來	本来	6B
P			
to para-chute	跳傘	跳伞	5B
to partici-pate	參加	参加	5A
to pass by (a place)	路過	路过	7B
to pay a visit	拜訪	拜访	4A
people upon people	人擠人	人挤人	7A
Persia	波斯	波斯	6B

English definition	Traditional Characters	Simplified Characters	Lesson
physique	體質	体质	8B
pineapple cakes	鳳梨酥	凤梨酥	9B
pitiful	可憐	可怜	6A
to plan to	計畫	计划	1B
plastic sheet	塑膠布	塑胶布	3A
platinum	白金	白金	9A
plug	插頭	插头	1A
polite, courteous	禮貌	礼貌	2B
pork	豬肉	猪肉	2B
pollution	汙染	污染	3A
popular	流行	流行	3B
posters	海報	海报	10B
to pray for	祈求	祈求	4B
preference, what a person likes	喜好	喜好	8B
pregnant women	孕婦	孕妇	3B
to prepare	準備	准备	2B
press release	新聞稿	新闻稿	10B
price	價錢	价钱	3A

English definition	Traditional Characters	Simplified Characters	Lesson
priority seat	博愛座	博爱座	3B
product	產品	产品	9A
professional work, business	業務	业务	1B
to propose a toast	舉杯	举杯	2A
prosperous, thriving	興旺	兴旺	5A
protagonist, leading role	主角	主角	2B
to protect	保護	保护	6A
to publicize	宣傳	宣传	10B
pure silver	純銀	纯银	9A
purpose	心意	心意	9B
purpose, aim	目的	目的	10B
to put in order, to arrange	整理	整理	1A
Q			
Qin dynasty	秦朝	秦朝	6B
queen	王后	王后	6A
Qutub Minar	古達明納塔	古达明纳塔	6A

English definition	Traditional Characters	Simplified Characters	Lesson
R			
rainy season	雨季	雨季	8B
real people	真人	真人	6B
reason, condition	關係	关系	1A
to receive guests	招待	招待	2B
recipe	食譜	食谱	4A
red envelope bags	紅包袋	红包袋	5A
to register	報名	报名	8A
regrettable	可惜	可惜	6A
relative	親戚	亲戚	9B
relatively	相當	相当	3B
relaxed	輕鬆	轻松	3A
religion	宗教	宗教	1A
reluctant	捨不得	舍不得	5B
the remainder of a number	尾數	尾数	5A
to represent	代表	代表	9B
representation	代表性	代表性	9B
to research	研究	研究	6B

English definition	Traditional Characters	Simplified Characters	Lesson
research, study	研究	研究	8A
to reserve something for someone	留	留	3A
to reside	居住	居住	9B
to respect	尊重	尊重	1B
rice	米飯	米饭	2B
romantic	浪漫	浪漫	6A
round shape	圓形	圆形	1A
rule, custom	規矩	规矩	2A
rupee	盧比	卢比	5A
S			
safe	平安	平安	4B
sari	紗麗	纱丽	5A
scale	規模	规模	10A
scenic attraction	景點	景点	9B
season	季節	季节	8B
seats, a place to sit	座位	座位	2A
second	秒	秒	6B
secretary	祕書	祕书	1A

English definition	Traditional Characters	Simplified Characters	Les-son
to see someone off, to bid farewell to; seeing-off, send-off	歡送	欢送	10A
self-orga-nized free travel	自由行	自由行	3A
to sell a lot, sell well	大賣	大卖	10B
serious	嚴重	严重	3A
seriously	認真	认真	7A
to set up a stall at a market	擺攤子	摆摊子	7B
shape	形狀	形状	1A
to shed tears	流淚	流泪	6A
shopping mall	商場	商场	9A
shopping spree	大採購	大采购	9B
sightseeing	觀光	观光	7A
to sign	簽	签	3A
signifi-cance	意義	意义	9B
singing and dancing	歌舞	歌舞	10A

English definition	Traditional Characters	Simplified Characters	Les-son
situation	狀況	状况	8B
social cus-tom	風俗	风俗	1B
soon	不久	不久	9A
sound	聲音	声音	4A
souvenir	伴手禮	伴手礼	9A
to speak of something	說起	说起	6A
special characteris-tic	特色	特色	3B
specially	特地	特地	10A
specialty	特產	特产	9A
spices	香料	香料	7A
to sprout, to grow, to prosper	發	发	5A
Spring Festival	春節	春节	4A
stall, stand or booth in a market	攤	摊	7B
stewed meat with rice	滷肉飯	卤肉饭	7B
to stick	黏	黏	5A

English definition	Traditional Characters	Simplified Characters	Lesson
to stimulate, to excite	刺激	刺激	7A
story	故事	故事	6A
strange	奇怪	奇怪	3A
strong, thick	濃厚	浓厚	9B
style	風格	风格	9A
successful	成功	成功	2A
to suggest	建議	建议	1B
suitable	合適	合适	1B
Sure, my pleasure.	應該的	应该的	10A
sweets	甜點	甜点	4A
T			
Taipei World Trade Center	臺北世貿（臺北世界貿易中心）	台北世贸（台北世界贸易中心）	10A
Taiwan Jewelry & Gem Fair	臺灣珠寶首飾展覽會	台湾珠宝首饰展览会	10A
take advantage of 'opportunity, time, etc.'	趁	趁	3A

English definition	Traditional Characters	Simplified Characters	Lesson
Taj Mahal mausoleum	泰姬瑪哈陵	泰姬玛哈陵	6A
taste	味道	味道	2A
to taste	嚐	尝	2A
tea	茶葉	茶叶	1B
temples	寺廟	寺庙	4B
tempura (Taiwanese style)	甜不辣	甜不辣	7B
Terracotta Army	兵馬俑	兵马俑	6B
the convergence of the three rail systems	三鐵共構	三铁共构	3B
the fifteenth day of a month	十五	十五	4B
then	然後	然后	7B
the other party	對方	对方	1B
the second day of Chinese New Year	大年初二	大年初二	4A
thin	薄	薄	1A
thing, matter	事情	事情	10B

English definition	Traditional Characters	Simplified Characters	Lesson
to think	認為	认为	8B
through	透過	透过	10B
Tomb of the first Emperor Qin	秦始皇陵	秦始皇陵	6B
tool	工具	工具	3B
top-grade, first-rate	頂級	顶级	10A
top-notch kungfu, lit. "the technique of carrying things on one's head"	頂上功夫	顶上功夫	7A
tourist	觀光客	观光客	9B
transportation	交通	交通	3B
to treat	治療	治疗	8B
to treat as, to take as	當作	当作	10B
tricycles	三輪車	三轮车	3A
trouble-some	麻煩	麻烦	3A
U			
Unbeliev-able, in-credible	不可思議	不可思议	6A

English definition	Traditional Characters	Simplified Characters	Lesson
to under-stand	了解	了解	1B
to use as a reference	參考	参考	6A
V			
video games	電動遊戲	电动游戏	7B
visa	簽證	签证	10B
volt	伏特	伏特	1A
voltage	電壓	电压	1A
W			
to walk briskly; brisk walk-ing	健走	健走	8A
wash hands	洗手	洗手	2B
to waste	浪費	浪费	10B
water well	井	井	6B
ways of thinking	想法	想法	4B
wealth	財富	财富	4B
to wear on hand	戴	戴	7A
websites	網頁	网页	10B
wedding banquet	喜宴	喜宴	5A

English definition	Traditional Characters	Simplified Characters	Les-son
wedding candy	喜糖	喜糖	5B
wedding ceremony	婚禮	婚礼	5A
wedding feast	喜酒	喜酒	5A
to welcome the God of Wealth	迎財神	迎财神	4A
(grape) wine	葡萄酒	葡萄酒	2A
wisdom	智慧	智慧	4B
World Heritage	世界遺產	世界遗产	6B
worthy of, to be worth	值得	值得	10A
Y			
You are wel-come. Lit. "Where? Where?"	哪裡，哪裡	哪里，哪里	2A
yoga	瑜珈	瑜珈	8A
You have been work-ing so hard.	辛苦了	辛苦了	1A

English definition	Traditional Characters	Simplified Characters	Les-son
Z			
zigzaging in and out	鑽來鑽去	钻来钻去	3B

附錄三　簡體字課文
Text in Simplified Characters

第一课　印度我们来了！

A. 对话

周经理：去印度，我们应该带什么礼物？

王祕书：因为宗教的关系，我们不能送皮类和酒类的东西。

周经理：那应该送什么？

王祕书：我们多带几罐台湾乌龙茶好了！

周经理：好。现在新德里是春天吗？

王祕书：是的，不冷不热，带一件薄外套就好了。

周经理：电压是跟台湾一样是 110 伏特吗？插头是什么形状的？

王祕书：电压是 220 伏特，插头是三孔圆形的。

周经理：从台北到新德里要坐多久的飞机？

王祕书：台湾离印度有一点远，不过，大概七个小时能到。

周经理：最重要的是别忘了带合约。

王祕书：没问题。文件我都整理好了。

周经理：辛苦了。有人来接我们吗？

王祕书：放心，有人会来接我们的。

B. 短文

见面礼

　　周经理是台湾清华珠宝公司的业务经理。今年三月计划去印度谈合作案。这是她第一次去印度，虽然她的英文非常好，但是她对

印度文化不太了解，更不会说印地语，需要一位有经验的祕书一起
去，所以她找了王伟中当祕书。王伟中是位印度通，不但去过印度
44 次，还会说印地语，也非常了解印度各地的风俗文化。

　　这次他们要去印度谈珠宝设计的合作案，得带见面礼给对方。
周经理出发前在台北买了一些合适的礼物。为了尊重当地的宗教信
仰，酒类和皮类的礼物都不合适。所以王祕书建议买一些台湾有名
的茶叶礼盒送给对方。

第二课　　接风

A. 对话

韦经理：周经理，请您坐在门对面。

周经理：谢谢您的座位安排。

韦经理：哪里，哪里！您是主要的贵宾，按照礼节应该坐这个位
　　　　子。

周经理：这里也有这样的规矩啊，台湾也有。

韦经理：您想喝红葡萄酒还是白葡萄酒？

周经理：我们喝红葡萄酒吧。

韦经理：好。祝您身体健康，也祝我们合作愉快。

周经理：谢谢您。请问，印地语的干杯怎么说？

韦经理：我们跟英文一样，也说：「Cheers」。

周经理：各位请举杯，为我们的友谊和合作成功干杯！

韦经理：我们今天吃到的是新德里有名的奶油咖哩鸡（Murgh Ma-
　　　　khani）。

周经理：好，我尝一尝。

韦经理：周经理，饭菜还可口吧？

周经理：道地的 Murg Makhani 味道真好！

韦经理：那就多吃点。一会儿还有甜点呢。

周经理：谢谢。小王，你还想吃甜点吗？

王祕书：不好意思，我已经吃饱了，不能再吃了。

周经理：那你就看着我们吃吧！

【电话响了。】

韦经理：对不起，我先接电话。

喂，我们正在吃饭呢。吃完饭，就去找你。

B. 短文

在印度做客的礼节

印度人请外国朋友到家里吃晚餐，是一种热情的表示。印度人大部分信印度教，不吃牛肉；伊斯兰教不吃猪肉，所以羊肉常常用来招待贵宾。咖哩是印度菜的主角，非常好吃。

印度南方人和北方人吃的习惯也不太一样，北方人的主食是烤饼，用叉子，南方人喜欢吃米饭，而且觉得用手抓着吃更好吃。当然如果有兴趣，客人也可以一起用右手吃吃看。主人会把柠檬水放在桌上，给大家洗手。

台湾人请吃晚饭，一般都会约在晚上六、七点。但在印度，因为午餐时间是一点，所以九点左右，才是他们晚餐的时间。客人到得太早了，主人可能还正在准备，或穿着不太正式的衣服，这样就不礼貌了。

第三课　自由行

A. 对话

【周经理和王祕书趁刚签了合约比较没事，打算自由行，在新德里到处逛逛。】

周经理：签了合约，今天轻松一下吧！王祕书，你怎么安排？

王祕书：没坐过 auto 和地铁，就不能说到过印度，搭车逛市区吧。

周经理：auto？你是说那种黄绿两色的车？听说不杀价就会被骗！

王祕书：对，印度 auto 大部分是黄绿两色。价钱，有我在，请放心！

周经理：好，试试吧！印度每个地方的车，颜色都不同吗？

王祕书：是的，auto 是平民的腿，没了它很不方便，塞车也会更严重。

周经理：说着说着，就来了一辆，奇怪两边为什么都挂着塑胶布？

王祕书：先上车吧，您马上就能发现为什么了。

【王祕书杀价以后，两人坐上 auto 去地铁站。】

周经理：我懂了，有塑胶布，不怕风也不怕空气污染。地铁站到了。

王祕书：别急，班次很多，不过前面两节车厢只给女生坐。

周经理：现在不挤，我们一起坐后面的车厢。

王祕书：您看每节车厢还有特别留给女生的位子，男生得让座。

周经理：真的，坐在那里的先生让座了。对了，等一下饭店试试搭公车，怎么样？

王祕书：坐地铁能用旅游卡，公车又挤又得在车上买票，太麻烦了。

周经理：那可以坐火车玩玩吗？

王祕书：印度人说：「再等一下，火车一定会来」，所以「有事」别搭火车吧。

周经理：那回去我们坐坐三轮车。

B. 短文

台北的交通工具

每个城市都有它主要的交通工具。印度的首都新德里，地铁、uber、auto 和三轮车都非常重要，而台湾的首都台北，捷运差不多就像城市的血管，一张悠游卡，就能带你轻松地到城市的每个地方。另外，机车、汽车、公车、计程车、uber，在交通和这个城市的发展上，也相当重要。

每天上下班时间，捷运站挤满了人，三铁共构的大站，搭车的人多得可怕，附近房子的价钱也非常贵。捷运的「博爱座」更是一大特色，老人、孕妇、行动不方便的人，可以先坐，不过看到身体不舒服的人，大家也都会马上让座给他们。

机车族是台北另一个特色，每天一些重要路口的机车瀑布，让人看了难忘，还有这几年流行的外送服务，他们骑着机车在大街小巷里钻来钻去，更让城市热闹不少。

第四课　热闹的排灯节

A. 对话

【今天是印度排灯节，印度珠宝公司韦经理邀请周经理和王祕书到家里作客。】

韦经理：欢迎，欢迎，请进。这是我太太，她是台湾人。

周经理：你们好。在这里看到家乡的人，好开心！

韦经理：我太太看到你们更高兴呢！请尝尝她做的甜点。

王祕书：真不错！不同国家口味的甜点要做得好，不容易吧？

韦经理：我太太按照食谱做，她说一点也不难。

【外面传来很大的鞭炮声。】

周经理：外面鞭炮的声音好大！真热闹。

韦经理：这几天是排灯节，是印度教的节日，跟过新年一样。

王祕书：谢谢您邀请我们到你家吃饭。

韦经理：不客气。你们来印度，就像是我们的家人。

周经理：排灯节你们跟家人一起吃饭，还做什么事呢？

韦经理：这个节日大概三天到五天，我觉得最有意思的是点油灯。

王祕书：我看过！你们在家门口、河边…点着小油灯。

韦经理：是啊！意思是希望平安。我们也穿新衣、放鞭炮、迎财
　　　　神。

王祕书：我也看过我的印度朋友带礼物去她姐妹家拜访

韦经理：这跟台湾春节大年初二，我太太回娘家一样的意思吧！

周经理：没错！很晚了，我们该走了。谢谢招待，再见。

B. 短文

印度的油灯与台湾的光明灯

　　点油灯是印度排灯节的重要习俗，而点光明灯是台湾春节的重要习俗。

　　排灯节是印度的重要节日，也是着名的印度教节日。排灯节在每年的十月或十一月举办。在五天的庆祝活动中，最特别的是：很多人在家、在商店和办公室的门上，放着小油灯，希望「灯」的光明带给他们平安和财富。排灯节和台湾的春节一样，是和家人在一起的节日。

　　「灯」在佛经中是光明、智慧的意思。台湾人点光明灯是为了祈求光明与平安。大概是过春节的时候，很多人会去寺庙付钱点光明灯，希望新的一年都平安健康、事事如意。点光明灯的方法很容

易，写好姓名、生日和地址就可以了。点完以后，每个月的初一、十五，寺庙的人都会为他们念经。

印度排灯节的「点油灯」和台湾的「点光明灯」虽然不一样，但是点灯的人，他们的想法是一样的，都希望年年健康如意。

第五课　去喝喜酒

A. 对话

周经理：王祕书，你再帮我看看，今天穿这套纱丽合适吗？

王祕书：都到了，您还在担心？纱丽是印度正式的礼服，不会错的。

桑　吉：看起来真是美极了！两位好，我是新郎的弟弟桑吉，替哥哥来招待贵宾。

周经理：您好！我们来自台湾，麻烦您了。（转身）王祕书，你看，我穿蓝色的礼服会不会跟新娘的一样？

桑　吉：不会的！印度新娘传统的礼服大部分是红的、白的加金色。

周经理：谢谢。对了，王祕书，等一下给新娘的红包和金饰带了没有？

王祕书：都带了，红包在这儿，一共是八千块，发、发、发，多吉利啊！

周经理：太好了，我们快进去参加婚礼吧！

桑　吉：慢点，先换个红包袋吧。

周经理：怎么了？为什么要换？

桑　吉：因为我们送尾数是「一」，不送尾数是「零」的礼金。

王祕书：对啊，我怎么忘了？只想到按照台湾的文化，「八」是最好的祝福。

桑　　吉：在印度「一」表示新人两人一心，从「一」开始，未来家
　　　　　运兴旺。

周经理：所以红包袋上黏一块卢比，尾数就一定是「一」了。

王祕书：快看，新郎新娘开始绕火堆了，听说得绕七次…。

桑　　吉：对，是希望平安、健康、永远爱对方。晚上喜宴能请两位
　　　　　一起跳舞吗？

B. 短文

台湾婚礼

　　台湾的婚礼有越来越多不同的形式，连跳伞、潜水或是骑着白马的古代婚礼，都能见到。形式越特别，年轻人越喜欢。不过大部分新人还是选在饭店举行婚礼。

　　结婚这天，在鞭炮声中，新郎一到新娘家，就得接受很多挑战，才能见到新娘。离开娘家前，很多新娘都会舍不得地哭了。车子一开，她就得把扇子丢出窗外，丢掉坏习惯，开始新生活。到了新郎家，新娘得跨火炉，把平安吉祥带到新家。

　　婚礼开始，新娘的父亲把女儿交给新郎，然后新人的父母说些祝福的话，再请大家举杯祝福新人。喜宴开始，客人吃着东西，看新人从小到大的影片。这时，新娘穿着另外一件漂亮的礼服，跟新郎和两人的父母一起敬酒。除了敬酒，新人还会跟大家玩游戏、送客人小礼物。最后新人拿着喜糖站在门口送客，客人开心地和新人照相，婚礼就在热闹的气氛中结束了。

第六课　古迹的故事

A. 对话

【桑吉陪着周经理和王祕书，一起到泰姬玛哈陵参观，周经理看着这座陵寝的墙。】

周经理：四百年前的建筑就知道用白色大理石和珠宝，真不可思议。

桑　吉：不过伟大的建筑，没有浪漫的故事，就不够吸引人。

周经理：你是说泰姬玛哈陵又是古迹，又有故事？

王祕书：我知道，这座陵寝是沙迦罕王为了王后盖的。

桑　吉：对！「泰姬玛哈」是结婚时，他给王后取的名字，「陵」是⋯

王祕书：「陵」是陵寝，它会因为日夜光线的变化，有红、蓝不同的颜色。

周经理：我听说国王后来被关在对面的阿格拉堡？

桑　吉：没错，沙迦罕王每天从阿格拉堡看着陵寝流泪，想着王后。

王祕书：他花了太多钱盖泰姬陵，所以儿子把他关了起来！

周经理：真可怜！不过只要来参观的人，就会说起他们的爱情故事。

桑　吉：要是有兴趣，明天再去古达明纳塔看另外一个伟大的爱情故事，怎么样？

王祕书：好啊！可惜现在古达明纳塔已经不能爬上去了。

桑　吉：对，为了保护古迹，也怕危险。

王祕书：胡马雍陵也该去看看，泰姬陵就是参考它盖的。

周经理：桑吉，谢谢您带我们认识印度文化。

B. 短文

皇家陵寝

　　中国秦始皇陵和印度泰姬玛哈陵都是皇家的陵寝，也都是世界遗产。从泰姬玛哈陵可以看到波斯和伊斯兰教的文化；而秦始皇陵的兵马俑对研究秦朝文化，也有很大的帮助。

　　「俑」是古代用土做的人或动物，放进陵寝去陪葬的东西，「兵马俑」是用土做的军队来陪葬。刚开始皇家陪葬是用真人，后来才改用土做的「俑」。

　　「兵马俑」被发现，最早是在 1932 年，西安附近挖出了一个跪着的俑，跟真人非常像。可是那时候，他们不知道是陵寝，还有人觉得俑是不吉祥的东西，就把它打坏丢了。到 1974 年挖井，才挖出这个古迹来。「俑」本来有颜色，可惜因为离现在的时间太久了，所以从地下挖出来才十几秒，很多俑的颜色就开始变了，后来也慢慢掉了，就是我们现在看到的样子。

　　在今天，我们能看着一支秦朝军队，多不可思议啊！除了激动，怎么能不感谢研究文化和保护古迹的人呢？

第七课　逛逛市集

A. 对话

【桑吉陪周经理和王祕书，逛印度传统市集。】

周经理：东西好多啊，连树上都挂着东西呢。

王祕书：对啊，有衣服、鞋子、饰品，还有传统香料和纱丽什么的。

桑　吉：这里人挤人，巷子又多，小心点，别只看东西，走丢了。

周经理：好的。天气真热，那里有鲜果汁和小吃，我们买一点吧？

王祕书：不行，一边逛一边吃路边的东西，小心拉肚子。

桑　吉：外国人刚来，还不习惯，真的得小心一点。

【在路上卖饰品的小妹妹，把一个手环很快地戴在周经理手上。】

周经理：小妹妹为什么把手环戴在我的手上？桑吉，你在跟她说什么？

桑　吉：我跟小妹妹说您戴起来很漂亮，可惜太贵了。所以她卖我三个五十五块。

王祕书：经理，您戴起来真的不错。桑吉，还你五十五块。

桑　吉：开玩笑，才五十几块，要是给我，就不是我的朋友了。

周经理：桑吉，你帮我们杀价，等一下我请大家到店里喝印度奶茶。

王祕书：太好了！前面那个人好厉害，头上放了好多衣服。

桑　吉：市集人多巷子又窄，货这么多，没有一点顶上功夫是不行的。

王祕书：虽然市集有点乱，不过看到印度人为生活这么认真工作，很感动。

周经理：没错，市集保存了传统，也刺激了观光，真了不起。

B. 短文

逛夜市

晚上去哪里玩？「夜市」一定是台湾人第一个想到的地方。

台湾小吃，种类多，味道好，是最能代表台湾人生活的饮食文化，逛夜市吃个蚵仔煎、大饼包小饼、大肠面线、甜不辣、肉圆、卤肉饭什么的，然后喝杯珍珠奶茶，多痛快！小吃摊，一摊连着一摊，什么都有，便宜又好吃，还能从「吃」发现当地的文化特色。

而卖东西的人常很有创意地大声叫着「走过，路过，不能错过」，也非常有趣。夜市还有一些好玩的游戏，像捞金鱼、射气球、电动游戏都很常见，还可以做脚底按摩。有时候外国朋友也会来摆摊子，卖些家乡食物，非常热闹。

　　台湾从南到北差不多每天都有夜市，跟西方国家只有在假日或节日才有市集不一样，跟印度市集比较像，不过夜市一定在晚上。约几个好朋友去逛夜市，开开心心地一边吃一边玩，真的是很快乐的事。

第八课　　养生的方法

A. 对话

王祕书：经理，您这几天看起来有一点累！

周经理：是啊！我们每天都有活动，还得准备合作资料。

王祕书：我建议您早上去新德里的洛迪公园慢跑。

周经理：我不太喜欢慢跑、健走这些运动。

王祕书：那瑜珈呢？洛迪公园的「草地瑜珈」非常有名。

周经理：瑜珈！我不但有兴趣，而且也常常练习。

王祕书：太好了！我们现在就去报名明天的草地瑜珈课吧！

【第二天，在洛迪公园草地瑜珈课后，有一位对印度养生颇有研究的人跟周经理聊印度的瑜珈和养生。】

印度人：印度瑜珈种类很多。现在大家比较常做运动瑜珈。

周经理：我们今天早上练习的就是吧？

印度人：是的，在草地上跟大自然沟通，让我们身心健康。

周经理：您对这方面真有研究。

印度人：哪里，哪里。

王祕书：我听说印度的阿育吠陀养生方法很有名。

印度人：对！我们会用瑜珈、按摩、食物和草药来养生。

王祕书：这跟传统的中医很像。

周经理：不早了，我们有事得先走，希望有机会再聊。

B. 短文

食疗

从以前到现在，每一个人都希望健康，没有人想生病，所以养生很重要。

中国人认为：「食物是最好的药物」。只要吃对的食物，就会对身体有帮助，也不容易生病。知道吃什么对身体好，就是食疗养生。

中国传统的食疗养生，是按照不同的年龄、体质、疾病和季节，吃一些让身体健康，或是能治疗疾病的食物。跟一般的食物比起来，这些食物比较养生，所以现在吃的人就多起来了。

印度的阿育吠陀跟中医一样也有食疗养生。按照不同的体质，吃不同的食物。但是阿育吠陀比中医更注意「季节饮食」，一年分春天、夏天、雨季、秋天、冬前和冬天六个季节，每个季节有两个月，每一季有不同的食疗方法。但是现在很多人是按照个人喜好或是家庭的状况，决定吃什么。

第九课　伴手礼

A. 对话

【印度珠宝公司韦经理、周经理和王祕书谈去新德里市集买伴手礼。】

韦经理：时间过得真快！不久你们就要回台湾了。

周经理：是啊！回国以前，想买一些这里有特色的东西。

韦经理：对！来印度一定要带我们的特产回台湾当伴手礼。

王祕书：经理，我带您去逛新德里有名的市集跟商场，顺便买些礼物。

韦经理：王祕书是印度通，在这方面更有经验吧！

王祕书：我认为逛市集，除了能买到当地的特产以外，还能看到不同的文化。

韦经理：说得好！阿萨姆红茶、香料、手工鞋、首饰⋯，都有我们的文化。

王祕书：我建议买草本的喜马拉雅产品，更有特色。

周经理：好建议。这次我不但要买伴手礼，而且想欣赏欣赏印度的珠宝设计。

韦经理：没问题。明天我陪您去参观我的珠宝公司。

【韦经理带周经理去参观珠宝公司，谈到黄金。】

韦经理：这些是黄金首饰，这些是黄金加上不同宝石的流行设计。

周经理：又美又有创意！而且都是一套一套的，有耳环、项鍊、手镯。

韦经理：这是我们的传统风格。现在也流行白金和纯银的首饰。

周经理：不过，看起来还是黄金首饰比较多。

韦经理：没错。因为在印度人心中，金色是最高贵的颜色。

周经理：听您这么说，我决定买一套黄金首饰了。

B. 短文

伴手礼的意义

　　当台湾人旅行或是回家乡的时候，总是想买一些旅游地或是居住地方的特产送给亲戚朋友，这些东西就叫伴手礼。台湾人觉得只

有这样做，才能表达对朋友的心意，所以伴手礼也代表华人社会浓厚的人情味。

来印度，台湾人带台湾特产乌龙茶、凤梨酥；回台湾，当然带印度的特产阿萨姆红茶、香料、喜马拉雅产品，还有文化特色的手工鞋、耳环、项链、手镯等。台湾人常说：「礼轻情意重」，意思是虽然送的礼物不贵，但是它表示台湾人对朋友的心意。

除了心意以外，伴手礼还能代表当地特色，也能给商家带来财富，又能对国家经济有帮助，所以各地都积极发展一些有代表性的产品，让观光客开开心心地逛完景点以后，也高高兴兴地大采购。

第十课　欢送会

A. 对话

【印度珠宝公司韦经理为周经理和王祕书举办欢送晚会。】

周经理：韦经理，谢谢您特地为我们举办这个欢送晚会。

韦经理：应该的。除了欢送你们，也让你们体会一下印度人的热情。

王祕书：体会到了。晚会不但有印度美食，还有印度歌舞。

周经理：是啊，道地的口味，华丽的歌舞，这趟印度行真值得。

韦经理：周经理，您觉得我们的咖哩，味道怎么样？

周经理：很特别，我喜欢上你们的咖哩羊肉了。小王，你呢？

王祕书：除了咖哩，我也爱上印度歌舞了。

【晚会结束以前，周经理邀请他们来台湾参加珠宝展览。】

周经理：韦经理，很高兴，我们的珠宝设计第一次合作就成功了。

韦经理：这要谢谢你们准备了这么好的合作方案。

周经理：明年十一月，台北世贸要举办「台湾珠宝首饰展览会」。

韦经理：我知道，规模很大，听说会有很多顶级的珠宝参加展览。

周经理：你们公司的珠宝设计很有特色，想邀请您参加。

韦经理：我对这个展览很有兴趣，但是得好好地计划计划。

王祕书：欢迎欢迎。我们一边吃一边聊吧，菜都凉了。

韦经理：真舍不得你们离开，什么时候回台湾？

周经理：后天。谢谢您今晚的安排，明年台北见！

B. 短文

珠宝展览会怎么宣传

　　珠宝厂商举办展览会的目的，当然是希望商品能大卖，而想卖得好，得先让人有兴趣买，所以商家怎么宣传才能吸引客人，是展览会最重要的准备工作。

　　现在是网路时代，一切透过网站宣传。在主要的网页上，一定要有几张有特色又能吸引人的珠宝照片，让从来不买珠宝或是对珠宝从来没兴趣的人，都想去看看！这些照片同时也可以当作宣传海报。

　　主要网页上要有和展览资讯有关的连结，如：展览会简介、参加展览和参观展览的联络方式、参展的资料，比方说为什么要参展、参展费用什么的。另外，展览哪些系列的珠宝、展览会的影片、宣传的新闻稿、交通、签证和旅游应该注意的事情。

　　网页上和展览会场上，最重要的是都要有清楚的展区图示，让参观的人很容易就能找到自己需要的商品，这样才不会浪费他们的时间。

附錄四 跨文化延伸中文版
Cross-Cultural Extension in Chinese

第一課

女性就業

你可能有點好奇，要來印度談生意的周經理竟然是位女性啊！其實在臺灣男女的工作權大致是平等的。在臺灣很多女性，學校一畢業就開始工作了，幾乎每一種職業都有女性從事，如：女工程師、女經理、女公車司機或是女導遊…等。

根據統計，每十個臺灣女性中就有一位是大學畢業生，加上新的服務業越來越多，所以女性有了更多的工作機會，政府也因此注意到她們的福利。比如說，為了讓女性員工安心養育子女，生產後有八個星期的產假，而且是有薪資的。產假後，也可以申請留職停薪的育嬰假。甚至於，有一歲以下嬰兒的女員工，在工作場所每天有餵奶或集奶的時間。因為有這樣的福利，讓已婚的女性能安心工作。

印度從 2005 年到現在，15 歲以上有工作的女性不但沒有增加，反而越來越少。有些研究指出，這跟印度的傳統文化有關。印度是一個「男性做主」的社會。還有報告提到，要是印度女人跟印度男人的工作機會一樣多，未來印度的產值將會大幅提升。

第二課

臺印社群媒體使用差異（Line vs. WhatsApp）

到印度經商或旅遊，臺灣和印度用的通訊軟體不同。臺灣現在

最常使用的是 Line，有一些國家也是以 Line 為主要通訊軟體。使用 Line 可以隨時隨地與好朋友免費聊天和互動。它不但支援一對一的聊天，還可以群組聊天。Line 提供免費國際語音和視頻通話，讓用戶跟親人輕鬆保持聯繫。Line 還有又方便又安全的 LinePay，可以讓你隨時在網路上安全購物。

在印度 WhatsApp 擁有很多用戶，功能跟 Line 差不多。WhatsApp 的一個優點是即使在 WiFi 訊號不太好的地區，像只有 3G 的地方，也能收到訊號。目前 Line 和其服務都是免費的，WhatsApp 也是免費下載。但因為 WhatsApp 來自美國，而且是用英語的通訊軟體，所以在印度很受歡迎。

第三課

三輪車跑得快

「三輪車，跑得快。」這首兒歌，描繪了臺灣早期的交通狀況，因為巷弄狹窄，大家經濟又不寬裕，所以帶著孩子，買了大包小包的媽媽，只好叫一輛三輪車，全家擠上去，所有重量交給車夫的兩條腿。這跟載著購完物的一家老小，滿街跑的印度人力車非常相似。

隨著時代進步，有了計程車，三輪車成了臺灣觀光景點的懷舊工具。臺灣的計程車都是黃色，所以又叫小黃，而印度每個城市的 auto 顏色不同，但兩者都是為了方便辨識和管理。

臺灣受到中央山脈阻隔，早期東西交通不便。50 年代政府帶領退伍軍人，炸山築路、犧牲生命，終於開通了東西橫貫公路。「太魯閣國家公園」，就在這條公路的起點。現在臺灣西部有高速鐵路，東部有火車和巴士，已經非常方便了。

印度地大人多，目前火車是貫穿全印度的主要交通工具，不過一般來說，擁擠、經常誤點，是人民最感不便的。雖然也有設備好又準時的火車，但是貴得不得了，所以又便宜又舒服的火車是人們最大的期望。

第四課

中文的祝賀語

「祝賀」是慶祝、賀喜的意思。「祝賀詞」是在特殊的節日或日子，祝福恭賀對方時，所引用的詞語。這些詞語都有針對性，也富有濃厚的感情色彩。

中國人很注重人際關係，都希望在適當的時機或場合，比如：春節、公司開幕、搬新家、結婚、生日等，適切地表達關心祝賀之意。這些祝賀的詞語，大多是「四字格」（Four-Character Idioms）。

「四字格」是由四個漢字組成的成語結構，有固定的意思。常用的結婚四字格賀詞，如：天作之合、永結同心、百年好合、白頭偕老。新年賀詞，如：恭喜發財、歲歲平安、心想事成。生日賀詞，如：長命百歲、平安健康、一帆風順、幸福快樂。其中，任何時候都適用的是：「萬事如意、心想事成」。

第五課

婚禮昏禮

中式婚禮，有很多特別的文化，像婚禮原來叫「昏禮」；「洞房」、「丟扇子」、「過火爐」，也各有意義。

　　古代沒有正式的婚禮，新郎看上哪家姑娘，趁黃昏，抱了就跑，躲進山洞成了夫妻。新娘的家人田事忙完，才發現女兒被搶，等找到女兒，已經是第二天了，只好同意。新郎家黃昏多一女，因此改稱婚禮；而結婚的第一夜，因為在山洞裡，所以稱「洞房」。

　　另外新娘「丟扇子」，除了「扇」和「散」音差不多，父母也希望女兒一出嫁，就把不好的習慣丟掉；「過火爐」，則是求火神破除厄運，並把火一樣「旺」的好運帶進夫家。

　　印度也非常重視婚禮，有新郎、新娘「繞火堆」七圈，求火神祝福平安、健康、永遠相愛，及貴子興家的文化。這跟我國「早生貴子」、「百年好合」的意義相似。臺、印雖然語言不同，卻有相似的文化，是不是挺有意思？

第六課

古蹟的科學

　　中國、印度雖然是古國，但是都有運用科學建造的古蹟。西安秦始皇陵的兵馬俑和大雁塔；印度古達明納塔的鐵柱、胡馬雍陵，以及倒金字塔型的月亮梯井都是代表。

　　在印度，古達明納塔鐵柱的製造技術，讓鐵柱屹立了 1600 年毫無鏽蝕；胡馬雍陵是印度早期波斯和伊斯蘭教文化的建築，戶外水池跟室內的設計，讓這些建築冬暖夏涼；月亮梯井在沙漠附近，早就具備了水庫的雛型，不論天旱、天雨，水位高低，居民都可以順著井邊的 3500 級階梯走下去取水。

　　臺灣山多河流短，許多現代水庫的興建也是相同儲水的概念。另外，秦始皇陵的科技讓兵馬俑被保存下來；而大雁塔據說是玄奘從印度取經回來後請求興建的，用來保存佛經。在當年沒有雲梯的

科技下，64.1 公尺的高塔，到今天科學家還無法解開怎麼蓋出來的謎。我們不得不佩服這些文明古國祖先的智慧。

第七課

臺印的素食文化

「吃素」在臺灣是一個很普遍的現象，也很方便，因為到處都有素食店。除了少數人是為了減肥而吃素，其他大部分是因為宗教的關係或為了保護動物而吃素。有人初一、十五吃素，有人天天吃素，有人吃早齋，要怎麼吃，可以按照自己的想法。

臺灣有的人吃「全素」，有的人吃「奶蛋素」，就是可以吃奶蛋類製品，但這兩種素食者都不吃辛辣的蔥、蒜、韭菜。另外，有一種很特別的「鍋邊素」，就是食物中可以有葷的，但自己只挑素的吃。

世界素食大國—印度，香料的種類非常多，印度教徒吃素可以放香料和蔥、蒜，但一定是吃全素。不過，印度男性即使是肉食主義者，每週仍會選擇在自己信仰的主神所掌管的那一天吃素，例如信仰象徵力量的猴神者，就會選擇在每週二吃素。其實不論哪種吃素的方式，「營養均衡」和「心誠」最重要，因為「心誠則靈」，「營養均衡」則健康啊！

第八課

中醫與阿育吠陀

中醫和印度的阿育吠陀醫療，是兩大古老的傳統醫學，也有很多共同點。

　　阿育吠陀的意思是「生命的科學」，它是一門醫學，也是一種健康的生活方式。這種醫療注重人的特性，比方說：體質、年齡、居住環境、社會及文化背景等。診斷方式有觸摸、檢查和交談等，並利用藥草、推拿及瑜珈三種療法，恢復器官的功能。

　　中醫的診斷方法有望、聞、問、切四個步驟。醫生先觀察病人外觀，再聽聲音和聞氣味，接著問病情、病史，最後把脈。常見的治療方法是：中藥、針灸、推拿及理傷等。中醫在臺灣很普及，連醫學中心也設中醫門診。中藥材更經常入菜，從根本上改善人們的體質。

　　這兩種醫療方式都重視「治本」及正確平衡的飲食方式，促進身心健康。它們在醫學上都有很大的貢獻，更融入了人們的生活。

第九課

中國的玉文化

　　中國人重視玉，就像印度人重視黃金一樣。玉是中國傳統文化的重要部分之一，深深影響古代中國人的思想觀念。

　　玉是一種美麗的礦石，通常指的是硬玉和軟玉。常見的軟玉有白玉、黃玉、碧玉、墨玉等，而硬玉就是大家熟悉的翡翠。玉在中華文化中，認為有趨吉避凶的作用，古代常作為象徵身分地位的裝飾，中國皇帝的印璽就是用玉刻造的。現代除了當裝飾之外，也常當作平安符隨身佩戴。

　　玉的文化內涵極為豐富，最具特色的是「以玉比德」的用字觀念，存在於漢語的字、詞及成語中。這些字詞的意涵大多表示美好、尊貴、典雅，如：玉手、玉容、玉體、錦衣玉食，也常作為人的名字，如：玉玲、清玉。

總之，在華人社會中，從古至今，仍保有愛玉與尊玉的文化傳統。

第十課

臺印不同的商務談判方式

　　臺灣與印度文化不同。臺灣受到中國文化的影響，而印度是由獨特的社會制度、歷史和宗教交織而成的國家，文化比較多元。不同的文化及市場環境，影響到做生意的方法與技巧。

　　一般來說，印度人在進行商務談判或是購物時，一定會殺價、討價還價。這是被國內市場鍛鍊出來的本能。印度市場競爭非常激烈，同一個產品常有幾十家進口商，而最後的談判手段當然是價格談判。

　　臺灣人溫和禮讓的思維，形成了「不好意思」的文化。但是應對殺價，在第一次報價的時候就會預留空間。面對過分還價，態度就變得強硬，也常用到中國人「打太極」的方法。如果客戶說以後會有很多訂單，希望再便宜一點，就會反過來對他們說：「價格是不能變的，已經是成本了，但是下次再買的話，一定會比這次更便宜的。」

　　話說回來，談判技巧並沒有對或錯，最終目的就是雙贏。

Note

國家圖書館出版品預行編目資料

Incredible Mandarin（不可思議華語）／陳
淑芬主編. 陳慶華，劉殿敏，張箴著.－－
初版.－－臺北市：五南圖書出版股份有限
公司，2021.12
面；　公分
ISBN 978-626-317-434-4（平裝）

1.漢語　2.讀本

802.86　　　　　　　　　110020387

4X26

Incredible Mandarin
不可思議華語

總 策 畫 ―	王偉中
執行策劃 ―	印度臺灣華語教育中心―國立清華大學計畫辦公室
主　　編 ―	陳淑芬
顧　　問 ―	信世昌、鍾鎮城、周湘華
審　　查 ―	顧百里、葉德明、張莉萍
編寫老師 ―	陳慶華、劉殿敏、張箴
英文翻譯 ―	張箴
英文審查 ―	顧百里
文化顧問 ―	王潔予
校　　對 ―	陳淑芬、林怡秀
行政支援 ―	蔡恩祥、鍾睿婕
插　　畫 ―	菊箱工作室
圖片提供 ―	陳姿靜、劉殿敏
錄　　音 ―	王政渝、歐喜強、陳慶華、劉殿敏
發 行 人 ―	楊榮川
總 經 理 ―	楊士清
總 編 輯 ―	楊秀麗
副總編輯 ―	黃惠娟
責任編輯 ―	吳佳怡
封面設計 ―	韓衣非
出 版 者 ―	五南圖書出版股份有限公司
地　　址：	106台北市大安區和平東路二段339號4樓
電　　話：	(02)2705-5066　　傳　真：(02)2706-6100
網　　址：	https://www.wunan.com.tw
電子郵件：	wunan@wunan.com.tw
劃撥帳號：	01068953
戶　　名：	五南圖書出版股份有限公司

法律顧問　林勝安律師事務所　林勝安律師

出版日期　2021年12月初版一刷
定　　價　新臺幣420元